DARLING, THERE ARE WOLVES IN THE WOODS

THE WICKED WOODS CHRONICLES BOOK ONE

L.V. RUSSELL

Independently published.
Second Printing.

CONTENTS

To all of you who wander the woods

PROLOGUE

*L*uthien stared out into the writhing mass of faeries. She did not dance or allow the music of the old trees to call to her. A smile twisted upon her full lips, though it held no warmth. From beneath the waves of bitter chocolate hair, her dark eyes shone hard and joyless.

"One day, I shall rule," she said. "You will see."

The faerie standing beside her only nodded, his own smile playing at his lips. Stealing a kiss from her, he turned back to the dance.

"Niven," he called, voice soft and gentle and wonderful. He watched as each impossibly lovely creature parted for him, revealing a tired and bruised looking girl. He outstretched his hand and waited. "Come with me."

Luthien watched them leave, remaining under the deep shadows of the oaks, seeing the point in the distance where the trees merged, a disturbance in the air that belonged to both mortal and fey. There were places just like it all over the world, a weakening of the veil between worlds, where if one was not careful, it was easy enough to slip through.

She lingered for a while, closing her eyes as the last of the music drifted away, leaving nothing behind save whispers of broken songs and lost promises. Slowly she turned, her voice a sweet and subtle poison.

"Did you think I had forgotten you?"

Luthien crouched beneath the ancient oak, its huge trunk rotted through, countless strings of ivy choking it from within. The little girl hiding in the shadows nodded, flame-red hair slipping over her face. Tears slid down her cheeks, the dirt on her face running with them.

"You wanted to see the faeries, didn't you?"

A nod. Then a sniffle that made Luthien recoil.

"Then why are you sniveling?" she asked, lip curling. "I gave you what you wanted, you danced with my fey, and I took what I wanted."

"Where's Niven?" The words were little more than sobs, but they stirred up no compassion...no empathy with Luthien. Only disgust, as she reached forwards to swipe one away.

"She is with us."

"When...when can I have her back?"

Luthien bit back a laugh, allowing a cold, terrible smile to settle on her lips. "She belongs to me now."

"You can have me!" the girl cried, desperation leaking into her little voice. Even Luthien had to admire the audacity. "Take me instead."

"I do not want you." Luthien said simply, rising to her feet. "We do not want you."

Luthien walked away as soon as the rain began to fall, causing her gown to cling to every perfect curve of her body. She smiled to herself...a rare, real smile at the thought of the hands that would free her of the silk later.

As the sounds of sobbing girls drifted further and further away, Luthien raised her finger to her mouth and tasted the sweetness of that lone teardrop. She held it upon her tongue for a moment as if it were a fine wine. The taste of innocence soon faded away, leaving behind the headier flavours of fear and hopelessness.

For the almost queen of Seelie, nothing tasted more divine.

CHAPTER ONE

a darkness so deep, I could hardly breathe. The sound of the wind as it sang through the trees, lifting their leaves so they danced as the fey had...a frenzied waltz I didn't know the steps to. A flash of teeth, a flicker of wings, the echo of a hundred things laughing and jeering...pulling and scratching. The nightmare lingered, hovering darkly in my memory, where even the faint light of morning couldn't quite chase it away. I lived with it always. A terrifying reminder of what I had done, of what was out there, hidden so very cleverly by shadows and dancing trees.

It was my penance for giving Niven to Them.

I knew I had to get up—lying there I could already hear the faint footsteps of my mother walking towards my door, her wheezing on the landing.

"Teya? Are you up? If you need me to drive you to college then I need you ready in twenty minutes."

The nasal whine of her voice penetrated through the thin wood of my door. My screams would likely have woken the neighbours, so my mum knew very well that I was awake. I counted to three before mum barged on in anyway.

"Are you meeting Moira later?"

"I don't need to meet Moira, Mother," I replied with a sigh at the mention of my therapist. Moira was a nice enough person, a woman lingering somewhere in her early forties with bouncy brown hair and an even bouncier smile. Moira wanted the world to be happy, and was working on achieving that with one helpless person at a time. Moira was sunshine in a bottle, the type of person always with a song on her lips.

I did not like Moira.

"I could ring her..."

"No, I'm fine."

Moira had been there from the beginning, happily jotting down my stories, searching for the metaphors within my words. Her perkiness had wavered slightly when she realised I meant actual monsters, the horned kind, with tails. Not the human type of monster that preyed on small children. I think she would have coped better with perverts.

I had learned quickly that mentioning the word 'faerie' too often around people resulted in uncomfortable questions. I had also learned that insisting monsters had abducted my sister would indeed result in a spell in hospital. I learned to perfect my smile, to say that I was coping better, and that I was slowly moving on. I told Moira that it was not my fault Niven disappeared and that there were no monsters lurking in the shadows, waiting for me. I could lie pretty well when the threat of a soft room was hanging over my head.

"I'll be down in five," I muttered to my mother.

"You'd better be." My mother reached out to touch my face, her hand curling for just a moment around the duvet. She had sent me to a clinic to deal with Niven's disappearance, but used a more direct tack when dealing with her own feelings and had swiftly divorced my father.

Deciding against the shower, I pulled on jeans and a t-shirt and quickly ran a hairbrush through my hair, leaving it to hang loose over my shoulders. The pale winter light caught the soft strands and highlighted the different shades of reds, golds and browns that ran through it.

"Have you got any lunch?" Mum asked as I slid into the front of her battered Micra, driving off before I had a chance to answer her.

"I have money."

"You sure?"

I shrugged as I fumbled with the seatbelt, cussing when I couldn't get it to click into the socket.

"Be gentle with it, Teya, you need to be patient."

"Or you could just get a better car," I retorted. "One that won't explode if something nudges against it."

"Hurry up and finish Art school and earn me money."

I really wondered what my mother wanted me to do with a degree in Art; I was a mediocre artist at best and not talented enough to earn a living through it. For me, it was escapism and nothing more.

My mother had higher dreams for me, and was nothing if not deluded. Though to be honest, I knew they were not truly dreams for me...they were what she dreamed for Niven.

They had scanned the woods for my sister. Teams of policemen with dogs that strained at the leash all went out looking for her, turning over every stone and stepping into shadows that I still feared to tread.

Niven was on the news, her beautiful face plastered over all the newspapers, alongside the wretched faces of my parents. Women fitting the pathetic description of Luthien I had given were taken in for questioning, and were released soon after. No one was ever arrested. Niven, it seemed, had just walked into the woods and vanished, leaving nothing behind to help us find her.

As the months went by, my broken family slowly stopped being front-page news. Without any leads on Niven, there was simply no story to tell.

"Do you want me to pick you up later?"

I turned my head to the grey sky out of the window, the sun barely strong enough to penetrate the gloomy clouds, and nodded my head slowly. It would be getting dark early.

"I'll see you around six then? Are you okay to stay on for a bit?"

"I'll be fine."

She pulled up to Griffons College, nearly knocking into a couple of students who lingered at the gates. She kissed me gently on the cheek before I was able to leave, trapped in her car by the damned seatbelt.

"I know you will, sweetheart."

We were both good at lying to each other.

I didn't watch my mother drive off, but walked through the gates and towards my locker, my heart sinking when the key jammed. Bending down, I tried to prise the dried spaghetti from the keyhole, fighting the urge to slam my fist against the metal. It was just another thing I dealt with...the endless taunts and pranks that had followed me into college.

It is worth noting that if you mention faeries often enough, not only will you be forced to talk to people you'd rather not, you will also be socially shunned. Forever. It will not matter if later on, you change your story, there will always be that stigma around you. You will be labelled for life as the girl who believes in faeries. Throw in a crippling, piss-yourself fear of the dark and you may as well go buy a load of cats and enjoy life living in a hovel.

I didn't attend College for my love of art, or a foundation

degree, or a thirst for knowledge or even to broaden my life skills so that one day I could escape the village I grew up in. I went to escape from my mother, without actually having to leave her completely. I couldn't leave the woman who still wrapped Christmas presents for Niven in the futile hope that one day she'd come home. The woman who, after ten years of waiting for Niven and a messy divorce, still set the table for four people, only to sit and stare at the empty spaces.

"Ah, Miss Jenkins!" Mrs Reynolds called out to me as I wandered into the art studio. "I need to talk to you about your final pieces..." She hesitated for a moment, trying to find the right words to describe the work I had handed in. She faltered. "They are very..."

"Odd?" I finished for her. "Peculiar?"

"Well, yes," Mrs Reynolds agreed, her little eyes narrowing beneath her glasses. "They are not your best work."

I sighed, scrubbing a hand over my face, and I watched her expression soften. She looked at me with pity. Her glasses were at least three times too big for her face, and yet she pitied me.

"Do you need to talk to someone?"

"No."

"I know life can be difficult, Teya. I know you still miss her..."

"I don't." The words fell from my mouth before I had the chance to pull them back. Nasty, truthful words that caused the heat of guilt to flame up my spine.

"It's okay: there is no time limit on grief."

There is no time limit on grief. Taken straight out of one of those awful self-help books, words that were supposed to comfort me but just left me wondering if I would feel miserable for the rest of my life. It would be better if there were a set time limit, almost like serving a sentence. You would just wake up one day, and poof! Happiness, sunshine...hope.

I turned away from Mrs Reynolds quickly before she could see me roll my eyes. I told her that I would re-do my work and that I would try harder, that I really did want to be there. I did not tell Mrs Reynolds how much I had hated Niven.

I spent the rest of the day in the studio, re-doing one of my paintings so I had something that would at least be accepted, that didn't scream crazy.

It was easy to paint undisturbed, remaining alone with just the splatter of paint on canvas for company. Despite the teasing and cruel remarks, there were a few students who had reached out to me, their smiles wide and genuine. There may have once been a place for me in their group, a spot for a fellow misfit. Friendship and belonging.

If not for my mother.

Because no one truly wanted to have tea with ghosts.

When I had finished, I watched the colours as they seeped from the paintbrushes, the blues and greens flowing under the cold water to merge into a muddy puddle in the basin. My fingers numbed against the cold, stained the same colours as the acrylics that bled from the brushes. I enjoyed the sensation, the dull burn at the tips of my fingers as the skin slowly felt nothing, but it ended at my hands. The rest of my body still felt everything. I gazed at my masterpiece and knew it was beautiful.

Picking up a fresh brush from the collection on my desk, I dipped the head into thick paint and splashed it onto the still wet canvas. I erased the beauty much faster than I had created it, hiding the rich chocolate of Luthien's hair behind unforgiving black. In one brutal stroke, the melting gaze of her eyes was gone. I continued until the entire board glimmered with new paint, until there was not a trace of the beautiful witch to be seen.

I glanced at the clock, noting the time with both relief and anxiety, knowing that I would soon be collected from my purgatory, only to be forced into another when I arrived home.

CHAPTER TWO

I waited in the car park for Mum, the evening dark and cold as I stood beneath one of the overhead lights. The orange glow caught the raindrops so they looked like little sparks falling against the black sky. My hands balled at my sides, my fingernails leaving little semicircles against my palms. I scanned the road for passing cars, fighting hard to keep my breathing calm. In and out...deep and slow. No need to panic over a drizzly winter's night.

A cry gurgled from my throat as the sound of a car horn swore through the night, disturbing some nearby crows. They flew overhead, a flurry of shadows nearly sending me to my knees. I jumped back instead, smacking against the wall. My feet landed in a puddle, soaking my jeans with freezing, muddy water.

"You couldn't pull into the car park?" I hissed, slamming the door to the Micra as I slumped in the seat, my heart still whacking against my ribcage. My hands shook in my lap, and I squeezed my eyes shut in an attempt to calm down. It was a car horn...not monsters, not faeries. My mother's car horn.

"If I go over the speed bumps, I might stall the car and I'll never get it started again," Mum said apologetically, glancing at me as she wrenched the handbrake down. The car lurched forwards rebelliously before it warmed up. "So how was your day?"

"Same as usual," I replied, offering nothing else so the journey home was finished in silence. We didn't talk about Niven, and we didn't mention my father. We simply sat as if it has always been the two of us, ignoring the fact that we could hardly hold a conversation, and that we felt like strangers.

"I'm doing Lasagne for tea," Mum said finally as we pulled into the drive. The once perfect white slabs outside our house now lay cracked beneath a forest of weeds, somehow managing to push up through the concrete. I had to admire their determination.

"Sounds good."

"It's a frozen one from Tesco. They had a deal on: any three for the price of two. I stocked up while they were so cheap."

I pictured the freezer brimming with cheap boxes of discounted Italian food and shook my head. "They've always got those deals on, Mum. It's a way of making money."

I hung back slightly as I watched her fumble in her handbag for her keys. Old receipts and sweet wrappers darted to freedom, swirling up in a chaotic mess before the wind caught hold of them and stole them away.

"Don't be silly, Teya," my mother replied, twisting the key into the lock and swinging the door open.

I slunk in after her, breathing in the oddly comforting smell of fabric conditioner and cigarette smoke that hugged the house like a security blanket. Kicking off my shoes and shrugging off my jacket, I escaped upstairs.

The deep carpet gave way beneath my feet, a luxurious cream that snaked up the curling stair and along the narrow landing. It had replaced the old beige one after Mum spilled red wine over it. The wine glass had slipped from her hand as I watched on from the railings above, splattering crimson all the way down to the bottom of the stairs. She hadn't attempted to stop it rolling, her gaze only fixed on my father as he lingered by the front door.

On the evening of the red wine disaster, my father did not come upstairs to kiss me goodnight, but I did hear him flick the catch on the front door as he walked out, allowing the frigid wind to sneak past him and chill me instead. My dad never came back for us, and it took only three days for mum to rip up the old carpet and dump it outside with the rest of her husband's belongings.

I had barely placed my hand on my bedroom door when I heard the microwave ping and I was called down to dinner. There used to be a time when dinner would take at least an hour—there was cooking involved and much less plastic wrapping. It was only out of habit that I went to my room before I ate.

The smell of tomatoes and melted cheese wafted around the kitchen, mingling with the swirl of bluish smoke around mum. She smiled as I walked in, her lips twitching up at one end, her teeth still clamped around the cigarette dangling from her mouth. I took my place at the table, so used to seeing the two empty places beside that I barely glanced at them.

"I was wondering, Teya," Mum began, digging the end of her cigarette into the ashtray at the centre of the table, snuffing out the vile smoke in one violent stab. I looked up, my fingers curled around my fork as I worked at turning my food into mush. I waited.

"It'll be your birthday soon." She paused and caught my eye, her mouth forming a tired smile.

"And?"

"I wondered if you wanted to do anything special? You'll be twenty-one."

I watched as the bubbling cheese swirled into the red sauce, the layers of pasta congealing as it slowly cooled to a sticky brown mess. "What did you have in mind?"

Mum moved her fork to her mouth, wincing slightly as the cheese burnt her lips. She didn't wait to swallow before she answered me.

"Anything, Teya. Maybe you would like to go out for dinner? Somewhere nice, invite some friends and have a great night..."

"I don't have any friends," I cut her off, my eyes fixed on the red blob stuck to her bottom lip, watching as it bobbed up and down every time she spoke.

"You've got to have someone," she replied, and the blob slid off her mouth, trailing down her chin and falling back onto her plate. I watched as she scooped it back up with her fork and shoved it back into her mouth. "No one is that lonely."

I bit my lip to stop the torrent of things I wanted to yell at her, staring down at my plate of uneaten food.

"So?" she pressed. "What do you say? Shall I book somewhere?"

I swallowed and looked up. My mother's eyes were beseeching, shining with a vain hope that maybe she could fill a gap that over the years had become cavernous.

"Okay." I pushed the words through gritted teeth. "Let's have dinner, but don't go overboard and book something too fancy. It'll just be the four of us."

"Four?"

Something inside me snapped, an instant uncoiling of hurt

and frustration that felt so good in the moment, but left me empty and broken after. "Just you and me..."

"Teya."

I glared at her as I swept my hand in a gesture over the two empty chairs, their places perfectly set. "...Niven and Dad. Just family."

I ignored the spasm of guilt as my mother's face darted to the vacated spaces before finally settling on me as I made to storm out.

"Please, Teya."

Grabbing at one of the clean plates from the table, I flung it against the wall where it shattered with an encouraging smash. I snatched up the other just as Mum's fingers swept across it, desperate to save it. It hit the wall like the other, crashing against the wallpaper before landing in unfixable pieces on the floor.

"I'm that lonely!" I screamed at her, closing my eyes against the pathetic look on her face. She turned away from me, and calmly, without a word, she moved over to the shattered plates and began to clear them away.

"It's okay, Teya. Don't worry about it: I'll get some more tomorrow. It's okay."

My hands darted to my mouth as I desperately tried to force down the sob that tried to break free. I turned away from her and bolted upstairs. I knew I wouldn't be disturbed in my room by Mum. Oh, no, I would be left until the morning where we would both pretend that nothing had happened. I would eat my breakfast, and so would she, and we would be joined by two bowls that continued to remain empty.

Later that night as I reached to turn off my lamp, I fought my usual urge to check under the bed for monsters, or in the cupboards for ghouls. Partly because I knew I was far too old to believe in bogeymen, but mostly because I was terrified that I might actually find something.

My dad had always been the one to chase the imaginary monsters from under bed, all with just a wordless lullaby at his lips. It had been a soft, sweet tune that had been passed down from his mother from her grandmother, for generations. It was an old song, and because I had never found monsters in my room, I believed it really worked. Though that fateful day, so long ago, that same tune had been tingling at my lips, and still the monsters had come.

Closing my eyes against the darkness, I waited for sleep to come. Dreading it...needing it, fearing the crippling nightmares as much as I hoped for them. I slipped into sleep easier than I thought, turning my back against the heavily curtained window on the far wall. They always remained closed, no matter what light shone from behind them. It blocked out the view of the silhouetted trees, and the beautiful creatures I knew danced under their enchanted boughs.

CHAPTER THREE

The nightmare flowed like a river through my sleep, dark and cold and oh so frighteningly real. Music played on, a haunting melody that forced the feet to move when the heart and soul forbade it. Within the darkness, the monsters danced. A flash of fang, of horn, of skin and naked breast, as they moved they sang, and the shadows joined them. The trees followed as did the wind, while shards of light skipped down through the leaves, all of them swaying to a song that carried like a whisper and stayed like death.

Niven twirled like a dervish, frenzied in the hands of beasts and beautiful creatures with cold eyes and colder hearts. She smiled, I wept. She cavorted.

I wouldn't...

...couldn't.

Laughter joined the melody, enriching it further with the sound of folly and carelessness, bewitching the woods with notes that were almost tangible. The pace quickened, the fey a blur beneath the swaying oaks. Laughter turned to shouts and jeers, a wild call that was as feral as it was beautiful, echoing across the woodland in a cacophony of fear and wonder.

Music played on...

...as did the song...

...the singing and calling and crying and shouting...

Until...

...it stopped.

The trees ceased their manic sway, and the wind grew quiet, leaving nothing behind but the dark beauty that crept beside me and tasted my tears.

I woke with the threat of my cry against my lips, swallowed quickly down before it could truly surface. It was always the same nightmare, the same dancing, the same song...always watching as they took away my sister, while I did nothing. Repetition did nothing to quell the sense of hopelessness and fear it left behind.

With a quick, scribbled note to Mum I left, noting that the plates had been washed and stacked on the draining board in the kitchen. The shards of broken china had been bagged up and thrown in the bin along with my uneaten lasagne, everything was neat and tidy, everything put back in its place. The events of the night before had been carefully swept beneath the mounds of all the other unwanted memories. It really was a marvel that we both hadn't been committed.

The early morning chill bit against my skin, and despite the heavy coat I wore, it still managed to creep under the layers of wool, making me shiver. The sky was cloudless, an endless span of whisper pale blue, lit by an October sun that gave out only weak light and no warmth. Mist curled up around the distant hills, flooding over the fields past the nearby houses to coil around the naked trees that lined the road.

The village of Hazelminster lay deep within the Dorset

Downs, nestled neatly between many villages, hamlets and winding lanes that seemed to lead nowhere. Fog and mist always descended upon it like a blanket, concealing it. It was always somewhat charming when I was younger...almost magical, until I discovered what was beneath the ethereal tendrils of winter morning mist.

Perhaps it was morbid curiosity, or simple stupidity that I found myself standing under the looming shadows of the old oak trees that morning. The dilapidated wooden fence, the only barrier between me and the woods I hadn't stepped foot in since I was eleven. There was a stile further down the fence, leading onto a winding path that cut through the woods and down into the fields that lay beyond them. Come spring there would be a cascade of beautiful bluebells under the tree-tops, and daffodils would huddle along the entire length of the fence.

Even then, with winter nipping at my toes, I could hear the early morning dog-walkers deep in the thicket. The excited yelps of those lucky enough to be allowed off the lead echoed back at me, no fear in their throats as they bounded under the branches. It was a place just like any other, not so different from the hundreds of other woodlands that graced the country. Even my mother walked through sometimes, finding some short-lived peace in treading the last steps that Niven had taken. It seemed that it was only me who could sense the sinister nature of that patch of earth, who could hear the hushed voices of the trees as the wind whispered past.

Gripping my coat tighter, I swung my leg over the fence and hopped down the other side. Instantly my feet were lost in the cold mist that swirled around my ankles, though I could feel the knots of ivy that snaked out from trees beneath my shoes. I took three big steps forwards, feeling the unpleasant sensation in my chest as it started to tighten. My heart slammed inside me. My fear threatened to choke me. With sweating palms, I reached out to the ancient branches in front of me, daring myself to touch them and see them for what they really were...trees.

Glancing back over my shoulder, I breathed a sigh of relief to see the fence just yards away from where I was standing. It wasn't too far away, the wire netting below the wooden railing tatty from too many sheep trying to nibble their way through. It was built to keep the sheep from going into the woodland, I reminded myself, not for keeping the faeries in. With my head held high I strode past the trees, ducking past strings of ivy to clamber over the rotting corpses of fallen oaks. The sweet smell of mulch and forest spice filled my nose as I walked. The chill of the unrelenting wind dug in a little deeper, and I shivered.

I stopped walking when I reached a small clearing, the hazy sun above filtered down through bare branches, causing the shadows to coil around my feet. I closed my eyes, and for just a moment I could see Them, holding my sister as they pulled her away from me. I remembered the glimmer of iridescent wings, the flash of sharp teeth, the sound of an impossible song too enchanting to exist in any world but Theirs. Niven had joined so willingly. Completely charmed by beautiful strangers, she had fallen into their arms with abandon.

I opened my eyes to the sound of nothing...

No wind, no biting chill, no dancing shadows. The echoes of the early morning dog-walkers had gone with the whispers in the trees. There was nothing but stillness, as if everything around me was holding its breath and waiting.

Watching.

Fear snaked up my body, constricting around my throat so I could hardly breathe, crushing any hope of a decent scream.

The cracking of twigs underfoot echoed lightly as I stepped back, crashing through the silence as if an entire tree had fallen. I didn't know why I had come. Perhaps a part of me wanted to see a flash of perfection that would prove to me that They were real, that They still lingered out there somewhere. Perhaps I wanted to feel the same tiny glimmer of hope my mother felt, believing that despite the odds, Niven was out there and safe.

The fragment of hope I grasped at didn't come, but the growing fear that maybe...just maybe, something out there was watching me, clutched painfully at my chest. Stepping back, I scanned the trees for signs of movement, but even the wind had not picked up to stir the bare arms of the oaks above me.

I ran.

The forest mulch squelched beneath my shoes as I darted back to the fence without once looking behind me. Throwing my hands out in front, I grabbed the wood and hauled myself over it in a shockingly graceful jump, feeling splinters break off and bury under my skin.

Pressing my hand over my chest, I felt my heart race. My heaving breaths blew out in clouds, and my lungs ached from the cold air I was sucking back in. I clutched at the fence as my legs wobbled, grimacing as I felt the sharp splinters dig further into my palms.

"You alright there, love?"

My head snapped up to the left, locking eyes with the old man who worked in the local shop. Beside him sat his fat Labrador, muzzle streaked through with blades of grey showing he was as ancient as his master.

"Spot of asthma?" he continued, stepping towards me. "My granddaughter has it. I think you know her: little Matilda?"

I swallowed and stood straight, forcing a smile onto my face as the old man chatted to me. "I know Matilda. She's just got a new puppy; she walks it past our house every afternoon."

He nodded and gave me the same odd smile I received so often from others. He didn't do the little sympathetic head tilt though which was something. My family's story was well known in the village, and it was a quiet enough place to live that no other news had quite topped Niven's disappearance. The cards and casseroles and sympathetic words had long stopped, the glances and whispers had not.

"Ah, that'll be her. New puppy yes...yappy little bugger. You caught your breath yet?"

"I'm fine," I replied politely, moving away from the fence and therefore the barren woodland I had just fled from.

"You take care then." He tipped his flat cap at me and slapped his thigh gently, calling the dog to his heel. I watched as he walked on, chatting happily to his four-legged friend.

I slumped back home, knowing Mum would have left for work and that I would have the house to myself. She worked a full day on Thursdays as a receptionist at the doctor's surgery, and she usually stayed on later to catch up on the village gossip with her friend Margery.

My footsteps left little footprints on the frigid ground, exposing the lush green beneath that was crying out for winter to end. I liked it. The cold, broken season that left everything in its wake shivering and barren. There was always fragility to the world beneath the ice and snow, one that was not always apparent with the rumours of spring.

Once home, I tossed my keys onto the hall table, closing the door behind me quickly to lock out the cold that was trying to push past me. Shrugging off my coat, I hung it up and made to go upstairs, but my foot had barely touched the second step before I heard my mother shout at me from the living room. My heart sank.

"Teya? Is that you?"

"Of course it is! Since I am the only other person with a set of keys to this house."

I walked into the living room, jumping back slightly as Mum leapt off the sofa towards me.

"Where the hell have you been?"

"I went for a walk..."

I stopped talking at the look on her face, noticing the red rims around her eyes and the crinkles in her once neatly ironed blouse. It looked as if she had been wringing it.

"I called your mobile and you didn't answer. I rang college and they said you hadn't showed up."

"I forgot my phone..."

"Where were you walking?"

I shrugged, and sat back into one of the armchairs. "Nowhere really."

"In the woods? You were walking in the woods, weren't you?"

"So?" I snapped back. "You go walking up there all the time, and I don't snipe at you."

"You've not stepped foot up there since..."

I curled my lip as she failed to finish her sentence, and we both stared at each other for a moment. More tears leaked up over her eyes and trickled shamelessly over her cheeks.

"Seriously, what is the matter? I didn't go to College. I am an adult, not a child bunking off school."

"This is the matter!"

She shoved the piece of crumpled paper under my nose, her voice rising to an unpleasant octave as I snatched the note from her.

"I left this for you this morning," I said, confused at the anger she was launching my way.

"I thought...I thought, for God's sake, Teya, can't you see how this looks?"

I glanced down at my writing, the black letters spidery on the white page linked together in my usual messy scrawl.

Sorry for last night, it was out of order and I lost my temper. I guess I'm still struggling. It's just been too long since I felt much of anything, I can't keep shoving these feelings down and hope they go away. That's not how life works. Forgive me?

Love Teya. Xxx

P.s. I won't need a lift home tonight. ☺

I waved the note back at my mother, my mouth opening and closing in disbelief. My tongue stumbled over the words it wanted to snap at her.

"You thought this was a suicide note?" I pushed through gritted teeth, rising from the chair to face her.

"That's what it looks like."

I threw the note at her, watching as it floated pathetically to the floor, and wished I had balled it up first. "You think I would put a smiley face at the end of my suicide note?"

"You have a funny sense of humour, Teya."

I choked.

"I should bloody well think so too! Living all these years with you, you crazy woman! It really is a wonder that I've managed to put up with you for so long, why after all this time I haven't done myself in. Wrapping creepy presents for people who aren't around to open them, setting places for your dinner party of the macabre! They are never coming home! One of these days you have to accept that in the end, everyone will leave you!"

The palm of her hand forced my head to the side; the sound of skin slapping skin cut through the silence my rant had left behind.

"I received a phone call this morning," Mum said quietly.

"Oh?"

"I've been trying to get hold of you, Teya. He killed himself last night, and I thought you had done the same. Your dad hanged himself, and I couldn't find you!"

My eyes flickered to hers, my heart pausing for just a moment as her words began to penetrate, hurting so much more than her slap had.

"No..."

Mum said nothing as she wrapped her arms around me, stroking back my hair as I wept into her shoulder. In the very back of my mind, I had always hoped that one day he would come back to us. Return to tie up the broken strands of our family so we could move on together, finding some comfort in each other—I knew Mum felt the same and I knew deep down that she had yet to give up hope of him returning. You didn't set the table for four people you knew were never showing up.

I guessed it was one less imaginary mouth to feed.

CHAPTER FOUR

I sat next to Mum in the car, taking her hand in mine as she gazed out of the window at the blue skies. I wondered if she too was wishing that it rained. We pulled up to the church far too quickly, and I had to force myself to get out and step into the bitterly cold graveyard. Most of the mourners had already gone inside, most likely to escape the cold, but I watched as a few more trickled past. I didn't know them.

They gave Mum and me sad smiles as they walked by, wanting to share in the grief that I was not sure I really felt. I didn't know the man in the coffin. Dad had kept to himself, choosing a life of loneliness and misery, rather than sharing it with his long-suffering family.

"Mother!" I exclaimed, watching as she took a cigarette from her purse, lighting it before taking a satisfied drag.

"Well, obviously I can't smoke in the church dear, I'm just having one for my nerves. It's going to be a trying day."

"I hear lung cancer can be awfully trying too."

Mum sucked on her cigarette like an oxygen mask before

dropping it underfoot and stubbing it out with the heel of her shoe.

"Wonderful," I muttered. Mum shrugged.

I knew about half the people who had turned up, and even those were relatives that we barely spoke to. I felt like a stranger at my own father's funeral.

We entered the church together, our footsteps echoing loudly on the flagstones beneath us, sounding almost loud enough to wake the dead. Though not quite. I felt fraudulent sitting in the front pews reserved for his closest family, almost as if I were intruding on someone else's funeral.

To know that after so many years, we were still his closest family was heartbreaking.

Whilst I sat there listening to the vicar talk about what a wonderful person my father was, I hummed to myself. The wordless lullaby vibrated almost silently against my lips, so quiet that no one else could hear me. I no longer believed in the magical powers it was supposed to have, I simply wanted to sing it for my Dad.

We both watched with a growing numbness as they lowered the coffin into the ground, remaining silent as we tossed roses into the hole. Afterwards mum clung to my hand as we made our way out of the churchyard and down the lane to the local pub, I didn't pull away.

"I loved that man," Mum said finally, stroking my fingers as we walked down the winding path that led to the Rose and Crown.

"We both did, Mum. I just don't think it was enough for him."

She stopped suddenly, jolting my hand back before crushing me in a powerful embrace. She rarely hugged me anymore, and it made me more than a little uncomfortable.

"You will fall in love one day, sweetheart," she breathed against my cheek. "Make it enough for him."

I smiled genuinely against her, enjoying the comforting mix of smoke and perfume that could only belong to her. "Is this where you tell me no man is worth my tears?"

Mum unfurled herself from me and dabbed at her eyes. I raised my finger to wipe away the smudge of mascara that had bled down against her cheekbone.

"Wouldn't that make life easier? But no, Teya, that would be a lie. Love is painful, and when it is at its very best, it's excruciating. You are not really in love unless your heart aches and your body wishes it to stop, but your very soul refuses to let go."

I kicked at the little stones dotted along the pathway, not knowing what to say next. I had to wonder if that was how she had always felt about my father, with her heart beating only for him, as her rational sense begged her to move on. With a sigh I reached for her hand, continuing the short walk to the pub.

The Rose and Crown was a grotty place, with water stains on the ceiling, and beer stains on the carpets. My shoes made soft squelching noises as I walked to get drinks. The stools along the edge of the bar were threadbare with their stuffing leaking out, standing motionless like gutted pigs.

"Two Vodka Lemonades, please." The barmaid poured my drinks with only a fleeting glance at me. Fumbling through my purse, I handed her the money and waited for my change, grinding my teeth as she clicked her black nails along the counter. I took my change with one hand and poured the vodka down my throat with the other, enjoying the burn it left behind.

"You're Teya, aren't you?" a woman asked, stepping up to the bar. She looked to be in her early thirties with ash-blonde hair that was cut just a little too severely for her face. "I'm Cathy; I used to work with Jack."

I smiled politely at her, noting her red rimmed eyes. "I used to be his daughter."

Her eyes widened, a flush spreading across her cheeks. "I know...I'm sorry for your loss. He was a good man."

I winced. "I'm sure he was."

Cathy placed a hand on my arm, a gentle squeeze that took every ounce of strength I had not to flinch away from. "He never told me he had a daughter."

"He used to have two."

Her blush deepened. "I didn't know, I am sorry."

"It's okay," I said, relieved that she was no longer touching me. "I mean, it's not okay, but I understand why he wouldn't tell anyone. You knew a different Jack than me."

"Can I get you another drink?" Cathy offered, relief relaxing her face. "Not that I'm recommending you drown your sorrows in vodka."

I smiled, accepting her offer. "You can't drown misery, it won't die, but a drink would be great all the same."

I left Cathy at the bar and walked over to where Mum was sitting, huddled with a few relatives that were all staring at me. Clear liquid sloshed onto the table as I jolted the drinks down. I sat beside Mum and stared into my lap, feeling the heat of everyone's gaze bear down on me. I busied myself by going through my bag, calming my breathing by counting out its contents that, no matter where I went, always stayed the same. One purse, one chewed Biro, a shockingly old hair-brush, three tampons, my phone and a loyalty card for a free coffee with six more stamps to go.

My lips twitched slightly as I thumbed over the small zipped compartment, where lying in wait beneath some old receipts was a condom. It had been forced upon me by Mum, despite my assurances that I wouldn't need it for the near future. I did not have a boyfriend. I had never had a boyfriend. I was still waiting for my first kiss, but Mum wasn't having any of it. So I kept it with me, a sad reminder every time I opened my bag that no one really wanted me.

"Will you fetch me some sandwiches, sweetheart?" Mum asked, breaking away briefly from her conversation with Mrs Dustin, our next-door neighbour. Shrugging, I swallowed the last of my drink and moved to the sad table in the corner where the buffet was laid out. Someone had spilled their drink down the paper tablecloth, causing it to rip and hang down in a pulpy mess over the fake wood. I grabbed a paper plate and gazed over the spread of soggy sandwiches and stale crisps, shaking my head at the paper doilies that were scattered over the table in a poor attempt to add some class. I bundled a few egg and cress rolls on top of a ham and pickle sandwich, took a handful of crisps and a few very anaemic looking sausage rolls. I decided to avoid the shiny, slightly mottled cocktail sausages like the plague. I picked up a slice of pizza for myself and watched as the napkin soaked up the excess grease like a sponge. I left it on the table and slumped back to Mum.

"Are you not eating anything?"

"If I found something edible, I would eat something."

Mum glanced away from her food to give me a look, eyebrows disappearing into her hairline as she silently begged me not to make a scene. "Go get yourself another drink, and one for me."

She slid a note across the table, and I silently took it and pushed my way through to the bar.

"I'm so sorry about your father, Teya."

I glanced up from my drink, watching as some cousin I

faintly recognised sidled up to me. I said nothing, wondering why people wouldn't leave me alone.

"Our family prayed for Niven to come home, we really did. The loss of a child is unbearable, unthinkable. We never gave up hope that she would be found, maybe... if perhaps there had been some trace of Niven, some answers...closure."

I snorted into my glass, relieved that I wasn't the only one that thought Niven would have been better off dead. Maybe we could have all coped with that.

My cousin Maria stayed beside me and for a brief, uncomfortable moment, she placed her hand upon my arm, on the exact spot where Cathy had rested hers.

"If you ever need to talk, Teya..."

I shrugged off her arm, gulping back a large mouthful of Mum's drink. "Oh? So where have you and the rest of this miserable family been for the past ten years?"

Maria opened her mouth to say something, and I noticed she had lipstick smeared across her two top teeth. "I..."

"You abandoned us, Maria, just like Dad did."

"I'm so sorry," she said, repeating the phrase I had been hearing a lot of, the words becoming meaningless. "You're right: we should have been there for you both. We didn't know what to say, what to do."

I shook my head, sighing. "There was nothing you could do. It's not your fault, Maria."

"It's not yours either," she said softly. "You know that, right?"

I eyed up Maria's drink on the bar, giving her a small smile as I reached for it and swallowed it back. She grimaced.

"That was a whiskey for my Pops."

"Order him another on me." I coughed, giving her the change I had in my hand. I started to walk away, but she caught my arm.

"Don't blame yourself, Teya. That's what your dad did—it won't help anyone."

I nodded, pulling away and feeling the floor beneath my feet wobble. "It's a little bit my fault."

I walked away and stepped outside, feeling the cold air against my too hot cheeks. It was getting dark, the winter sun sinking early behind the hills, setting the sky on fire before the frost crept in.

I was going to sit at one of the benches and clear my head, but I carried on walking instead, my mind numb. There was a part of me, deep, deep down that wished I had turned back to the pub and continued eating dinner with ghosts. That small part of me wanted nothing more than to wake up in the morning with a hangover, and the relief that I wasn't completely insane. It was easy, safe, and strangely comfortable.

But I didn't go home, I went into those woods.

CHAPTER FIVE

$\mathcal{I}$ stood against the fence and stared through the dark shadows, standing still with the absence of breeze, and waited. Goosebumps prickled against my arms, and something deep inside remembered the cold, making me shiver. I had left my coat behind with Mum, and the frigid wind bit through the black silk of my dress with razor sharp teeth. It was nothing less than a miracle that I didn't succumb to hypothermia. After so many years of fearing the woods and the monsters within, I thought how anticlimactic it would be to die from my own stupidity.

I clambered over the fence with very little grace, landing in an undignified heap on the other side with my dress crumpling high around my thighs. As I stood, I felt the silk catch on a nail in the rough wood, and I closed my eyes as the fabric split, revealing the hem of my black knickers. Standing at the edge of the woods, I took in a shaking, furious breath and shouted.

"You did this to me! I'm wearing this because of you!" I jumped as my echo screamed back, but spurred on by anger, I stepped forward. A bitterness clouded over the fear that usually bubbled through me when I glimpsed those trees, an unpalatable blend of hate, guilt and loss finally set free amongst the waiting trees.

"Can you hear me?" I screeched. "Why didn't you take me?"

The trees began to sway as the wind picked up, the whole wood suddenly moved as if taking a breath. It carried with it no beautiful voices, no answers to my questions, only my echo as it faded through the branches.

"You had me!" I continued as my breath caught. Angry tears burned against my eyes, and I dashed them away quickly before they could fall. "Why wasn't I enough for you?"

I choked on a sob and rested my back against one of the oaks, feeling memories flood me as I remembered taking Niven's hand and leading her into the woods. I sincerely doubted whether all the substances in the world could dull the constant presence of my guilt.

"I need my sister back," I breathed, hating myself for not saying I wanted her back. Despite everything she was, Niven held our family together, it hadn't survived without her. I had to wonder if perhaps it would have survived without me.

My voice had barely carried past my lips, and therefore it did not echo. There was nothing around me but quiet.

Silence.

Even the wind, for just a moment, stopped screaming, and the trees became still. My anger faded as quickly as it had come, leaving me trembling. I was alone in the darkness, my pounding heart the only sound.

I nearly ran home.

I came so...so close to running home.

Every muscle in my body ached as I braced myself against the urge to flee.

I could taste the coppery tang of blood as I bit my lip so hard it bled. I stood still, peering into the black, allowing the spicy scent of fallen leaves to fill my senses. I took a step forward, pressing my hand against a low branch to steady myself while reaching out to grasp another branch with the other. Slowly I dragged myself deeper into the trees, forcing my protesting body onwards until I could no longer see a way out. I was surrounded by woodland, completely lost within its darkness, and the only thing I could hear was my own voice inside my head telling me what a fool I was. My drink-induced bravery was fast wearing off, leaving me alone with a swirling sick feeling in my stomach. I lowered myself onto the log of a fallen tree, feeling the moss damp against my legs, and closed my eyes.

When I opened them again it was staring at me.

A naked, thin creature had perched itself two feet away from where I was sitting. Its huge eyes were an unnerving black, and seemed to shine despite the darkness. It watched me stare, cocking its long neck to the side. As if it sensed I was no danger, it crawled closer, stretching its rake-thin body over the ground, clawing at the earth as it moved.

"Jesus," I muttered, slowly pushing myself up from the log as I braced myself to run. The log refused to take my weight, and my fingers crumbled through the ancient wood, my hand swallowed by the rotting hole. I swore loudly and the creature, just inches away from my face, recoiled like a snake. It rocked back and forth, drawing its blue-grey lips over its teeth, and hissed.

Frantic, I tugged at my hand, but the log refused to surrender and I remained stuck. The imp-like thing remained where it was and smiled at me, revealing a mouthful of needle-like teeth. I watched as it leant back upon its haunches, widened its mouth and let out an oddly beautiful cry. Its head snapped back to me the instant the echo died away, tossing its blanket of silvery hair over its shoulder, revealing the surreal womanly body that was hidden beneath it. There was haunting, strange and delicate beauty about her, a wild thing...feral.

She inched closer to me, and I could only look on dumbly with my heart crashing against my ribcage. From the cold smile on her face, I knew she could hear it. Sweet, cloying breath swept over my skin as she leant over me, tracing my cheek with her fingertips. Her touch was like ice, and I suddenly knew what it felt like to be touched by something with no soul. She moved her hand to mine, wrenching it from the decaying wood with such force that the jagged splinters tore at my skin.

"Ow! Christ!" I snapped through gritted teeth, watching as blood pooled to the surface of my arm, and trickled down. Her head turned down to my hand, still grasped in her own, and she watched as red slithered down over my fingertips. She licked her lips.

"Lily!"

Her head spun around to stare into the shadows; I followed her gaze but could only make out the faint outline of the trees in the darkness.

"Drop it."

She snatched her hand back, her long fingernails grazing my skin as she did so. She snarled at me before she skulked back towards the shadows, to where the voice continued to call to her. I stood up, brushing off the moss that covered my dress, and scanned the tree line. I knew something else was out there, and I didn't like not knowing where it was. Nothing moved within the shadows, nothing disturbed the under-growth...I swore that nothing was behind me until I felt the hand upon my shoulder.

"Did I frighten you?"

I jumped about a foot in the air, my scream echoing back at me, breaking the silence with the sound of my terror. I scrambled away, forgetting the old log that was directly behind me, and flew backward over it. I landed in a heap, instantly tangled in the knotted strings of ivy that covered the floor. I looked up, and for a moment every coherent thought vanished from my mind, leaving me slack-jawed and dumb.

I knew he wasn't human: no human could have looked like he did...so utterly beautiful that he made Luthien herself look plain. His eyes were deep violet, framed with thick dark lashes that were striking against his pale skin, and they were ageless. He looked as if he lingered in his late twenties...but those eyes betrayed that apparent youth, and I didn't wish to take a guess at how many years they were hiding. Dark hair curled against the nape of his neck, not quite black, but a vast hue of browns, golds and espresso blending against each other to create a colour I had no name for. The wind caught the midnight strands, lifting them away from his face to reveal delicately pointed ears. He towered over me, lean and strong and agile, his full mouth twisted into something almost like a smile...though not quite. My heart hammered away within my chest, and he tilted his head, lips curving as he listened.

I knew that I was staring, I knew I was staring with my mouth open, but my brain had all but melted and I could do nothing about it.

"Are you lost?" he asked, his voice soft with a hint of an accent I couldn't quite place. "You seem like you are to me."

I opened my mouth to reply, but nothing came out. I could do nothing but reach for his hand as he held it out to me, helping me to my feet.

"I'm not lost," I said, finally finding my tongue, and kick-starting my brain. "I know where I'm going."

"Do you now?" he replied, keeping hold of me.

"I need to go through the woods, I need to get something back." I wanted to pull my hand back, but something told me that he wouldn't let me go if I tried.

"What are you looking for?"

"Something that was taken from me."

"Why don't you go home instead?" He let go of my hand and shoved me in the direction I had just walked. "Keep going and stay on the path."

He pressed against the small of my back, I could feel his fingers through the thin fabric of my dress. Despite myself, I leant into his touch, and with little force, he pushed back and I stumbled.

His voice was soft and warm. A gentle lull to it made me want to please him...as if everything he said was solely to help me, to keep me safe. His words enticed a heaviness in my mind, a fog that dulled everything else, erasing the fear with a whispered word. Like an obedient pup, I placed one foot in front of the other and began to walk away.

"Wait!" I spluttered, shaking the sudden fog from my mind. "Don't do that!"

"Do what?"

I spun around and stood on my tiptoes to meet his eyes—I doubted I looked half as intimidating as I had hoped. "Whatever magic you are doing! Stop it."

"It is called a Glamour," he smiled, showing teeth. "I am not making you do anything you do not wish to do."

"I want to go into the woods."

His smile vanished, and he stepped closer, closing the small gap between us. I backed up, dropping my gaze at the sudden darkness glinting in his eyes. "Do you indeed?"

"Please leave me alone."

"Do you want me to leave you with Lily?"

I glanced at her, shrinking back as her black eyes met mine. "No..."

"So, you want me to stay?"

"No...I..."

He outstretched his hands, a grin lifting his lips. "I cannot do both, either you wish me to go or to stay."

"Can you not go and take her with you?"

"No."

"Why?" I asked, frustrated at the circles I found myself going in.

"I do not want to."

"You're one of them, aren't you?" I began. "A faerie?"

"Are you asking me or telling me?"

"You're a faerie," I said again. I swallowed, remembering fragments of faerie lore I had researched over the years. I guessed there had to be some truth hidden amongst the stories and role-play games. "You can't lie, can you?"

He obviously didn't like me pointing out a weakness, because his entire stance changed, evolving into something far more dangerous. He raised an eyebrow, inviting me to point out more, and never one to turn down a dare, I continued.

"I know that cold iron will kill you."

I jumped as he laughed at me, the tension dispersing as quickly as it had come. "Do you even know what cold iron is?"

My cheeks heated as he mocked me. "No."

"I thought not, else you would have possibly armed your-self with some before wandering through these woods. Why not just go home, girl, and stop pretending you have the courage to continue. I can smell the fear on you."

"I'm...not going home!" I snapped, and silently cursed myself for spluttering.

"Go!" Not a request, but a demand, and one that nearly had me fleeing the woods. His tone resonated with impatience, barely concealed violence showed beneath clenched fists and I knew I was really pissing him off.

"What do you want from me?" I asked quietly, wondering if I could out run him if it came down to it. I glanced down at his long legs. I sincerely doubted it.

He glanced down at Lily, who was sitting near his feet, and kicked her away with his foot. She hissed at him, drawing her knees close to her body, and turned her eyes to me, hatred burning within them.

"I guess I am bored," he replied wistfully, reaching up to run his fingers through my hair. I stiffened at his touch and raised my hand to push him away, but he caught it in his own, gripping it tight. He squeezed, and I felt my skin bruise. "Today, I am helping you find your way home because I am bored. Perhaps if you had found me tomorrow I would have led you further into the woods and watched you die."

"You're hurting me..." I said as I took a breath, feeling it shudder all the way up my throat before bubbling from my mouth as a pathetic gasp.

"Good," he sneered, leaning closer. "But I am by far not the scariest being out there."

"I need to get my sister," I pleaded as a cruel smile broke out over his face. "Please let me go."

"She is in the woods?"

"Yes."

"When did you have the misfortune of losing her?"

"I was a little girl, and..."

He cut me off with a quick bark of laughter, a sound that rebounded off the bare trees and seemed to mock me with every echo. Angered, I pushed him off me and he took a step back, grinning.

"It has taken you half your life to get this far into the woods? You really are foolish are you not? Go ahead, little girl, wander into the darkness and something with sharp teeth will hunt you down and shred the skin from your bones. Whatever is left of you will be ground down and sold. Your very soul will be gleaned from your remains to be bottled for those rich enough to enjoy such things."

"Is that what She did to my sister?"

His eyes narrowed, "Who?"

"A faerie called Luthien took her..."

He shoved me roughly back against a tree and pain shot through my body. One hand tightened around my throat as the other wound in my hair to force me onto my tiptoes. His eyes were black, and he was too close to my face. I could feel his breath against my cheek, warm and filled with the scents of the forest.

"What did you say?" he snarled, forcing my head back hard so my teeth clattered in my skull. "Answer me!"

I opened my mouth, desperately trying to free my hands so I could free myself from his. Dark blobs floated before my eyes, and I could do nothing but gasp soundlessly as he choked me. With my coherent thoughts fleeing, I did the only thing I could think to do and brought my knee up hard, sinking to the ground beside him as he snarled in pain.

"What...what the fuck is wrong with you?" I gasped, clutching my bruised neck, gulping in air as if I would never get enough again. "You nearly throttled me!"

"Does Luthien have your sister?" he snapped back, pushing himself up gracefully from the floor as if I hadn't just forced him to his knees. His dark eyes were livid, and he towered over me with Lily creeping closer to snake around his legs. She drew her lips back and snarled.

"Why..."

"Does she?" he interrupted sharply, his voice laced with the promises of cruelty and dark things. "Is that where she is?"

I pushed myself to my feet. "Yes..."

He grabbed at my arm, and I tried to force him off as he pulled me back through the forest. I dug my heels in, clutching at his fingers as I desperately tried to prise him off me.

"Go home! Your sister is too far out of your reach."

He dumped me at the edge of the woods. I could see the rickety old fencing, and the soft glow of the lights in the nearby houses. I glared up at him. "Who the hell are you?"

I shrank back as he crouched beside me, dominating my personal space with his presence. He caught a strand of my hair as the wind flicked it towards him, and forced me to bend closer. "Do you know how boring eternity can be? It gets so tiresome, watching the things you take wither and crumble away, to spend so long picking the right one only to watch as it weeps itself to death..."

"You didn't answer my question."

"You demand my name and yet have not given me yours," he said softly, releasing my hair and leaning back. "Stop pursuing what is lost, girl."

"My name is Teya," I said as he made to walk away, and I grabbed his arm as I desperately clung to any hope of finding Niven. "Help me find her! Please!"

I dropped his arm instantly at the look he shot me, knowing instinctively that very few people grabbed him and remained with all four of their limbs attached. Beside him,

Lily looked ready to lunge at me, held back only by a sharp kick.

"I believe I have helped you enough, more than you deserve, you ungrateful girl. I have no reason to care if you live or not."

I pulled back the strap on my dress as it slid down my arm, shivering against the cold wind and wishing for my coat. He watched the movement with violet eyes, his gaze lingering over the naked skin just above my neckline.

"Why show me the way home then?" I demanded, "If you care so little about my life, why help me? And stop looking at my boobs!"

"You don't even have a jacket," he sighed, suddenly sounding exasperated and for a fleeting moment, the coldness surrounding him lifted.

"I'll find her," I said, pleased that my voice held. He only shrugged and gestured towards the trees. I stepped away from him with the expectation of him grabbing me back, but he let me go.

Lily, however, moved closer, twisting herself around my legs like a dog. She opened her hand to reveal a mushy pile of squashed berries, their juices tainting her fingers. They should have repulsed me, but my mouth overflowed with saliva and I had to swallow hard to stop myself from dribbling. They oozed a strange oily juice, blackish in colour with blobs of green that dripped through Lily's long fingers and onto the floor. I shouldn't have wanted to lick them, taste them, shove them in my mouth until I choked upon them, but I couldn't remember why.

I moved to take the fruit from Lily's outstretched hand, my own fingers trembling with anticipation, but he took them first. Without taking his eyes off me, he pressed a berry to his mouth, sinking his teeth into the flesh until it popped. Juice bled over his lips, and it was a hard internal battle on my part not to lean forward and lick it off.

"We shall see," he whispered, breathing the strange and intoxicating scent of the berries into my face. He then took hold of Lily's sticky hand and walked away, disappearing into the vast shadows of the oak trees.

CHAPTER SIX

I watched him leave, watched as the trees and darkness swallowed him up—unlike me, he wasn't afraid. I turned to face the way I had come, the way he had pointed out with his cold smile. I really did contemplate going home. At the very least, I could have popped back and changed my clothes, perhaps grabbed a bag that contained more than loose change and an old hairbrush. I could have nabbed a coat whilst I was at it ...put some trainers on...

Ah, but I knew if I stepped out of those woods, I would never again have the guts to go back in. For all I knew, they would not let me back in. Not everyone who wandered the woods found themselves in Faerieland.

I walked on, keeping straight even though there was no true path to speak of, only a twisting clearing where the vines and shrubs held back. The semi-frozen ground beneath my feet crunched with each step, and the silly heels on my feet slipped around on the frosted mulch. I had to keep my hands outstretched to catch myself from falling flat on my face. I was bloody freezing. Every hair on my arms stood up, desperately trying to retain heat as I trembled helplessly. My

breath ghosted in front of me, teeth chattering, heart thumping, body shaking...every fibre of my body fought to stay
warm and failed. It fought to dampen the fear that bubbled up
within me, to give me the courage I thought I had to go
on...and failed.

My chest felt too tight, the puffs of breath floating out in
front of me were too quick, too erratic...it was just too dark,
and unknown and frightening and I had no idea where I was
going. There were things lingering in the shadows that I had
no name for, echoes of creatures I had not heard before
screamed through the branches. The trees watched, the wind
listened...and...and...and there was no way in hell I was going
any further.

"Oh, shit," I cursed, my heart sinking as I stared at the
mass of knotted branches that barred my way back. "Bloody
hell!"

The wind pushed the trees forward, causing them to look
as if they were bending low to listen to me. Their ancient
branches creaked in the breeze, gnarled arms outstretched to
forbid me my right to leave. With my way back blocked, I
breathed deep and forced myself to walk on. I tried to ignore
the little voice in my head telling me how stupid I had
been...it annoyed me that it had assumed the tone of the faerie
who tried to show me the way home.

As I walked, I began to notice subtle changes in the trees.
Tiny buds grew upon their bare branches, blushing a pale
pink, shining with the hope of new life. Some of those buds
had already turned to lush leaves, growing furtively over the
apparently sleeping forest. I watched one expand as if yawning, unfolding wetly into a beautiful formed leaf. I looked
ahead, and noticed for the first time that the sun shone
through the canopy of full trees, all in various stages of
spring. Some bent slightly with the weight of their leaves,

while others rained down sweet smelling blossoms that bathed the ground in soft perfumed snow.

I had left the Rose and Crown on the brink of winter at eight thirty in the evening, so I could only marvel at how impossible it was to stand under the trees and watch as spring unfolded before my eyes. Even the air had warmed up, and I no longer had to wrap my arms around my body to keep the cold out. I kept them wrapped around myself, not for the warmth, but for the fear of falling apart if I let go.

It was so much more than beautiful, but as I stared open-mouthed at the scene before me, my mind lingered on the little fey creature named Lily, and I wondered what other dark fey waited beneath the perfection of the wakening trees. I felt myself being watched, I had that unnerving feeling at the back of my neck, a sharp tingle that caused my body to go cold. I knew that although I could see no other being around, I was far from alone.

As the sun rose higher, I found myself following the light into a large clearing surrounded by newly flowering saplings. Sunlight warmed my face as it filtered through the trees, leaving the chill of winter far behind. The sound of a little spring trickled nearby, banked by lush green grass covered in wildflowers. I could hear the waters roll over the rocks, smell the damp, glistening petals of the flowers that bloomed around its edge. It was a paradise, overflowing with scents and colours I had never known before.

Everything about it was bathed in perfect beauty...save for the odd metallic sound that seemed so out of place in such a glorious meadow. I heard the clink and creak before I determined where it was coming from. The sounds disturbed the soft melody of the water and echoed mechanically over the little paradise.

I turned and left the stream behind me, walking down to

where the noise was coming from, slipping on the dew covered lush grass. In the distance, I could hear bird song, bright and lovely as it slipped over the creaking sounds I was following. The noise jarred the pretty song, ruining it. As I moved closer, a new sound joined the strange creaking.

Tiny cries mewed from a cluster of trees, and I gaped as I took in the sight of dozens of small golden cages as they swayed in the wind. Each one was heavily ornate and glistened as it caught the sunlight. The chains they were strung by creaked and chimed and clinked against the branches, creating the metallic orchestra. At first, I thought the cages contained little birds, but when I looked closer I could see they were each packed with tiny, strange creatures.

They gazed at me through the bars, huge eyes sparkling with tears that rolled down their perfect faces. Many of them had curled their long, delicate fingers around those of its neighbour, clutching hands so tightly that their knuckles strained. One reached out for me, stretching its arm as far as it could through the bars, its face twisted with fear. Its other hand never left the one standing beside it. Deep black eyes beseeched me from behind the bars, milky blue cheeks damp with tears. Some shivered, their naked little bodies hairless and smooth, with iridescent wings that trembled behind them. I raised my hand to the latch on the closest cage, out of reach to those trapped inside it. I hesitated, fingers lingering over the lock and wondered...just for a moment...if there was a reason they were behind bars. I quickly shrugged off that thought as I spotted one of the thinner creatures. It stood near the back of the cage, staring up at me, arms wrapped around a tiny form that whimpered pitifully against its mother's breast. With my mind made up. I released the catch.

The door swung open instantly, releasing fifteen winged prisoners that all whooped in delight at their new-found freedom. My screams joined their delighted shrieks as they suddenly turned on me, the rest of them howling in their cages, rattling the bars with pained determination in a vain attempt to get out...and get to me. I swatted at them with my hands, grabbed them by their legs and pulled at their horns, desperate to get them off me. Tearing one from my shoulder, I gasped as it left its pointed teeth embedded in my skin. I tossed it to the ground and brought my heel down hard upon its squirming body. I felt it pop beneath me as I ground it into the dirt.

"GET OFF ME!" I screamed, thrashing my hands as the creatures flew down at me and latched needle-sharp teeth into my bare skin. I squashed three more, and they began to hesitate, watching from a distance and licking the blood...my blood from their blue lips. The infant in its mother's arms lapped red from her fingers, suckling deeply and greedily while its mother tilted its head and smiled at me. I wished I had squashed them all.

When they were done glaring at me, they threw back their heads and screamed into the sky, wings stretched wide as they flew away. The others still trapped inside their cages screamed too, a combined piercing screech that had me clamping my hands over my ears. They all reached through the bars on the cages, the sadness in their eyes replaced by a ravenous hunger that caused them to salivate green gunk down their naked bodies. I shivered and took a step back, pressing my fingers to the bite marks on my neck. With a trembling hand, I tugged out two slivers of teeth, held them in my palm and watched with a sickly feeling as they dripped a burning poison over my skin. I blinked and looked up at the cages that had grown suddenly silent. They all stood completely still, dark eyes fixed upon me, and each one wore the same frenzied grin. One stepped closer, and it smiled cruelly as it drew its finger across its neck.

I caught its meaning perfectly.

I backed away and wiped my sweaty hands down my dress, and I knew that it wasn't just the fear and vodka that was causing the sick feeling in my stomach. I ran towards the stream, the jeers of the caged little monsters fading as I left them behind, the bodies of their fallen friends crunched beneath my feet as I darted away. I slumped on the riverbank, hands shaking as I forced water down my throat, desperate to wash the acidic taste of bile from my mouth as I vomited into the water.

"Little bastard," I gasped, before I pulled myself weakly to my feet. The meadow spun, whirling and tilting around me and before I knew it, I was doubled over again, dry heaving into the grass. I forced myself up with shaking legs and stumbled through the trees. My stomach cramped and twisted, and all the while the world around me refused to stay still. I half crawled my way forwards into the cool shade of the trees, and I leant back against an old oak with a rattling sigh. I closed my eyes and felt sweat bead against my skin, slipping down my face to sting my eyes. My left leg cramped, and agony shot up my thigh as I twitched and groaned. I didn't dare call out...I was too afraid of what would come looking for me if I made too much noise. There was blood in my mouth, I could taste the metallic tang against my tongue. I wiped my trembling hand over my lips and winced as they cracked.

"Come with me."

I barely had the strength to look up as something hovered over me. The effort to care was simply dwindling away.

"You are to come with me now." The rough voice was female, her words crackling as if she seldom had use for them. It was not warm or kind or comforting. The voice did not bring me hope. I cried out when her fingers coiled around my arm, tight enough to bruise. Long fingernails raked at my aching skin and left trails of blood beneath her hands.

"No..." I protested, as I tried to pull my arm back, but I was unable to dislodge her hold on me.

She knelt down beside me, allowing sunlight to fall upon her papery skin, and I could see that once...a long time ago, she had been lovely. Eternity had not been kind, and had taken any trace of beauty with its passing years leaving her haggard and broken. Her eyes were a filmy blue, and no longer sparkled, though I guessed that men had fallen at her feet when they had shone. Matted hair hung unwashed over her shoulders, lying in knotted clumps that were tangled through with brambles, leaves and dead things.

"No, no, child!" she snapped, while I tried in vain to pull away. Her fingers tightened, and with her other hand she slapped me hard around the face. My head rocked back, and the world flipped...and for a moment there was nothing but pain and darkness.

"Leave me alone!" I begged. "I've done nothing to you!"

She smiled then, cracked lips splitting to reveal a mouthful of broken teeth. A waft of old breath brushed against my face, and I felt my stomach roll again.

"You freed my picksies!" she hissed, spraying me with a glob of spit. "Two moons it has taken me to catch those little foul demons. I finally have enough to leave to wither in the sunlight, and then you happen by and set them free! Do you know what Slimy Soo could have got for their dried husks? The juices from their eyeballs?" Her horrible smile broadened. "The poison from their little mouths?"

I shook my head, my panic rising like my nausea.

"No, you don't!" Slimy Soo snarled. "A damn fortune, little bird, that's what you've cost me! Now I'm taking you instead, fair's fair, don't you think? You really couldn't expect me to work for so long and go empty handed, could you?"

I had thought the question was rhetoric so said nothing, but she slapped me again, demanding that I answered her.

"No," I mumbled, only because it was the smallest word that I could push from my mouth.

"Good girl," Slimy Soo replied as she tugged at my arm and dragged me to my feet. "Now come with me."

It was only a short walk to Slimy Soo's crooked little cottage, but my legs screamed at me with every step I took, and my head pounded. My body burned, chilled, ached. I just wanted to curl up and die, but the hag wouldn't let me. She didn't let go of my arm as she hauled me through the forest and said nothing as she pushed me through the door of her house and onto the dusty floor.

The cottage was made up of one large room. A cooking stove and basin stood in one corner, with a creaky looking bed in the other. A fire burned in the grate by the far wall, warming a pot filled with steaming liquid that trickled up over the top and spilled down the tarnished surface to hiss in the flames. A skinny tabby cat stretched itself in front of the glowing embers, kneading the rug while six hungry kittens fed from her. I pushed myself to my feet, dragging the sweaty hair from my face, and nodded towards the cat. "Isn't she meant to be black?"

Slimy Soo just smiled and slammed the door behind us as I watched while she turned the key in the lock, placing it in her pocket. She made no attempt at hiding where she put the key. We both knew that I lacked the strength to fight for it.

"What do you want with me?"

"Oh, you'll see my dear." She grinned. "Now let's get you cleaned up."

I watched with growing dread as she picked up a wooden

bucket that sat near the fire, bracing myself for what was coming next. I still screeched when the water hit me, and I had to wonder how cold it would have been if it were not for the fire. I trembled with the sudden cold, Slimy Soo grabbed at my hair and yanked a comb through it, ignoring my yelps as she wrenched the teeth through the knots and tangles. When she was finished, she shoved me to my knees, and I simply lacked the will to fight her as she scrubbed my arms raw with a lump of harsh soap.

"For the life of me I can't seem to wash the stink off you!" she snarled.

"Have you no children to snack on?" I hissed back, wrapping my arms around myself.

"What do you think is boiling away in my pot, little bird?" Slimy Soo smiled as she tossed a bundle of damp smelling cloth at me. "Now get dressed."

With the old hag watching, I stripped off my ruined black dress, and pulled on the rough woven smock she had given me. Its hemline floated down below my knees, and the neckline was too high and itched. I picked at the faded red fabric, my fingers trailing the broken blue stitches that had once held the seams together. It was filthy: the grime had actually sunk deep into the material and had blended with the weave. It was the only thing keeping the thing together.

"It will do." Slimy Soo huffed. "Shame you're not much of a looker, I could have got a lot more for you."

"You're going to sell me." It wasn't a question, just a realisation that hit me as unexpectedly as the water from the bucket. I wasn't sure what I thought she was going to do with me...but whoring me out hadn't crossed my mind. Nothing much had crossed my mind except the fear that I was going to throw up on her red dress, and that I didn't think I could live through another icy bath.

"For scraps, little bird," she said, "nothing more."

"Please..."

"Don't you 'please' me, girl! I'll get some coin for you if I must gut you and bleed you myself, understand me? Now be good and get some rest, we'll be leaving for the Midnight Market in a few hours. Try not to waste my time and die in your sleep."

She pointed to a dark corner of her house, watching as I settled myself onto a blanket on the floor. She turned to her stew and ladled some in a bowl for herself, slopping some on the floor for her cat. I was unsure if there really were children simmering in her dinner or not, but I could only be thankful that for the time being at least, it was not me.

I pulled the blanket tight and tried to ignore the stink that had bound itself to the coarse fabric. I cried out in pain just once as my legs cramped, and then my arms before everything from my neck down slowly grew numb. I should have been terrified, but for just a moment, I could only feel relief that the pain had gone.

I burned that night. Sweated...shook...convulsed and dreamt of things so nightmarish I would never forget them. I shivered...trembled...wept...dreamt and burned again. I had no one to tell me that I wasn't dying, no one to comfort or soothe or fetch painkillers. I only had an old hag in the corner, telling me I hadn't better die, which wasn't the same thing at all.

CHAPTER SEVEN

*S*ometime during the night, the skinny cat had abandoned her brood and curled up with me, seeming to enjoy the feverish heat I was giving off. Her scrawny body vibrated with purrs, and she kneaded her claws against me painfully, though I just didn't have the heart to push her away. We both jumped when the hag woke up, snorting from the creaking bed in the corner. The cat's fur spiked, her ears lying flat against her head before she darted back to the fireplace. The hungry mouths waiting for her latched on the moment she lay down with them.

"You!" Slimy Soo barked, pointing a finger in my direction unnecessarily, for it was obvious she was speaking to me. "Get up."

I groaned quietly and stood, bracing myself against the wall as I swayed. The restless sleep I had been granted had done nothing to dull the ache or fever, which left me wondering how much worse I could possibly feel. I wondered how long it was going to take me to die.

I didn't want to die, not alone. With a desperate glance around the cottage, I searched for a way out, knowing the door was locked. The windows were barred, the panes nailed shut. Slimy Soo turned to where I looked, grinning at me with a mouthful of yellow teeth.

"The last girl who tried to flee out of the window had her hands chopped off," she hissed, kicking me so sharply I fell to my knees. "Brush your hair, little bird, and wash your filthy face. We are leaving soon."

"Where are you taking me?" I asked, panic flooding my body, causing my head to spin. "What are you going to do?"

Slimy Soo just smiled, her crooked teeth poking out from beneath her lips. "You'll see. Now ready yourself, or I'll shave off your pretty red locks and wear them myself."

I fumbled in my bag for my hairbrush, and did my best to remove the tangles from my hair, leaving it to hang limp and greasy over my shoulders. I splashed my face with cold water from a bucket, washing away some of the sweat and grime that clung to my skin.

"Wear this, it's chilly out."

My hands reacted too slowly to catch the bundle of red fabric that was thrown at me, so it landed on the floor with a soft thump. I bent low and groaned as I unfolded the filthy scarlet cloak.

"Did you murder Red Riding Hood?"

Slimy Soo grinned at me, placing a finger to her lips with a wink, as if we were sharing some daring little secret. I shuddered as I wrapped the cloak around my shoulders, not wanting my thoughts to linger on what unlucky girl had worn the clothes before me.

"Now, what am I forgetting?" Slimy Soo mused, glancing around her dingy cottage before counting off tasks with her bony fingers. "Windows closed, fire out, cat fed..."

"Broomstick?" I offered, earning a sharp clip around my head.

"Ah, that's it...that's it. Here we are, little bird, we don't want you running off and getting lost now."

I watched in despair as she pulled out a length of thick rope from a drawer. I shook my head and forced my hands beneath my cloak, knowing how futile an attempt it was to avoid being tied up.

"Give me your hands, or I will hack them off."

"Where do you think I would go? I can barely walk, let alone run off," I argued, but I held out my hands because I didn't want to have them forcibly removed.

"I'm not taking any chances losing you. You will pay off your debt to me."

"With my life?"

Slimy Soo shrugged, knotting the rope tight around my hands so it pinched my skin. "If it comes to that, little bird. You have no one to blame but yourself."

How true.

The old hag chuckled to herself while she pulled the key from her pocket and unlocked the door. She kept a tight grip on my leash and gestured for me to step outside into the moonlight. Without a word, she turned the lock on her miserable cottage. It was a small blessing to find the cart behind the hag's home, which she had bundled all her wares upon. Boxes of glass jars and bottles were packed neatly in wooden crates, all labelled with jagged writing to reveal what was in them. Ground fingernails. Basilisk poison. Semen of centaur. Saliva of goat (distilled in alcohol). Infants' first laugh, both girl and boy. Virgin soul. Baby teeth...

I stopped reading after finding the jar filled with bloodied teeth, and settled silently beside the crates as Slimy Soo hitched up an old knackered-looking donkey to take us to market. The rocking movement of the cart played havoc with my delicate stomach, and surrounded by the hag's gruesome collection, it was all I could do not to throw up.

"The midnight market is a sight to behold, little bird!" Slimy Soo called from the seat of the cart. "You're in for such a surprise. Everyone likes surprises."

"Does anyone actually like your surprises?"

Slimy Soo laughed. A light, almost musical note softened the edge of her cackle. It was the sound of a spoiled youth, of wasted beauty. Of lost love. I smiled back, hoping her blackened heart pumped in ruins beneath her withered chest.

It turned out the Midnight Market *was* a sight to behold. Slimy Soo was right about that. The cart slowed down at the edge of a great slope, the lush moonlit grass giving way to rock that had been smoothed over by countless feet over countless years. The effect was almost bowl-like, with the imposing edge of a cliff looming over the far side. Within the silvery grey rock, crystals glistened beneath the moonlight. Blues, reds and golds all twinkled like stars, priceless and perfect and ignored by the traders that crowded every inch of the ground below. Looking down, I could only see a patchwork of brightly coloured canopies that sheltered the people beneath them, but I could hear the cries and shouts and bargaining of hundreds and hundreds of faeries.

With a click of her tongue, Slimy Soo ordered the donkey on. The poor creature gave a weary snort of discontent before dragging the cart downwards, and I had to cling on for dear life as it pulled us down the sharp incline. We joined the bustling market seamlessly, with Slimy Soo knowing exactly where she wanted to go and able to get there without losing her way amongst the labyrinth of carts, tables, banners and people. I quickly lost track of where we were going and had no hope of finding my way out again on my own.

When we finally stopped, Slimy Soo pulled out a folding

table from the back of the cart and began to set out her trinkets. Thankfully, she didn't expect me to help, but instead
dragged me out by my bound hands and tied me to the table
leg. I tried to make myself as small and inconspicuous as
possible, hoping that if no one could see me amongst the
noise and chaos...then perhaps I could just curl up and die in
peace.

On either side of me were carts brimming with things to
sell. On the right, a tall pointed looking man sold wonderful
smelling fruit and sugared sweets. To my left, a pretty man
sold jars of fat little creatures with no faces. It seemed that
everything was for sale at the Midnight Market, from the
seemingly impossible to the utterly macabre. You could quite
literally sell your soul for anything.

I watched as the fey wandered by. Beautiful creatures that
barely glanced down at me glided past in silks and finery.
Some clutched at the dainty hands of children, whose glittering eyes shone with a cruelty no human child could ever
possess. One small girl crouched beside me, her pink eyes
twinkling with an almost innocent glee. Her lips curved into a
small smile that widened when she caught sight of the bruises
over my arms.

"Mama!" she called. "I want this one."

The elfin child poked me, prodded me and grinned as I
winced as she jabbed at my arm. I suddenly pictured myself
as one of those poor tortured Barbie dolls that you found with
bored toddlers and I shuddered. The child ran her cold finger
over my face, and without much forethought, I jerked my
head up and bit her hard. The girl screeched, and her mother
slapped me.

"Wretched thing!" snarled the woman, turning to Slimy
Soo. "If she has caught anything, you darkling hag, I'll have
your head!"

"Now, now my lady," Slimy Soo said quickly. "My sincere apologies to you and your child, have mercy, the girl will not go unpunished, I promise you."

The fey woman glanced from her daughter to me, her own pink eyes burning with fury. Her next words were quiet, though there was no mistaking the malice in her soft, haunting voice.

"See to it that she is. Leave her out to rot."

Slimy Soo nodded, and eager to appease the woman she pulled a shiny marble from behind her ear and held it out for the little girl.

"A gift for your beautiful daughter, madam," she said, holding it out for the child to snatch away. "Wish for something nice."

The woman had barely disappeared into the crowd before the old hag turned on me, clouting me sharply around the head.

"Don't you ever do that again!" she hissed, raising her hand and smacking me again. My head snapped back with the force of her blow and pounded sharply on the cart behind me. "I will sell you for scraps...so help me."

"Better that, than that little monster's plaything," I snapped back.

"Do you think?" she whispered, crouching low to face me. "Is it better to be harvested bit by bit by creatures you have never even read about? To watch as they reap your soul and bottle it for the rich. To spend eternity behind glass, gathering dust as you lie forgotten? Sometimes they like to watch you die, see how long they can draw it out, days...weeks...years."

I didn't even wince as she placed her wrinkled hands on my face, using her fingertips to catch the tears I no longer had the strength to hold in.

"Leave me alone."

Slimy Soo chuckled as she turned her back on me and returned to her table to sell a jar of floating heads to a gentleman with huge black wings. He looked down at me, his dark eyes narrowing as he took in my sickly appearance. He murmured something to the witch, pointing a bone white finger in my direction. I recoiled in horror when Slimy Soo mentioned a price, but mercifully he shook his head and walked away.

"Damn you!" she seethed. "You'll be dead before I get anything for you."

"Won't you be reprimanded for selling faulty goods?"

"Just keep quiet. I will hear no other words from you, lost bird, understand? I will not be taking you home with me. If you are still bothering me come sunrise, I'll boil your bones where you lie and have you for tea."

"There you go," I spat. "Now you sound more like a witch."

I sat in silence and watched as faeries came and went, thankful that no one seemed to want to purchase me. It was with a cold and hopeless realisation that I acknowledged I would never go home again. I wouldn't find Niven, I wouldn't bring her home and my mother would have lost what was left of her family.

I must have fallen asleep because I was suddenly jolted awake by an icy hand against my arm. I blinked several times to clear my vision, but the world around me tilted anyway, so I closed them again.

"Do you want that one, my dear?"

I forced my eyes open to see what horrible thing was trying to buy me, and my heart sank. Very slowly, I pulled my arm away but the ice-cold fingers only latched harder. Lily smiled, her black eyes staring deep at me as she reached for the cord that bound my hands together. She terrified me more than Slimy Soo, or any of the other creatures I had met. There was a haunted, wild quality about her, and she looked like death. Not like she had died, no… Lily looked as if she would feel comfortable harvesting souls.

"Not you," I breathed, recoiling. "Please."

Lily's smile widened, showing pointed teeth, and then she tilted her head back and chirruped her odd little call. My head flicked to where she had turned, and I allowed a small amount of my fear to turn to hope.

He moved painfully slowly towards us, running his long fingers over the glass bottles. He grabbed at Lily's hand and pulled her away without as much as a glance at me.

"What do you want for the girl?" he asked in a bored voice, not looking away from Slimy Soo.

"Three vials of blood and the memory of your first love."

"Come now, she'll be dead by morning." he replied laughing, cupping Lily's face in his hand and turning it away from him.

"She's cost me a lot more." Slimy Soo snapped. "That's my price."

Pushing Lily away, he stepped closer to Slimy Soo who scowled up at him. "How about one vial of blood and a month of dreams? That is a very generous offer, do you not think?"

My mouth dropped open as he openly haggled for me. It would have been tempting to tell him to stuff it, if I weren't quite so desperate.

"Do you want her or not?" Slimy Soo said, and a beautiful smile spread over his face.

"You see," he began, as he leant over the table to whisper to the old hag, "my servant seems to have taken a liking to the girl, and I am fond of her...loyalty, if you understand me? I am rather reluctant to displease her."

Slimy Soo drooped a little where she stood, and I remembered how I had all but melted when I had stared into those violet eyes.

"Two vials then," she gushed, a deep rose flooding the wrinkles of her cheeks, "and I want a decent supply of dreams from you. I don't suppose there are any nightmares lingering around in that pretty head?"

"None that you will be able to reach."

"Pity."

Slimy Soo held out her hand for his, and I watched as she closed her fingers around his wrist and sliced it open with her fingernail. Blood pooled over his skin, dripping down into a glass vial Slimy Soo held beneath with her free hand. She filled both vials to the brim and never spilled a drop. With a satisfied smile, she placed them beside the baby teeth on her cart.

"Now close your eyes," the hag ordered. "This may sting a little."

Whereas he had shown no reaction to getting his wrist cut, he tensed when Slimy Soo placed a hand on either side of his head. He closed his eyes, his fists balling at his sides as the hag began to pull a swirling fog away with her fingers. Blues and purples glimmered against the black, and then there were flashes of green...flecks of pink, all mingling together like an oil spill. She coiled the ghostly mist just like strands of thread, winding the fog tightly around her hands until I could barely see them beneath the dreams. She took a wooden box from the cart, and carefully lifted the lid to sweep the dark fog in amongst the other collection of dreams, and snapped it shut.

"That was more than a month's worth, witch!"

"And yet you are robbing me blind!" snapped Slimy Soo. "Now take her away before she keels over. I do not give refunds."

He finally looked at me, his eyes dark and cold as they travelled the length of my body. I wanted to believe that he was trying to help me, because the alternative was too much for me to think about. I couldn't dwell on what a man would want with a woman who was too weak to defend herself.

"Go home," he ordered Lily, grabbing her hand as she made to touch me again. She hissed, and he kicked her. "Now!"

Lily glared at me, her black eyes filling with tears before she turned her back on me and ran off into the shadows. I shuddered, knowing that somehow I had made an enemy. I was studying the shadowy trees where Lily had disappeared when I was suddenly lifted off my feet and scooped up into strong arms as if I weighed nothing.

"I think I can walk," I said.

"I doubt it."

He was right: with my head against his shoulder any fight I had left just vanished. I sighed, feeling the subtle sting of tears push against my eyes, and I swallowed a sob.

"Are you going to kill me?"

"I have no idea what I am going to do with you," he replied, sounding disappointed. "But no, I am not going to kill you, the picksie venom will probably do that."

"I think you may have overpaid," I smiled weakly.

"I think you should have gone home," he replied.

I didn't answer, allowing myself instead to be carried until the faint light of dawn began to creep through the trees, stirring the slumbering blossom into wakefulness. He set me down outside a house of pale stone, opening the door with a gesture for me to enter. I took a step forward and swayed, and if it weren't for his quick hands, I would have smacked the floor. My head swam when he pulled me to my feet, and my legs buckled. There was a glimpse of concern on his lovely face as he caught me, and before I sank into oblivion my stomach heaved and I vomited on his feet.

CHAPTER EIGHT

I screamed as he held me down. His hands found mine and yanked them behind my head so hard I could feel the skin bruise. I kicked him away, using the last of my strength to fight him off, but he was stronger...so much stronger. My head was forced back, my lips parted before a vile, hot liquid was thrust down my throat. I choked. Gagged. Then spat the treacle-like substance out, as my eyes and throat burned.

"Drink this!" he ordered, pushing the steaming liquid to my lips again. "Drink it, or you will die tonight."

Fog filled my brain, swirling shadows appearing in front of my eyes that I wasn't sure were there at all. Monsters in the dark clawed at me, bit me, strangled me and pulled at my hair...but when I turned my head and opened my eyes, they were gone. There was nothing in the darkness but him. And it was dark, so dark...too dark.

I panicked, and fear made me lash out. My fist connected with the side of his face, and I heard him snarl. The feral sound resonated through the darkness, and I made to bolt off the bed. He grabbed me, cursed and rammed his potion down my throat, holding his hand over my mouth until I finally swallowed.

"That's it," he said, his voice softer. "You can stop fighting me now. Get some sleep, and maybe you'll get to wake up in the morning."

Candlelight flickered on a table nearby, heavy furs covered me, smelling of pine and moss. I fell against the pillows and closed my eyes. Exhaustion dragged me under before I could fight it. Sleep came quick and unforgiving, bringing with it nightmares and monsters and all the other demons that had chased me throughout my life. There was no escape from it, and the dark, enchanted forest I slept beneath only further fuelled my terrors. I stirred a few times in the night, startled awake by nightmares, only to fall back under before I could take in where I was.

I caught a slight movement in the room just as my eyes began to open, and the constant fear of monsters in the dark had me wide awake again. I sat up, my eyes darting around the room as my spine prickled. I took a breath, feeling it shudder through my teeth as I found what had come uninvited into my room.

She sat in the far corner, her eyes glistening opaque as the light flickered across her face, her long arms stretched in front of her, cat-like and ready to strike. I stared and Lily stared back, her bluish lips pulled back against her teeth and twisted into a smile. She crept closer, slinking over the wooden floor with a strange sort of grace. Utterly silent. When she reached the edge of the bed, she pulled herself up and climbed toward me, her smile widening while my scream lodged uselessly in my throat. She lay over me, her haunting face just inches from mine. She was so close; I could smell the spice in her hair as it fell across my face. My heart whacked against my ribcage, my mouth too dry to call out, even when she placed her cold hand against my chest and listened to the song my fear made. Then with surprising gentleness, she ran those cold fingers down my cheek, trailing them down my collarbone to rest against my throat.

"He..." she rasped, her voice terrifying. "is mine."

I didn't move as she recoiled from the bed, slinking deep into the shadows. She turned once, her grin still on her face while she lifted one long finger to her lips, then she disappeared through the doorway, shutting the door silently as she went.

Shaking, I shoved back the heavy covers and stepped out of bed, reaching quickly for the bedpost when my legs refused to take my weight. It was then I noticed that I was no longer dressed in Slimy Soo's nasty clothes. Someone—I could guess who— had stripped me of the coarse dress, and had hopefully tossed it onto a fire and watched it burn. That same someone had then dressed me in a clean shirt that trailed past my knees and smelt vaguely familiar. All whilst I was sleeping.

With a deep breath I walked shakily to the doorway and ran my fingers over the keyhole, heart sinking as I realised there was no key. Sweat trickled down my back, my body exhausted by the journey from the bed to halfway across the room. I turned my gaze onto a heavy looking chair in the corner and smiled to myself at the thought of jamming it under the door handle, keeping any further creepy things from sneaking in. However, it was much heavier than I had anticipated, a solid antique with carved legs and headrest that shimmered with butterflies when the candlelight settled upon it. It was a beautiful piece of furniture, but it was a complete nightmare to drag across the room. I grabbed it and pulled, wincing slightly as the legs screeched along the wooden floor.

"What on earth are you doing?"

I jumped and turned around, seeing my saviour standing in the doorway,leaning casually against the frame.

"I couldn't lock the door, there's no key," I said, breathing hard.

"Because I do not need one," he said simply, then took a step toward me. His dark eyes flicked down to my hands clutching the chair, which were shaking with the effort of keeping me upright. I was never one for exercise, but I made a quick mental note to perhaps take up weightlifting...or yoga.

"I just wanted to keep the door shut," I mumbled, taking a heavy breath. "Don't panic, but I think I'm just going to sit down for a minute."

I sat with a sigh, tilting my head back as my limbs groaned in relief. In a flurry of movement that made me feel faintly sick, he was at my side, kneeling down so his violet eyes were level with mine.

I lifted my head. "Hi."

"You should not be up yet."

"Noted."

The sleeves of his shirt were rolled up, a few buttons left open as if he had quickly thrown it on. There were red marks down his arms, the signs of bruises that were already starting to heal. He watched as I raised my hand, not moving as I placed my fingers over the marks where they matched perfectly. I dropped my hand and looked away.

"Sorry," I said, not knowing what else to say.

"I wonder," he breathed, seemingly to himself as he tilted my chin up with a long finger.

"What?"

Keeping his finger against my skin, his mouth lifted into a small smile, his lips parting slightly in a flash of white teeth. "If I will regret saving you."

I jerked away from him, leaning back into the chair, and absently picked at the frayed velvet of the seat pad. "It would be a shame to waste blood and dreams on something not worth saving."

"I never said you were not worth saving," he countered. "I have yet to make up my mind."

"Would you have left me?"

He cocked his head to the side, his eyes unsure, as if he hadn't understood the question. The movement was fluid, purposeful. I had no doubts that he didn't move an inch unless he needed to.

I shifted in my seat, swallowing down my unease of the man in front of me. "If Slimy Soo wanted what she asked for me, would I be dead by now?"

He leant away from me, his hands curled tightly over the armrests, effectively trapping me in the chair. "I value my memories Teya."

"Is that a yes?"

"I don't know," he said with a subtle lift of his shoulders. He dropped his hands from the chair and stood up so he loomed over me.

"The way you move is so strange, did you know that?"

He raised an eyebrow. "Oh?"

"It's too perfect, too graceful, too..."

"Inhuman?" he finished for me, the word hissing through his teeth. I jumped and watched a look of satisfaction wash over his features.

"Yes," I replied, meeting his gaze. "You all seem to move like that, like there is a song you are dancing to and no one else can hear it. It reminds me of the monster that stole my sister away, she moved like the wind, finding a melody in the storm."

The candlelight flickered across his face, causing his eyes

to darken to an almost black as he glared back at me from the shadows.

"The way I move makes me a monster in your eyes?"

"Are you denying that you are?"

He did smile then, a cruel smile that made him appear just as inhuman as he said he was. "Not at all. I just wanted to hear your definition."

"And I wanted to know if your kind is capable of any sort of empathy, if there's anything beneath all that cold beauty that resembles a soul."

He bristled, all colour disappearing from his eyes. "My kind?" he sneered, and I flinched. "If I were not capable of empathy or pity, girl, you would be dead and don't ever forget that. If by some misconception you want me to apologise for what I am, then you will be waiting a long time, do you understand me?"

"Do you make a habit of tormenting your houseguests?" I asked.

"Is that what I am doing?" he replied. "Then I do apologise. May I ask you a question?"

I nodded, the tone of his voice making my body go cold.

"Do you make a habit," he began, "of sleeping in a man's bed whose name you have yet to learn?"

My skin flushed scarlet, cheeks reddening as I lost the battle to keep my gaze on his and I looked away. He caught my chin in his hand, forcing my head back to look at him.

"You are just a toy," he whispered, leaning closer so I could feel his breath against my face. The scent of spice and moss engulfed my senses. "A piece of meat, something to be bought and sold and broken. If we do not kill you, we forget about you, and then you starve. These woods are filled with wolves all too eager to devour you whole. The trouble is, many stand upon two legs and look too much as if they are helping."

"I'm not afraid of you," I said, and he laughed, the sound a cold, humourless bark that slid effortlessly from his twisted smile.

"Really?"

I recoiled when he came closer, shifting as he knelt beside me and began to wind my hair around his fingers. I tried to pull away, but he held tighter.

"You are a terrible liar."

"Almost as good as you," I countered, and he raised an eyebrow. "Let go of me."

He held my gaze, opening his hand to release my hair, fingers coming down to trail along my cheek. I held my breath, tensing as if he were a wild animal.

"You didn't tell me your name," I breathed, relieved and equally disturbed when purple seeped back into his irises.

For a moment I didn't think he was going to answer; he just stared at me with his head tilted to the side, taking up far too much of my personal space.

"Laphaniel," he said at last, the strange sound of his name lilting and soft.

"I read somewhere that your name has some sort of power. I'm guessing that's not true or you wouldn't have given it to me."

"It is a myth," he said. "One of many, conjured up when humans were only discovering flame. It is why humans have a middle name, so they would not have to disclose their true one, lest it gave someone power over them. Nonsense of course."

"So, words have no real power?"

"I never said that," Laphaniel answered, making my head ache. I suddenly felt very tired and incredibly vulnerable.

Barely stifling a yawn, I raked a hand through my filthy hair. My fingers caught in the matted tangles, and for one horrible moment I thought I was going to cry. All I wanted to do was crawl back under the covers and sleep. With a shaking hand I scrubbed at my eyes, quickly hiding the tears that threatened to fall. Laphaniel stood, disgust or pity, I couldn't tell which, shadowed his features.

"You should rest, you look..."

"Disgusting?" I finished for him, my voice wavering.

"I was going to say you look like you could do with more sleep."

"Your bed is rather comfortable." I tried to smile, but it was too much hard work and all I could manage was a lopsided lift of my mouth.

Laphaniel gestured to the bed, grabbing my arm quickly when I stumbled into him. "Try not to die in your sleep."

I sunk back into the soft mattress, enjoying the comfort before I registered what he had said, dread chasing the sleepiness away.

"Wait…wait!" I grabbed at him, my words heavy as sleep threatened to pull me under before I was ready. "My mum doesn't know I'm here…she won't know where I've gone…if I don't come back."

"What concern is that of mine?" he answered, pushing my hand off so it thumped down beside me.

"Please," I whispered, and he hesitated, waiting. "Six Mulberry Close…it has the roses at the front…they're nearly dead because she forgets to water them."

"Perhaps you should not have left her," he said, pressing the back of his hand against my forehead, his eyes narrowing. "Would you like me to return your broken little body to her?"

Tears spilled over my eyes as I nodded, and I no longer had the strength to keep them away, so they fell unhindered down my cheeks as I slipped back into blackness. Even as I drifted, I felt exposed, lying in his clothes, beneath his blankets, in his bed. From the darkness I heard him mutter something that sounded vaguely like a curse, and then the blanket lifted over my shoulders, swamping me in warmth.

"Can you lock the door?" I mumbled, my words barely coherent even to my own ears.

"It doesn't lock."

Fear gripped me, lifting me from sleep, the thought of Lily creeping back in when I was sleeping made my chest constrict in panic. I forced my eyes open, the room a blur. "Can you keep her out? Please?"

Laphaniel's head snapped back to me. "Was Lily in here?" he demanded, a sharp edge entering his voice, cutting through the darkness like shrapnel.

"That's why I dragged the chair over..." I slurred, blinking back sleep as it began to crawl back over me. "I was going to...push it under the handle...sorry about the marks on the floor."

I heard him say something as I closed my eyes, but the words became jumbled before they entered my brain. I could make no sense of them. Just before I drifted, I felt his hand brush against my face again, sweeping away my hair with cool fingers, leaving an echo of his touch on my skin as I slept.

CHAPTER NINE

I woke feeling rested, though whether I had been
sleeping for hours or days, I didn't know. The
heavy curtains had been pulled back to allow sunlight to
stream through unhindered, flooding the bedroom in warmth.
I shifted in the bed, reluctant to move from beneath the furs
and throws that covered me.

The fragments of nightmares still clung to my mind, a
lingering sense of guilt and dread and horror that was such a
part of me, I doubted it would ever go. Niven twirled in those
dark dreams as she always did, uncaring...unafraid, her
bright eyes alight with something I could never place. Among
the nightmares, beneath the heavy darkness, I had sensed him
standing over me. There had been the feel of cool water
against my face, at my lips. Then nothing, not even a whisper.

I blinked the last clinging fragments of sleep away and
rubbed my eyes, stretching until I felt my bones click. Reluctantly I sat up, glancing at the bedside table where fresh water
and a plate of food all covered with a glass dome waited for
me. My stomach growled just looking at it.

I drank the cold, crisp water until there was nothing left

and then I turned to the food. With the covers still snug around me, I lifted the glass lid and breathed in the delicious scent of warm bread, little cakes and cold meats. I hesitated for a moment, my fingers lingering over the plate as I remembered the stories about eating faerie food. I had to wonder what would happen if I took a mouthful, would I ever want normal food again? Would I starve to death when I returned home, unsatisfied by the ashen meals that failed to quiet my hunger. What would I do when the food my body craved was too far out of reach?

My stomach grumbled loudly again, and I remembered I hadn't eaten since my father's funeral, and I really didn't know how long ago that was. Too long, it seemed. With all that had happened, I forced my grief for him down into the black space where memories of Niven lingered, although he didn't deserve to be placed there, amongst the taunts, bullying and cruelty that were my memories of my sister.

No, I had happy times with my dad. We had holidays in Devon, down by the beach with a dripping ice cream in hand. We used to watch old films curled up on the sofa together, and we would mouth along to the words, knowing every line because we had seen them so many times.

Before Niven was taken, my dad was what every dad should have been to his daughter, he was my hero, and I was his baby.

I took one of the little cakes, deciding that I wouldn't be able to get much further in my quest to find Niven if I ate nothing. I bit into it, feeling the warm honey that ran through the middle trickle down my chin. It was easily the most delicious thing I had ever tasted. I took one of the warm bread rolls and nibbled on it while I gazed around the room. In the soft sunlight, I could see that the ceiling was criss-crossed with the branches of a living tree. They knotted over each other, growing through the stone walls and up over the window. It was a never-ending twist of bark and root that seemed to envelop the entire room, and I had to wonder if it grew around the whole house. Pale pink blossoms sprouted from green buds dotted along the length of the smaller boughs, with leaves gracing most of the larger ones.

I untangled myself from the covers and wandered over to the wooden armoire nestled neatly under the winding branches. With curious hands I flicked the ornate latch, opening the carved doors to a neat row of soft shirts and trousers, all roughly woven, all in various dark earthy tones. One drawer held thick socks, the other empty save for a handful of loose copper coins. No drawer for underwear...curious.

Turning my curiosity away from Laphaniel's clothing, or lack thereof, I moved to the huge window at the far side of the room, and my breath caught as I stared at the beautiful world outside. Just beyond the thick stretch of trees was a lake so clear, I could see the shadows of the creatures that swam in it. The surface reflected the sunlight like a mirror, its waters almost still, save for the odd ripple as the wind blew over it. Graceful willows stood at the edge, winding their long fingers over the water, disturbing the calm where they touched. All of it was bathed in warm light, a soft early morning glow that gently roused the sleeping things, and it was then that I marvelled that not one...but two suns burned in the beautiful blue sky.

"I see you are up."

I jumped and smacked my head on one of the lower branches, raining down pretty blossoms onto my shoulders. "Don't you knock?"

Laphaniel lifted a casual shoulder. "It is my house."

"I know that," I said, flicking the flowers onto the floor.

"But I could have been changing." Or rummaging through his drawers, not that he needed to know.

"Changing into what? You have no clothes," he said, a hint of that wicked grin at his lips. "Who do you think dressed you in that?"

Laphaniel pointed to the shirt I was wearing, and I quickly wrapped my arms around myself. He took another step into the room and sat down on the edge of the bed. I backed further away, wishing I had a big jumper.

"Were the picksies locked in cages?" he asked, picking up one of the cakes I had left and taking a bite. "Were they swinging from the trees as if someone had purposely put them there?"

"I'm guessing you already know the answer to that."

"Why open them?"

He watched me, waiting patiently on the bed for me to answer. I was trying to think of something that wouldn't make me sound like an idiot.

"Well, I didn't think they would attack me."

Laphaniel laughed at me, and I was taken by surprise at just how musical his laughter sounded. "You are really not going to last long here."

"I'm a fast learner," I snapped. "From now on, I'll just assume that everything is trying to kill me."

He stood up and crossed the room in two strides, once again far too close to me. "That is the first smart thing you have said," he replied. "But accepting you are going to get ripped apart will not make it any less horrifying."

I turned my face away before he could touch me. "I just need to find my sister."

"Do you want to die here?" Laphaniel asked. "Because you will."

I shrugged, the movement much more carefree than I

really felt. Of course, I didn't want to die...but I didn't want to go back to the life I had just left either. I couldn't do that.

"How many girls have you forgotten about and left to die?" I asked, daring him to answer me and at the same time wishing he wouldn't.

He hesitated for a moment, sucking the honey from his fingers. "Too many."

"Is that what happened to Niven?" I pictured my sister alone and broken beneath some whispering tree.

"It's what happens to a lot of girls."

I sighed. "Do you know where Niven is?"

"Yes."

"Where is she?"

"Somewhere I truly hope you'll never find," he said, a gentleness entering his voice, softening it.

I said nothing as I turned again to the window. With my arms resting against the cool wood of the windowsill, I stared out at the lake. It should have been a relief to find out that Niven was alive, but it was no consolation to me. Perhaps it was the thought of my sister trapped under Luthien's cruel gaze that stopped me...I didn't wish that for her, no matter how much I disliked her. I had to wonder what would be left of a person after ten years in hell. Perhaps I should have felt some form of relief if she were dead.

"What am I supposed to do now?"

"Just go home," he said, like it was the easiest thing in the world to do. "Live."

"I have nothing to go home to," I said soberly, twisting around to lean against the wall, and felt the cold stone against my back as I slid to the floor.

"Your parents?" he offered, angling his head as he regarded me. "Friends? Boyfriend? Isn't that something human…girls, value so highly?"

I laughed and shook my head, seeing out of the corner of my eye how his almost black hair fell over his face as he watched me. He looked curious, as if my sad little life had piqued his interest. With a silent grace he sat down beside me, waiting for me to answer.

"Luthien tore my family apart, I guess that left me too messed up to really get close to anyone. Moira says I push people away because I'm scared I'm going to lose them too."

"Who's Moira?" Laphaniel asked, leaning closer to me, his voice taking on a gentleness that made my heart pause.

"She's someone I was made to talk to after Niven was taken by faeries...and I kept telling people that Niven was taken by faeries." I laughed again, a bubble of hysteria making it sound a little manic. "People don't really like it when children start talking like that. My mother would cry every time I mentioned the word, so I stopped talking altogether. They liked that even less."

I paused and glanced up at him, expecting to see boredom in his eyes, but he was just sitting there, watching me.

"I can't cope with my mother anymore. I can't stay in that house and watch as she waits for her family to come home." I squeezed my eyes shut, and felt hot tears against my cheeks. "My father killed himself, hence the black dress I was wearing when we met. I have nothing left but this...to find Niven. Without that I have nothing,"

I am nothing.

More tears fell and I covered my face, not wanting him to see. There was no comforting hand on my shoulder, no kind words. Silence save for the sounds of my gasping sobs as I wept into my hands. My mother had never been good at hugs either, and I had learnt not to need them. To want them. I hugged my knees, snot running down my face, and waited for the ache in my chest to go.

Laphaniel said nothing as he rose to his feet, not looking at me before he started to walk away.

"Have I made you uncomfortable?" I asked, staring at his back. I swiped my eyes with my sleeve, leaving black marks behind. "Do you even give a second thought to the people you leave behind? They waste away too, you know, hoping that one day their loved ones will return to them."

"Do you love your sister then, Teya?"

"What kind of question is that?"

"A simple one," he replied, turning to face me again.

"I don't think it's any of your business," I snapped, pushing myself to my feet so he was no longer peering down at me. "I know you saved my life, and I am thankful for that, but you're a complete asshole."

"An improvement on monster, perhaps?" He smiled, a disarming innocence betraying the wicked streak lingering beneath.

"I guess." I found myself smiling back. "Just a little."

The breeze from the open window teased against my back. I shivered and moved away, holding my arms around myself. Petals slipped from my shoulders, pale pink and delicate, the edges curling inwards as I held one up.

"Are you cold?"

I nodded and released the blossom so it spun lazily to the floor. "I'm cold, filthy and I think I have old sick in my hair."

"Okay," Laphaniel said quietly, leaning away from me. "There is a bathroom down the hall with hot water and clean clothes, take as long as you need."

I nearly slumped in relief. "That would be great."

Laphaniel nodded and turned away from me, and I caught his arm when he made to leave. He looked down at my hand before flicking his gaze back to me. I didn't let go.

"I am really grateful for what you did." I said, keeping my

hand on his arm. "I didn't want to die with that witch. I didn't want to die on my own."

"And yet you repay me by going back out there, and likely dying anyway?"

I sighed and went to take my hand back, but he caught it with his quick fingers and held it for a few moments before letting it drop.

"Enjoy your bath, Teya."

I watched as he left, feeling my fingers tingle where he had held onto them. They had been soft and cool, I stared down at my hand as if I could still feel his touch. I shuddered, though it had nothing to do with the cold or any lingering effects of the poison. I touched my fingertip to my mouth and wondered what it would feel like to have his lips against mine.

It was a thought I really could have done without.

CHAPTER TEN

I walked down the winding corridor that led to the bathroom, fingers trailing along the branches that crisscrossed over the walls. I allowed them to linger over the blossom that peeked out from behind the knotted wood, snaking around the candleholders on the walls, dripping pale flowers onto the floor below.

I was thankful there was a lock to the door as I closed it behind me, guessing Laphaniel wanted Lily spying on him in the bath as much as I did. The bathroom was a small stone room, with a window that looked out over the forest towards the lake. A basin stood in one corner, a shaving brush and straight razor occupying the alcove set above it. A wooden toothbrush sat in a glass tumbler upon the sink, a lidded jar of what I presumed was toothpaste beside it. Normal things to find in a bathroom that was so very far from normal. The exquisite bath had been carved from frosted green glass that stood away from the wall, sheltered by a screen decorated with emerald dragonflies. Copper piping flowed from the bath and down through the floor. It was a relief to discover that Faerie had indoor plumbing.

I turned on the tap, watching the water rush from it to pour down the smooth surface. Steam quickly filled the room, clouding over the mirror and hiding away my ragged reflection. I took another glance around the room before slipping out of my borrowed shirt, placing it neatly beside a stack of wonderfully fluffy towels.

It was then I noticed the swirl of bruises on my arms, a mess of purple and green that throbbed up my shoulder, the mottled skin covered in teeny-tiny bite marks that had yet to scab over. They didn't hurt much anymore, but it did make me wonder what other things lurked out in the woods, hiding under the guise of innocence.

It made me suddenly very afraid of Laphaniel who had never made a pretense of being anything near innocent.

Slowly, I lowered myself into the bath and enjoyed the feeling of the hot water sliding over my skin, melting away the aches and pains in a way only a bath could. I took the bar of green soap resting on the side and lathered it between my hands. It smelled earthy and didn't sting my sensitive skin as I rubbed the bubbles over my legs and arms. I soaped up my hair and scrubbed it until I was sure it was clean, and then sank back until I was fully submerged and could hear nothing but the whoosh of water around my ears.

I came up for air, drained the water, watching as the murk and filth that had clung to me pooled down the plughole. Knowing that I had just dissolved the grime, I popped the plug back in and refilled the bath.

After my second soak, I wrapped myself in the thick towel and picked up the clean clothes Laphaniel had left out for me. I shook my head at the fresh shirt with sleeves already rolled back and trousers with the hems rolled up. I slipped into the clothes and fastened the belt he had left as tight as I could, but the trousers still slipped past my hips and I had to keep hitching them back up. Pulling on the worn black boots, I looked at myself in the mirror and smiled. I was clean, my hair was clean, but I looked like a small pirate.

Feeling much better and refreshed...much more human, I unlocked the door and made my way back to the hall and to a staircase that seemed to twist down from the walls like one huge branch. Ivy covered the banister, snaking around it, trailing down over the steps, just itching to trip me up. I gripped the wood and took a careful step, pausing for a moment to take in the amazing window just above the front door. Its stained glass cast a warm pinkish hue over the pristine white stone. The lean branches of a sapling tree grew elegantly over the window frame, its thin adolescent boughs winding down over the glass before joining the arm of a larger tree on the far wall. I watched as its fragile blossom slipped free and floated to the floor, joining the petals that had fallen before, coming together to create a sweet-smelling carpet. It was so utterly otherworldly that, for just a moment, I felt homesick.

My breath caught when I noticed Laphaniel waiting at the bottom of the stairs, leaning casually against the wall with his face turned away from me.

"I think I've used up all your hot water."

He twisted his body in my direction, a smile itching at his lips as he stepped closer. I froze as he raised a hand to my collar, tracing the edge of my neckline before fastening a button I had missed.

"The water comes from a spring beneath the house," Laphaniel explained. "There is endless hot water whenever you want it."

"I won't be staying much longer." The echo of his touch lingered on my skin after he dropped his hand. "I don't want to outstay my welcome."

Laphaniel took a seat on the stone bench nestled neatly into an alcove to the left of the front door, reaching up onto one of the shelves above him. He began to thumb through a worn book, and I raised my eyebrows when I noticed the title, *Jane Eyre*.

"'I am no bird, and no net ensnares me.'" I reached to take the book from him, shaking my head as I looked inside. My brows lifted. "This is a first edition."

"Would you like it?" Laphaniel asked, surprising me. "I've read it many times."

"This is worth a fortune," I said. "Even in this condition. I can't accept this."

I passed him back the book, and he shrugged, folding the page back to mark his place. I winced.

"So, where will you be going?" he asked.

"You know where," I replied. "Don't roll your eyes at me."

Laphaniel sighed. "Do you know how to get there?"

"No, but..."

"But what?" he replied. "Are you expecting me to tell you?"

"Would you?"

"Okay, Teya," he said with a laugh, the sound mocking and suddenly cruel. "Go north through the woods for about a night and a day, take a left past the three lakes on the eastern side for about a day and a half, and then left again before taking a right into the marshlands. Pack some food, don't drink the water and try not to talk to anyone."

"Laphaniel..." I began and ducked when he threw the book at me, wincing as the spine broke and pages fluttered across the floor.

"Get out!" he hissed. "Go into the woods, you foolish

girl, I am done trying to help you. Go wander the shadows and die somewhere else."

I yelped as he grabbed my hand and threw me out of the door, slamming it shut behind me. I stood alone on the doorstep, my mouth open in shock, strangely hurt that he had thrown me out. I turned to face the surrounding trees, the narrow pathways all covered with brambles or fallen logs. Even with the sunlight glittering through the canopy, it looked dark...dangerous...stupid.

I sucked in a breath, allowing it to hiss through my teeth while I slammed my fist against the door. I cursed him loudly, screaming obscenities that I had no doubt he heard with his stupid pointy ears. I kicked the door for good measure, my boots making a decent thumping sound, as I seethed on his doorstep.

"You are looking for your sister, yes?"

I jumped at the sound of her voice, a soft whisper that sang from her bloodless lips. She sat near the shadows of the giant oaks that shaded Laphaniel's house, her body curled up like a cat.

"What is it to you?" I said, taking a wary step toward her, tensing when she sat up.

Lily blinked and stretched, hands reaching up high, stretching the white of her skin so her ribs were shockingly visible. "I know where she is."

"Are you offering to take me to her?"

"Would you follow me?" she answered, cocking her head slowly to one side, silvery hair swirling around her like mist.

"I'm not going into the woods with you."

Her smile was a nightmare, revealing the row of sharp teeth she had hidden behind her ghostly mouth. "Are you going to stay with him then?"

I glanced back at Laphaniel's door. "No…"

"He won't let you go, you know that, don't you? He never does. There are silly girls just like you buried all over these woods."

Cold prickled down my spine. "Where's Niven?"

Lily outstretched her bone white hand. "Follow me."

I hesitated before taking her hand, her sharp nails digging into my skin. When she wasn't looking, I slipped a fist-sized rock up my sleeve...just in case. I knew it was foolish to trust a creature like Lily, but I couldn't wander the woods without knowing where I was going. That hadn't worked out well before, and I was unlikely to find a map that would lead me to my sister. I was getting nowhere with Laphaniel, who had made it abundantly clear he was not going to help me. I couldn't stay and hope to change his mind, and then there was a shameful part of me that was starting to like the way he looked at me.

I followed her through the winding pathways, the sunlight overhead piercing through the treetops to settle upon the lush leaves below. Flowers awoke as the sunlight touched them, uncurling to reveal a rainbow of blooms that covered the paths and hid away our footprints.

"Where are you taking me?" I demanded as Lily led me over mounds and down rocky paths that I slid down in my too-big boots. "Stop!"

She turned to me, as swift as a snake. "Do you want to find your sister?"

"Yes…"

"Hush then."

"What do you get out of this?"

She closed her eyes for a moment, looking almost wistful. "I want him back."

"Laphaniel?"

"He looks at you strangely," she said, the words hissing

through her teeth. "Like he believes there is something beneath the skin you wear that is worth something."

"Which you don't." Not a question, but Lily nodded…a quick tilt of her head that was all I needed from her.

"I miss the taste of him," she purred, closing her eyes as she ran her tongue over her lips.

"If it's any consolation, I don't think he likes me much," I said, unable to dwell on what kind of relationship Lily had with Laphaniel.

Lily blinked, her nose flaring as she scented me, a low growl shuddering past her lips. "He wouldn't come to me, instead he was at your side ensuring that you still drew breath."

She paused, squatting back onto her haunches as she trailed her eyes down my body, her disgust plain on her other-worldly face.

"I didn't know…"

"Three nights you festered away in his bed," she continued, cutting me off. "In the room I am forbidden to enter. He finally emerged when at last you stopped your infernal thrashing and screeching, and he reeked of sweat and bile, you foul little thing."

I had no idea. I had sensed someone over me while I slept…as I fought off the nightmares, but I couldn't comprehend that I had been sleeping for days…that he hadn't left me, that I was sick all over him…again. Fear, along with a dreaded realisation crept down my spine.

"Where are we really going?"

Lily straightened, a flicker of glee flashing over her pallid skin. "Somewhere no one will ever find you."

"You lied to me."

Lily shook her head, a smirk creeping over her mouth.

"You don't ask the right questions. I do know where your sister is, I never said I would take you to her."

Lily launched herself at me with a piercing cry, scattering the restless birds overhead towards the skies. I swung quickly and the rock I had been carrying since I began following her collided with her face. There was a sickening crack and a spray of blood as Lily fell to the moss-covered ground and didn't move.

"Fuck," I spluttered, dropping the bloodied rock and trying vainly to get a sense of my surroundings. I backed along the way I had come…or thought I had come, I wasn't sure anymore for everything looked the same…but was so, so different.

The ground beneath my feet was damp, inclining downwards into a murky swamp that writhed and moved with unfathomable creatures beneath the green waters. Something crunched beneath my feet and, looking down, I noticed dozens and dozens of bones littered over the ground, all picked clean.

I looked back to where Lily had fallen, my heart freezing when I realised she was gone.

"Bitch," I hissed, creeping away from the swamp, scanning the swaying trees for any sign of her.

Something else was waiting.

Something bigger.

I could feel its eyes upon me, sense the trees around me grow quiet, the chatter of birdsong dying out until there was nothing but silence. Then a low, soft hiss.

A heron shot out from the reeds, its sharp cry drowning out mine as a huge black shadow launched forwards, passing over the terrified bird to disappear back into the shadows.

For a moment I thought it had missed its prey, but the heron fell to the ground with a soft thump, eyes wide and strangely white. It jerked before folding in on itself, feathers decaying as it withered at my feet.

With my hands clamped around my mouth, I dragged myself behind a cluster of skinny trees just as the long shining form of a giant snake slithered back out of the shadows, its monstrous face scanning the woods. I looked away, not daring to meet its gaze after what it did to the bird.

Sucking noises filled my ears, the wet lapping of flesh that should have been solid but no longer was. I swallowed quickly, willing myself not to throw up as I slipped away.

I knew it followed me before I heard the hiss, and without looking back, I ran as fast as I could through the forest, not giving one damn where I was headed. I clambered over rocks and slid down moss-covered banks, splashing through the shallow waters of the swamp and disturbing creatures that dwelled beneath.

Teeth sliced at my skin, tiny fish-like creatures flung themselves at my legs, gaping mouths stretched wide to clamp down and suckle at me. I tore them off, yelping when my skin came away too.

Behind me I heard the trees snap. I scurried up the bank as the writhing mass hunted me, its black scales seeming to suck in the light. With a loud thwack it lashed out with the tip of its long, long tail, catching me on the back of my legs so I was sent flying.

I rolled, sprang back to my feet, not daring to look as it lunged again and caught a frightened doe that ran across my path instead. The deer froze, frightened black eyes milking over while it bubbled, skin sinking against its bones, its flesh turning into jelly as the monster loomed over it and sucked it dry.

With stinging, bloodied legs I ran, clawing my way up over the slick ground and back around to the shadow of the thicker trees, away from the swamp. I spotted Laphaniel before he saw me and, not having enough breath in my lungs to call out his name, I slammed into him instead. I had no time to be grateful that I had found him, nor to wonder at the look of relief that passed over his face as he caught my arms.

"No!" I gasped. "Just go…run!"

"What…"

"Shut up and run!" I shoved him forwards, dragging him by the arm when he hesitated.

"What is it?" he called to me, dragging me up as I stumbled. "Teya?"

"Giant snake." I managed to gasp, "Lily lured me to it."

He spun me around, his hand tight on mine, his breaths coming out as sharp as mine. "Why would you follow Lily?"

"I thought she was taking me to Niven."

"You really are stupid…"

I tugged on his arm hard, forcing him to turn down a winding path, thick with brambles, instead of the one he had chosen. "Not that way!"

"My house is this way!" he snapped.

"Do you really want that thing in your back garden?"

"No…"

"Didn't think so," I panted, leaning back against a tree to catch my breath, feeling it burn against my lungs.

"Did you look at it?" he asked, raising a hand as if to touch me, but seemed to think better of it, and allowed it to drop back to his side.

"Since I'm not a pile of mush, I guess not."

His eyes narrowed, the violet darkening while he glared. "Do not snap at me."

"I'm pissed off," I hissed, turning to scan the surrounding trees for any signs of movement. "I'm a little tired of things trying to eat me."

"I told you…"

"I'm tired of you telling me all the ways I'm going to die, okay?" I said, angry tears threatening against my eyes. "Just stop it!"

"I was trying to help."

"No," I said softly, taking a breath as the trees around us remained still and calm. "You're trying to frighten me."

For a moment he said nothing, his own eyes darting at the shadows the trees made, head tilting slightly while he listened. "I didn't think you would run off."

"Were you hoping I would sit and wait on your doorstep like a little puppy?" I said. "I'm not yours to order around… to manipulate and torment."

"Yes, you are," he replied, his hand reaching out to grasp my wrist. "Don't forget that."

"I don't think you'll let me," I hissed, wrenching my hand away. "Keep moving, I don't fancy having the flesh melted from my bones today."

"Give me your hand."

"Why?"

"Because the snake has your scent, and it will not stop following you unless we can lure it elsewhere."

I hesitated before reaching my hand out, eyeing the little knife in his hands warily. I barely had time to react before he sliced the blade over my arm, cutting deep enough that blood pooled down over my fingers.

"Ow..."

"Hush!" he snapped, crouching low, one hand still clamped around mine. He closed his eyes, going very still while I looked on. His free hand shot out, moving before I could blink, to grab the screeching body of a terrified hare from the bushes. He held it by the scruff, and hastily rubbed my blood all over it, until the soft brown of its coat was sticky with red. I couldn't help but pity the poor creature.

"Wait," he said, taking a breath, his voice softer. "Tie this around your arm."

He tore a strip of his shirt for me to use, wiping his own hands over the frantic animal, his eyes darting to the trees, head cocked as he listened.

"We should climb up." I said, peering up.

"Good idea…go."

I didn't need to be told twice. I forced myself up onto the lower branches of a looming oak tree, hoisting myself up deep into its canopy, my arm throbbing. I looked down as Laphaniel released the hare, just as the coiling form of the mighty snake slithered into view. It stilled, waiting, watching. Laphaniel climbed noiselessly behind me, a strong arm coming around to steady me on the branch.

We both stood tense while the snake tasted the air, and I didn't protest as Laphaniel guided my head against his chest, forcing me to look away. I was trembling, my heartbeat whacking against my ribcage, echoing the thump of Laphaniel's. My fingers gripped his shirt, but I didn't care, I didn't dare move, holding my breath until it was forced through my lips in a shuddering rasp.

"It's gone," Laphaniel whispered. "It's following the hare."

I pushed away from him, my breaths coming out sharp and panicked as I fumbled back down the tree. He landed gracefully beside me, placing a concerned hand on my shoulder, hurt flashing over his face when I jerked away.

"Don't," I murmured, swallowing the lump in my throat. "Unless you want to see what hysteria looks like, please just give me a minute."

I sucked in a shaky breath, rubbing away the stray, frightened tears that trickled over my cheeks, suddenly feeling weak and useless.

He gave me space, eyes narrowing as he watched me.

"What?"

"I didn't say anything."

"You're staring at me," I said, drawing a steadier breath. "This is a human reaction to nearly being eaten, take note."

He didn't take his eyes off me. "I am."

"Shall we go back, then?" I said, uncomfortable under his scrutinizing gaze. "You're not going to slam the door in my face again?"

"Probably not," he replied. "The snake won't bother you again if you don't come back to the swamp. In its mind, you're already dead."

"Good to know."

He held out a hand, waiting with a smile as I hesitated. Sighing, I took it and his long fingers folded over mine, cool and soft. Without another word, I let him lead me away from the swamp and back to his house.

CHAPTER ELEVEN

*W*e walked the long way back in silence, my nerves simply too frazzled to engage in conversation. Laphaniel seemed uncomfortable, dropping my hand and walking a little way ahead of me, only glancing back now and again to make sure I was still behind him. He asked if my arm was okay, stopping at a clear stream to help wash away the dried blood and grit and bound it tightly with another strip of his shirt.

I almost sighed in relief when his house came into view… but I stopped myself. I didn't want the safety of his house…it wasn't safe, and neither was Laphaniel. It was getting all too easy to forget that.

"You're strangely quiet," I said finally, unable to bear the silence any longer. "Are you still pissed I ran off?"

"I'm tired," he said, and I was surprised at the honest, simple answer.

"Can I ask you a question?"

He nodded, waiting.

"Do you enjoy tormenting me?"

"Yes," he answered without hesitation.

"Why?"

He sighed and reached up to brush a stray strand of hair from my face. "Because you are so beautiful when you are angry."

I opened my mouth to utter a retort, but nothing came out, so I just stood there and gaped at him like a fish.

"That's not a compliment," I said finally, trying to wrap my mind around how the words made me feel.

"It was not meant to be," Laphaniel replied, confusing me more.

Wrapping my arms around myself, I took a step away from him and wandered to a little garden at the side of the house. I didn't look around until I had sat upon one of the stone steps, but I heard him follow me.

I leant forward with my head against my knees, waiting until the burn in my chest eased up. I rubbed at my stinging legs, the grazes over my knees just filthy.

Tilting my head back, I let the warm breeze brush over me, carrying with it every scent of the surrounding forest.

There were roses everywhere in Laphaniel's garden, creeping up vines and blooming from huge shrubs and bursting from hedgerows. Every colour flower imaginable blossomed in his garden, but the reds were simply breathtaking. Vivid scarlet and velvet soft, they filled the garden with a perfume that was unlike anything I had ever known.

Laphaniel reached out and plucked one of the red roses and offered it to me. I hesitated before I took it, eyeing the beautiful bloom with distrust.

"Will it turn into a snake if I touch it?"

With a quick twist of his hands and a sly smile at his mouth, the rose vanished, and in its place, a writhing snake coiled around his arm. I jumped as it reared back, baring its fangs and hissing at me.

"Don't!" I cried, recoiling from him and the snake. Laphaniel swiftly moved his hand again, turning the snake back into a rose, and held it out to me once more.

"It is just a flower, Teya. It has never been anything more, and never will be anything else."

"It was definitely a snake just then."

He laughed, and my rebellious heart danced at the sound. "Only because I wanted you to see a snake. You could have just as easily seen a rose."

"Oh, really?"

Reaching forwards, he carefully took my hand and placed the rose between my fingers. "In the woods when I tried to get you to turn back, you resisted me. You have a sharper mind than you give yourself credit for."

"So, you used magic?"

"Glamour," he clarified. "An illusion, it's only real if you believe it is."

I laughed then and shook my head, allowing the rose to fall at my feet. The petals broke away from the stem when it hit the ground, and the gentle wind swirled them away like confetti. Laphaniel watched the petals dance, his face unreadable as the red shapes teased at his hair.

"Can you hear that?" he asked.

"Hear what?"

"I think the wind is singing to you. Listen."

Laphaniel took my hand and drew me closer as I closed my eyes and I strained to hear what he was hearing. I could hear his heart beating, the sound of his breathing...my own heart thumping out an erratic beat, but there was no music in the wind. "I can't..."

"Try harder," he whispered, his words tickling the edge of my ear.

I smiled and took a breath and really listened, remembering that I was in a world where the trees could sway to music that the wind sang for them. I heard it then, subtle at first, but it grew louder as the breeze picked up. It was an orchestra of fallen leaves, of blades of grass and the creatures that trampled across them. It was the sound of laughter, of wild things...the sounds of screams, all carried together on the breath of a breeze, and I was lost within it.

"Now can you hear it?"

"Yes!" I laughed as Laphaniel grabbed my arms and swung me around, forcing me to dance. My feet moved, stepping with his in a frenzied dance that I didn't know the steps to, but my soul seemed to know by heart. The world became a blur, the feral choir joined by the sounds of my laughter pushing itself from my lips. I could have danced forever, laughed forever and forgotten everything that needed to be remembered.

His hands were warm against mine, curling around my fingers while he led me in a waltz between the roses. I rested my head against his chest and closed my eyes, letting my feet move without thinking. Laphaniel's hand came around my waist, his other lifting my arm so I could twirl and twirl until I laughed with dizziness.

His fingers traced my cheeks, his touch as gentle as the words he spoke to me, ghosting past his lips so that I barely heard them. His eyes flashed wicked, betraying the softness of his hands on me.

"You're almost as good a dancer as your sister."

My head snapped up, all music suddenly forgotten. "What?"

He stared at me, all gentleness melting away to reveal what I already knew lingered just below those pretty eyes. I froze, wondering if maybe I had misheard him...hoping I had misheard him.

His thumb moved along my hand, a soft caress before he pulled me closer, his lips against my ear. "Niven was a wonderful dancer for such a spiteful creature."

I tried to pull away, but his hand tightened, keeping me close. His words whispered like kisses against my skin, their meaning spiked and poisonous. I squeezed my eyes shut, willing him to stop.

"She wasn't afraid," he continued. "But you were, weren't you? While Niven swirled around us, you huddled and wept."

"You were there when Niven was taken," I said, realisation hitting me hard and leaving me breathless.

"Oh, I was there, Teya," he said. "And when I took her hand, she skipped beside me as I led her into the woods."

I tore myself away from him, choking on a scream as I fled away from the garden and collapsed at the edge of the woods, not daring to go any further. Beneath the lengthening shadows of the trees, I broke down and wept until there was nothing left but the sounds of my ragged breath. I had never felt so utterly desolate in my life, and the terrible - the most awful thing was, I cried for the loss of a friendship I believed was blooming, more than the horror of losing Niven.

atching the slow sunset catch the sky alight, I tried to name some of the constellations as the stars began to shine in the deepening black, but everything looked different in the alien sky and there was no comfort to be found within it. I wondered if the sky I was looking at was so different from the one at home, if the stars wished upon up there were the same as those that fell over our skies.

A long time ago my father and I had spotted a shooting star and we had both wished upon it. He had wished for Niven back, I wished Luthien had taken me instead.

I had envied my sister for dancing so boldly under the enchanted trees while I only trembled from their shadows, and I hated myself for envying her...for wanting to be more like her. Closing my eyes against the sparkling night, I remembered Luthien's smooth touch against my shoulder, the way her lips sang poisonous whispers to me under the old oaks. I remembered Niven's name on those lips, along with the bitter taste on my tongue as I sold my sister so I could dance with faeries.

Perhaps she deserved it.

As perhaps I deserved the nights of broken sleep, the gnawing guilt in my stomach, and the aching, crippling fear of the dark that threatened to tear me down even as I stood under the moonlight. It was that very fear that stopped me from running into the woods, even though I didn't feel safe lingering in the shadows of Laphaniel's home. I was stuck in a limbo, trying vainly to determine what—or who—I was more frightened of.

I watched as a star flew across the sky, racing past the others as they remained stuck in the midnight. I didn't make a wish; there was nothing to gain from wishing on a memory of dead light. I leant against the garden wall and slowly slid my body down until I was sitting on the ground. I fiddled with a loose thread on my borrowed shirt and fought the urge to start crying again. Cold settled around my body like a disease.

He had taken her.

Charming, beautiful, cruel and dangerous Laphaniel had taken Niven away as I huddled out of sight. All this time, it had been him. I had slept in the bed of my sister's kidnapper, had imagined how his lips would feel against mine...and I should have felt something like hate, but I could feel nothing but a deep and pathetic wish that it had been anyone...any-thing, but him.

I slowly rose to my feet when I noticed Laphaniel walk toward me, his feet barely making a sound as he moved. He made no attempt to stop me as I slapped him hard across his face, and with my palm stinging, I made to hit him again.

"No," he said, catching my hand. "Strike me again, and I will hit you back."

"I don't doubt you," I hissed, yanking my hand away. "Leave me the fuck alone."

"Wait. Teya."

"Why?" I spun around, taking a step towards him,

watching with a bitter smile as he took a single step away from me. "What have you got left to say to me? Do you think I have anything left for you to destroy?"

"Please..." He moved closer, taking my other hand. "Would you just..."

"No!" I spat, struggling against his hold. "Let me go!"

"Just wait..."

"Leave me alone!" I screamed at him. "You stole my sister away; you tore my entire family apart and left me to sift through the remains. What on earth do you think you can say that will make me hate you any less?"

Something resembling regret flickered over his face and for just a moment all traces of his wicked confidence vanished. He shifted, lifting a shoulder.

"Could *you* say no to Luthien?"

I turned away from him, closing my eyes as I remembered how desperate I was to please her, how I wanted nothing but to see Luthien smile at me...and she did. She lit the world alight with that smile and beneath its welcoming glow, I didn't think twice about handing over my own flesh and blood. I could still remember the melody of Luthien's voice as she sang my name and asked for my sister. She promised me music and dancing and tiny sprites that would braid my hair with wildflowers. She would show me a glimpse of her magical world, in return for a dance with Niven...and I didn't think twice.

"There was nothing you could have done, Teya," Laphaniel said from behind me. "She would have taken her, with or without your help."

"She could have taken me."

"Luthien didn't want you."

No one wanted me.

Though he was blunt, there was no coldness to

Laphaniel's voice, he was just stating a fact that I had known all along. Though the unintentional cruelty didn't make it sting any less. I wasn't enough for Luthien, not enough to keep my family together, not enough for my mother, not enough for my father to live for.

Not enough.

"Can I ask why?"

"You can."

I sighed as he dodged my question. "But you won't tell me?"

"If I told you, would it make you stop looking for her?"

I caught his gaze and tried to hold onto it, though it was me that broke away first. "Yes."

"You are a shocking liar."

My rebellious lips twitched into the ghost of a smile and my heart danced a little faster against my ribs, but all the while my brain screamed at me to stop...

"Where the hell is Niven?" I blurted over the mess in my head. "Please?" I added hastily.

"Luthien has your sister, Teya, and she will be keeping her. There is no way for you to get her back now. I'm sorry."

"Why tell me?" I asked, bitterness creeping into my voice. "You could have carried on without me knowing what you did. Did you do it just to hurt me more?"

He took a breath, not meeting my eyes, and I wondered if he regretted telling me at all. "I didn't do it to hurt you. Would you believe I simply wanted to ease some of the guilt I feel?"

"That's pretty selfish," I bit back, recoiling from him. "You knew it would upset me, and you still did it."

"I wanted you to trust me. That would not work if I were hiding something from you." He paused, looking uncomfortable. "I wanted to see your reaction, to see if you would stay or run."

"I have nowhere else to go," I snapped. "I'm actually a little less afraid of you than I am of the monsters in the woods."

Laphaniel placed a hand carefully on my shoulder, and I leant into his touch, moving against him until I was wrapped in his strong arms. It wasn't okay...it was so far from being okay, but as he ran his hand over my hair, I allowed myself a moment before I pulled away.

"We're cursed."

I blinked. "What?"

"Please just come back inside, and I'll explain everything," Laphaniel said, giving my hand a little tug.

"Why can't you just tell me out here?"

"Because it's getting dark and cold, and I'm hungry."

I hesitated, weighing up whether or not it was safer to go back inside with him, or stay out as night began to fall. Laphaniel dropped my hand and walked away, shooting a quick glance into the nearby trees.

"The wolves will be out soon."

"Oh, for Christ sake!" I growled, storming beside him. "This had better be a good story."

"I'll even cook for you."

I held my hand over my heart and sighed deeply. "Dinner and fairytales, what more could a girl possibly want?"

"Not to be strung up and left for the dogs?"

I couldn't tell if he was joking or not, and I wasn't keen to test him, so I followed behind as he led me back into his house and into the kitchen.

It was an oddly rustic space, with huge bare beams stretching along the ceiling, with pots, pans and dried herbs hanging from hooks. The room was dominated by a fireplace set deep within an inglenook, a heavy pot hanging over the grate. A worn leather armchair sat in the corner, a tatty blanket hanging over the back. I could imagine him curled up there, book in hand…I stopped myself; I didn't need to think of him as anything but a cold, heartless monster.

Sitting down at a weathered old table, I watched while Laphaniel prepared dinner, plucking the vibrant feathers of some strange bird he had hanging from the rafters. He cleaned it with skilled hands before adding it to the pot, alongside an array of deliciously scented ingredients that made my mouth water. I really hadn't realised how hungry I was until the prospect of a proper meal was in front of me.

"Do you cook often?" I asked, feeling the awkwardness of the silence that lingered over us.

"If I want to eat."

"And you need to?" He gave me a funny look. "I mean, you don't live off sunlight or the nectar of flowers? Perhaps the laughter of children?"

"Why would you think I lived off the laughter of children?"

"Their screams then?"

Laphaniel laughed, and just like that, some of the tension between us lifted away. It made eating with him much more bearable. It was almost less awkward than sitting to dinner with my mother and her ghostly dinner guests, though not quite.

"Smells good," I said, as he handed me a bowl filled with enticing food. "What is this?"

"Marsh bird, they flock down by the lake in their hundreds."

I barely noticed I had finished my bowl until Laphaniel re-filled it, and I smiled guiltily before I wolfed that one down too. It tasted amazing, creamy and spicy and filled with flavours I had never tried before. The meat was tender and perfectly cooked and had a delicate sweetness to it that balanced the warmth of the spices. Feeling wonderfully full, I pushed my empty bowl away and leant forward towards Laphaniel. He gazed back, chewed and swallowed before lifting an eyebrow.

"So....cursed?" I asked.

"Yes."

"Do tell me."

Laphaniel sighed. "How much do you know about faeries, Teya?"

"Not much."

"Did you know there are two Courts?" I shook my head, and he continued. "The Seelie and Unseelie are the two Courts of Faerie. Brianna ruled over the Court of Light...the Seelie with her Consort, and Soren, the Barren Queen, ruled over the shadow Court of the Unseelie. There had been no wars for centuries, the boundaries between each court were clear, and as long as each court remained on its side, no one was killed."

"What Court are you from?" I asked, flinching when his eyes blackened at the question.

"If I were Unseelie, you would have been flayed alive," he said, a chill seeping into his voice.

"Right. Good to know," I said. "Please continue."

Still glaring at me with narrowed eyes, Laphaniel poured himself some wine before offering me the blood red liquor. I took a wary sip, tasting ripe blackberries dance on my tongue alongside the subtle warmth of chocolate. I could have easily drained the cup.

"Ciaran, the King of Seelie, went missing. The Queen was desolate and sent out searches that spanned as far as the northern mountains. Most of the parties never returned, most likely picked off by giants or caught by the ice witches up in the caverns. She sent knights into the Unseelie lands, some refused to go and were executed in the courtyards, the ones that did go never came back either." Laphaniel poured himself more wine. "I have no idea why Ciaran would trespass into the Shadow Court; perhaps he was so arrogant that he believed he would be left untouched, and that the Unseelie wouldn't peel him apart and send him back to his beloved in bits."

"They chopped him up?" I asked, closing my eyes against such brutality. "Oh, God."

"The Unseelie have an incredibly talented surgeon, and she would have made sure he was kept alive and knew exactly where he was being posted to."

"She?" I shuddered at the thought of such a monster, silently praying I would never be unlucky enough to meet her.

"Charlotte is the demon that fey mothers warn their children about. They whisper stories around the fire of the Spider that can carve you up without the use of a blade."

I shuddered. "A faerie bogie-woman that scares even the likes of you?"

"Don't creep past the old oaks when the moon is full, else the spider-witch will eat you." Laphaniel grinned, and I found myself smiling back.

"So, she killed the Seelie King?" I asked, taking another sip of my wine, enjoying the warmth it left behind.

"Eventually. His heart was the last thing to be sent to the Queen," Laphaniel replied. "She didn't take it well, and strung herself up from the willows down by the lake with Ciaran's heart in her hands."

"What a beautiful love story," I said dryly. "So why did you need Niven?"

"Will you let me finish?"

"Okay, go on. What happened after your King and Queen died?"

Laphaniel poured himself yet another drink, giving me a look when I held out my own empty cup. With a small shrug, he filled mine to the top.

"The Queen had two daughters, Teya. We were left with two princesses, the eldest was Sorcha and naturally destined for the throne. And then there was her sister."

"Luthien," I breathed. Laphaniel nodded.

"There were many that felt that Luthien was better suited to rule, myself included. So the Seelie went to war amongst ourselves."

"For how long?"

"Too long."

Laphaniel closed his eyes briefly, losing himself to a memory I played no part in. His fingers played with the cup, and for just a moment he looked uncomfortable...almost restless.

"War ravaged on for years," he continued, flicking his fingers over a candle stub and instantly bringing the flame to life. "Though finally, Luthien's army began to get an advantage, and a few of us were able to take the Castle. We tore our way through the corridors, merciless...exhausted...bitter, and finally found Sorcha in the west tower, unguarded and alone save for a human child she bounced on her lap.

"Sorcha barely looked up as we surrounded her, but she was smiling. Then she reached up, took the crown from her head, and placed it upon the child, whilst whispering words none of us understood. She then cut her own throat before we had a chance to stop her."

"Why?" I couldn't keep the horror from my voice, unused to so much violence.

"Because she knew she had lost."

"What happened to the child?" I asked.

"The enchantment Sorcha uttered before her death had made the child our Queen. Knowing she was outnumbered and was losing the war, she chose to curse her own people with a human ruler, not caring that it would weaken them. Just as long as her sister never gained the throne."

"What did you do with the little girl?" I asked, not sure if I really wanted to know the answer. I wasn't really expecting a happy ending to his story.

"Luthien killed her in the vain hope it would allow her to rule. Obviously, it didn't work, and soon we had Unseelie sniffing over our borders, picking off the weaker fey. Sorcha ensured that only a human girl would rule the Seelie Court, but they would wither and die every fifty years and would always need replacing. We would always try to source those that had some potential at creating a stronger court...a certain coldness or detachment from those around them, a lack of empathy..."

"Cruel and heartless, just like Niven," I blurted out, and smacked my hand over my mouth as if I could just shove the words back in. "I didn't mean that. Niven could be a bully, but she wasn't heartless."

Laphaniel looked at me, and I scowled back at the pity in his violet eyes. "We wouldn't have taken her if she was anything less."

"You made my sister your queen?"

"Now can you understand why we cannot give her back to you?"

I dragged my hands through my hair and rubbed at my eyes, feeling the weight of a few too many drinks press against my temples. I took a breath, trying to take in everything he had told me, but I couldn't...I didn't know where to start. I was tired, emotionally and physically. The whole story had left me with a pounding headache.

"Perhaps it's all the wine you have had," Laphaniel offered when I complained, grinning slightly before he tipped back the last of his drink.

I glared up at him, his story whirling around my mind, revealing a few answers I had been seeking, but leaving me with so many more questions. "You said you lock the human queens away, where?"

"In the Castle of Seelie. We abandoned it long ago, nothing haunts its rooms now save for the mortal Queen we dump there."

"Why? Why treat them like that?"

"Because they are practically useless to us, Teya," Laphaniel answered, not unkindly. "They are not fey, they don't possess the raw power a true queen would hold. We lock them away so we can forget."

I swirled the last of my wine around in my glass, spilling it over my fingers. "What kind of queen would Luthien have made?"

He was quiet for a moment, deep in thought. "She would have set this world alight, burned her enemies with a fleeting thought and rejoiced in the embers she left behind."

I swallowed. "And you wanted that?"

"In the end, I just wanted the war to be over."

"I don't know what to do," I breathed, allowing my head to fall against the table. "I need her back. I can't go home without her."

"Do you love Niven?" Laphaniel said, suddenly beside me. I looked up and noticed that the wine had stained his lips a deep red.

"Do you love Luthien?" I countered.

He reached up to tuck a stray strand of hair behind my

ear, the light from the candle flickering across his face and making his eyes shine. When he spoke, I couldn't miss the hint of regret in his voice, the note of sadness that added a haunting melody to his already alluring voice.

"I did once."

He didn't say anymore but walked over to pluck another bottle of wine from a shelf and brought it back with him as he sat down beside me, turning to gaze out at the stars that nestled against the night sky. With a quick glance to me, he topped up my wine before bringing the bottle to his lips to drink deeply.

"Are you trying to get me drunk?" I said, drinking from my own glass, enjoying the gentle numbness.

Laphaniel shook his head. "No, I just don't enjoy drinking alone." He paused, tilting his head to give me a sideways glance. "I am not going to hurt you, Teya."

"I wasn't implying that," I replied, the thought having never actually crossed my mind. I was oddly saddened that was where his thoughts drifted to.

I watched him as he watched the stars, noticing how his fingers absently moved up and down the near empty wine bottle. Without thinking, and feeling incredibly lonely, I rested my head against his shoulder. His body tensed for a moment, then relaxed as we sat in comfortable silence and watched while shooting stars raced across the skies.

Perhaps it was all the wine I had tipped back, or simply because of the new, strange companionship, but tears began to slip down my cheeks. Quiet tears that I thought went unnoticed until Laphaniel swiped one away with his fingertip.

"I don't usually cry this much." A lump formed in the back of my throat. I took another long swallow of wine, knowing it wouldn't help. "I'm a melancholy drunk."

He nudged my shoulder. "As am I."

More tears fell, not the gasping sobs like before that left me unable to breathe. I was like a well that was simply too full.

I stared out into the star-speckled night. "I don't want to be alone anymore."

"I am not used to company," Laphaniel began, swirling his wine before drinking. "Well, not the kind to sit and watch the stars with. To talk to over bottles of wine. It is not terrible."

I snorted into my drink. "Not terrible?"

"Pleasant then."

"I can hardly imagine why you don't have many friends." I said with a smile. He tilted his head as he looked at me, so close I could see the silver circling his pupils. "You're so warm and welcoming."

"I welcomed you into my home." He poured another glass of wine. "Are we not now friends?"

My stomach flipped. "I think we could be."

The rich wine settled over me like a blanket, and I didn't even realise I had fallen asleep until I opened my eyes to find Laphaniel lowering me into his bed. He turned to ignite the candle with a twist of his fingers. He made to leave, and with no conscious thought, my hand shot out to stop him, fear rising like a tide inside me at the thought of being alone in the dark.

"Please don't leave," I pleaded, dropping my hand instantly at how childish I sounded, but Laphaniel just sat down beside me, stretching his long legs across the covers.

"You're afraid of the dark?"

"Can you blame me?" I replied, somewhat defensively even though there was nothing mocking in the tone of his voice. I stared up at the twisted branches that swept across the room and dripped down the walls. "Imagine if you needed a nightlight just so you could sleep without screaming. The girls at my school found out and made my life miserable because of it. They cornered me one day, a group of them, like a pack of hyenas. Sam Black, Lizzy Taylor, Pippa McKinley and Rebecca Long all dragged me behind the school to where the caretaker kept all his tools and things. It was more of a cupboard really, damp and smelly and windowless, and they locked me in there until...”

“Until what?” Laphaniel asked, his voice soft in the dark.

I remembered the utter blackness, how smothering it was, how it enveloped everything. I remembered the feel of bruises on my arms as they shoved me in, pinching at me in a way only girls could.

I remembered thinking I would suffocate, and although I had scratched at the door until my fingers bled and screamed and screamed and screamed, they didn't let me go.

“Let's just say when Mrs Harkness found me, we needed to rummage through the lost and found box to find dry clothes.”

“What happened to the girls?”

I shifted to face him. “They were suspended, which was a small victory really. If I thought being the girl who was afraid of the dark was bad, being the girl who wet herself was a lot worse.”

“I sent Lily away.”

Relief coursed through me. “Thank you.”

“I thought perhaps I would give you one less reason to worry about the monsters lingering in the shadows.”

I was quietly touched. “Was she your...friend...or...”

“Are you asking me if she was my lover, Teya?” Laphaniel replied, humour warming his voice. “She was on occasion, but never anything more.”

“Did she sleep in here?” I asked, running my hand over

the worn furs that covered the bed, feeling them warm and soft against my skin.

"No. There has only been one woman to lie in that bed, and she's still occupying it."

"Oh." I felt a blush creep up over my cheeks, feeling a strange mix of happiness and fear wash over me.

"What will you do when you don't want me here any longer?"

Laphaniel chuckled, the sound deep and oddly reassuring. "Why? How long do you plan on staying?"

"Hopefully not much longer."

That was the truth. I didn't want to stay any longer. The more I stayed with him, the more I seemed to like him. I could feel the hate I should have felt for him ebb away, slowly turning into something else that made the guilt inside me rise up until I could think of nothing else.

Are we not friends?

"If you say so," Laphaniel said softly, leaning back against the pillows.

"Curses can be broken, you know," I said.

He paused before speaking. "They can."

"Laphaniel?"

"Yes, Teya?"

I shifted on the bed, pulling up a particularly furry throw and wrapping myself in it. "You live in a house made from trees, don't you get all sorts of wildlife in here? Like stray squirrels and errant deer?"

He huffed a laugh. "No, I don't have that problem."

"Why do you think that is? What's stopping them from nesting in here?" I asked, staring into the eaves, but I could see nothing save the odd cobweb in the far corners.

"It's likely something to do with the vast forest outside."

"Oh," I murmured, watching as the candlelight flickered

over the walls, making the shadows waltz. I enjoyed the quiet for a moment, there was no sound save for the gentle sway of the trees outside. "Laphaniel?"

"Hmmm?"

"I'm not going back home."

He said nothing, and I figured I had pissed him off again. I steeled myself, but I wasn't in the mood for more bickering. I turned, and his head lolled against the pillow.

He had fallen asleep beside me, lips slightly parted as he breathed deeply. Sighing, I grabbed one of the furs that covered his bed, pulling it over him, watching him stir slightly as I brushed the near black hair from his eyes.

"I was doing just fine not liking you." I whispered. "It would be so much easier if I could hate you, I should be able to hate you." I ran my finger over his cheek, trailing his jawbone and the edge of his mouth. He didn't move, looking utterly exhausted. "I don't know how you make me feel. You frighten me, but then you do this...you make me feel safe and it's making my head hurt."

I closed my eyes and I curled up beside him, smiling to myself as he mumbled something incoherent in his sleep. For the first time in years, I wasn't afraid to go to sleep, I wasn't afraid of the shadows that danced around the room. I even hoped that the nightmares wouldn't find me, and that instead of Niven filling my dreams, it would be him.

CHAPTER THIRTEEN

I woke sometime during the night, a weight against me, warm and comforting. I shifted slightly, and Laphaniel's arm slid over my shoulder, his hand coming to rest upon my stomach. He snored softly, his head resting against my neck, his breath on my skin. It was incredibly disconcerting.

I snuggled back under the blankets and closed my eyes, enjoying the warmth and absence of nightmares. I nestled against Laphaniel and slept until sunrise. He left as soon as the sun came up, slowly withdrawing his arm and untangling his limbs from mine while I feigned sleep.

I heard the latch on the door click as he left, and I reached out and spread my hand over the still warm sheets where he had slept beside me.

Guilt bubbled up like acid inside me, ruining the feeling of contentment I felt, as I lay there surrounded by blankets that smelled like the forest. A prickly warmth started at the base of my spine, creeping its way up to replace any happiness with shame and disgust.

It was a nasty feeling, being torn between an increased

longing to be with him, and the cold loathing I had for myself for wanting him. Why couldn't I hate him? Deep down I wondered if it was because I thought Niven wasn't worth saving, a thought that left me hot with shame.

Niven and I had never been close. We had never shared that sisterly bond that others seemed to have, and ever since I could remember, Niven had always frightened me. My mother tried to coax us into being friends, but Niven would stare at me with her periwinkle eyes until I shuddered and looked away. She was an unnerving creature, my sister.

Things would go missing around her, small items to begin with…a favoured doll, a cherished necklace, only to turn up much later. Damaged. My parents were oblivious to her sly smiles, the way she watched me as I was comforted over the broken remains of my belongings. She hid it so well, wrapping her arms around me while I cried, her fingers pinching where no one would see.

I stretched and slid out of bed, moving over to the cupboards to find fresh clothes, already missing my jeans and t-shirts. I found a deep blue shirt and another belt, fashioning myself a makeshift dress. I ran my fingers over the fabric, rolling up the sleeves so they didn't trail over my hands. It was warm, roughly woven and smelled like him.

Feeling suddenly awkward, I made my way downstairs, finding Laphaniel once again in the kitchen. He smiled as he tossed me an apple, taking a stride across the room to take my hand, tugging me towards the door.

"Come with me, I want to show you something."

Laphaniel pulled me outside, and I shivered slightly in the early morning breeze. I looked out over the trees, at some of the still sleeping blossom that unfurled against the gentle wind. The rising sun only just touched the edges of the branches, teasing them with kisses so the dew upon them glistened.

"Show me what?"

"It's a surprise," he said, pulling me towards the trees.

"I don't like surprises, Laphaniel," I replied, panicked. The last surprise had me sold at market, and I wasn't likely to forget that in a hurry.

"Am I not your friend?" he asked, turning to face me, his lovely features shining with innocence. "Don't you trust me?"

I looked at him incredulously. "Are you serious?"

Laphaniel was silent, revealing nothing as he looked at me. He dropped my hand and began to walk into the forest. I flexed my fingers, missing his warmth.

"Why on earth would you expect me to trust you?" I demanded.

"I don't expect you to do anything."

"You are infuriating," I snapped, bristling.

"Thank you."

"Do you know you've told me countless times that you've led people into the woods to watch them die?" I said to his back, while he carried on walking. "You can be charmingly sweet to me one minute, and the next you look as if you're going to rip my heart out. You danced with my sister when I was just a child, taking her into the woods never to be seen again..."

"Then why are you following me?"

"How the hell do you do that?" I gasped, looking around. I had no idea where I was. Damn my rebellious feet, I hadn't even realised they were moving.

Early morning mist circled around my ankles, swallowing my feet in a cloud of damp. I backed away from Laphaniel quickly, but he caught my wrist before I could take two steps. I thought my heart was going to explode through my chest as

I struggled against his hold. He tried to pull me into the shadows which danced and skipped across the forest floor, swirling up from the mist with ghostly fingers.

"I want to go back," I pleaded. "Now."

"Don't you want to know where I'm taking you?" he said, lifting his hand up so I was forced to twirl, my feet skidding over the damp grass.

"No." I kicked him hard, forcing him to drop my hands with a hiss of pain and I bolted. I ran back the way we had come, stumbling over in my haste to get away, clawing my way back up when I fell.

"Teya!" Laphaniel shouted, his voice too close for me to slow down, so I continued to trip and heave myself up as I darted through the oaks. "Stop."

I felt my foot twist on an exposed root, sending me sprawling into Laphaniel's arms. He clamped his hand over my mouth as I made to scream, but I choked down the noise knowing that no one would come for me.

"You will get lost," he snapped. "You're running the wrong way."

Laphaniel's hold was unbreakable as he began to drag me towards the shadows, his left hand still clamped firmly over my mouth.

"Don't scream," he ordered, before he slowly withdrew his hand from my lips. But panic and blinding fear overruled everything, and I screamed as loud as I could.

I bit my lip when his hand smacked against my mouth, muffling my cries instantly. The woody scent of his skin mingled with the coppery tang of my blood.

"You will scare them away, Teya," Laphaniel said gently, keeping his hand over my mouth. "Be quiet."

With my legs shaking, he pulled me along as I could only imagine what lay in store for me. Finally, he stopped, and my legs buckled as I sank to the floor. Leaning in closer, Laphaniel sank down beside me, almost tenderly taking my face in his hands. I was too terrified to move, too terrified to break my gaze away from his face.

With an affection that made my confused heart leap, Laphaniel slid his hand down my neck, twisting it gently so I could see the monsters he had waiting for me.

"Oh..."

They stood in a small circular clearing, surrounded by trees whose branches entwined in a knot of both ancient and young. A stream trickled nearby, growing into a faster flowing river that poured over the hillside, turning the water white as it crashed over the rocks. All was silent except for the rush of water. The soft sunlight streamed down through the still trees, casting elegant shadows that stretched across the ground.

"I told you not to scream," Laphaniel whispered beside me, slipping his hand in mine to help me up. I rested my back against one of the trees, giving me a better view of the clearing, keeping my hand caught up in Laphaniel's fingers. I pulled him with me as I crept closer to get a better look, feeling the warmth of his skin against mine. I couldn't find any words to say to him; though hundreds flooded my mind...none of them would do. A simple thank-you just wouldn't have been enough.

"Can I touch them?" I finally said, the words breathless against my lips.

"Yes."

I couldn't take my eyes off their gleaming horns, the wild blackness in their gaze as they noticed me, the clouds of breath snorting from flared nostrils as they pawed the ground. Swallowing hard, I stepped forward, praying that it wasn't all just a cruel joke. Laphaniel stayed where he was, and I could feel his gaze on my back as I walked into the clearing. I looked back once, seeing him sitting on the forest floor with his knees drawn up to his chest, his head slightly cocked as he watched me. From where I was standing, I could see the incredible colour of his eyes, shining bright amongst the shadows of the trees and I felt my stomach flip.

I took a step and then another, watching as they reared their heads as I moved closer, their horns snapping through the air in an almost violent movement, cutting through the swirling mist that curled up from the ground. You could compare them to horses as easily as you could a sparrow to a phoenix.

The sunlight danced over their coats as if drawn to them, barely touching their hides to make them glow. It was the purest of whites, shadowed only by the flecks of silver in their manes as it flowed over their graceful necks. Raising my hand, I reached out to touch the one closest to me, feeling my fingers tremble when they ghosted over the gap between us. It took a step closer, pushing its head into my trembling hand, forcing my fingers through the tuft of hair between its ears.

I gasped as my hand brushed against the base of its horn, startled by the odd chill that came off it. I entangled my fingers in its mane as it raised its head to rest against my shoulder.

"You are beautiful," I whispered, turning my head to breathe in the soft smell coming from its coat, a mix of rain and spice, the smell that comes just before a thunderstorm.

Shadows fell across me as the others crowded around, curiosity shining in their obsidian eyes. Their horns came shockingly close to my face, grazing softly over my skin as they gently nipped my clothes. I counted eight, each one as stunning as the others, each one nudging the other out of the way to get a better look at me. My face ached with my smile, my head spinning with the impossibility of what was surrounding me. I couldn't see anything but shining white, the shimmer of their horns and the fierce, wild black of their eyes. Their scent swirled around me like the forest mist, clinging to my skin, my hair...my memories. I couldn't remember a time when I had felt so happy...so alive.

All too soon it was over. A crash of thunder rolled in the distance, and they reared up as one. I narrowly missed being blinded by dropping to the floor with my hands clamped over my head. Before the echo of thunder had died out, they were gone, disappearing into the trees without so much as a whisper.

I kept my eyes on the empty clearing, watching as the newly broken stems of grass swayed in the breeze. I barely felt Laphaniel's hand on my arm as he gently pulled me back up, his fingers cold and damp where he had been sitting on the ground.

"I won't ever forget that," I said, standing on tiptoes to kiss him on the cheek, joining my hands behind his neck, so I could feel the soft thump of his pulse against my wrist. It quickened under my touch, my own heartbeat speeding up as my lips brushed over his skin.

Laphaniel's head turned down, just as mine turned up, my mouth grazing over his cheek to find his lips. His hands came up around me, entangling in my hair as he pulled me closer, crushing my lips to his with a kiss that forced any coherent thought from my mind. Laphaniel pulled away first, and my skin tingled where he had touched me. I could still taste him against my mouth.

"Sorry," I mumbled, as heat flooded my face. I noticed that a few of Laphaniel's shirt buttons were undone, and I couldn't remember undoing them. I guessed my hands were just as rebellious as my feet.

"Sorry that you kissed me? Or sorry that I kissed you back?" he asked, his voice a whisper against my neck, rich in the promises of tempting kisses.

"I dunno..." I breathed, rolling my eyes at the pathetic noise that escaped my mouth, wondering desperately where my resolve to hate him had toddled off to.

"You dunno?" The word sounded strange coming from him, his accent made the slang seem like something magical.

There was a smile hinting in his voice, but he dropped his hands from me, and stepped back, giving me space. Feeling suddenly fearless, I closed the gap, tilting my head up to meet his eyes. There was something deep within me that called out to him, a wildness I had yet to fully discover...to let loose.

"I would like to find out though."

Laphaniel's breath caught when I kissed him again, and I could almost taste the surprise on his lips as he kissed me back. I forgot that I wasn't supposed to like him...I made myself forget, because giving in was so much easier than I could have imagined.

I didn't care that the grass was damp beneath us as we sank to the floor, or how the dew soaked into the fabric of my clothes. There was nothing but the sensation of Laphaniel's hands against me, his careful fingers deftly freeing the buttons on my shirt. He moved his hand to my cheek, pushing it gently so that I was looking at him. I blinked and blushed under his burning gaze, returning his wonderful smile with my own shy one.

My hand stayed to the waistband of his trousers, not daring to go further. My fingers brushed against him, and I yanked them away.

"We can go back, if you wish," Laphaniel said, taking my hand and pressing a kiss to my wrist.

His breathing matched mine, erratic and harsh. His eyes

were black…the curve of his lips, wicked. He looked wild, with his hair mussed, and his chest bare. There was mud on his stomach…handprints. My handprints.

Something stirred in my belly that was definitely not fear, it slipped lower and I clamped my thighs shut.

Laphaniel froze, dark gaze slipping from my face down to lap. I didn't think he was breathing.

"Do you want to go back?" The words were slow, deliberate. He moved closer without seeming to realise it.

Perhaps I should have felt a spark of fear then, at the wild faerie hovering over me, black eyed and feral.

Instead, I felt powerful.

"I don't want to go back," I said, pulling him closer to me, my mouth finding his again.

His reply was a rough whisper, "Good."

He kissed me again, his mouth hard against mine, his hands trailing beneath my borrowed shirt to rest against my hip.

"I don't have…" I blushed harder as he stared at me, eyes narrowing. "I don't...you know...I'm not on the pill or anything...I don't..."

"Oh," he said, suddenly looking sheepish, and unfolded a small blue square in his hand. "Don't get angry."

"You stole that from my bag!" I snapped, ignoring his request for me to keep my temper. I jumped up, shoving him off me as fury and humiliation replaced any other feelings I had been enjoying. "Did you just assume you could show me some unicorns and I would sleep with you?"

"You are hardly proving me wrong," he countered, at least having the good grace to look wounded.

"Is that why you did it?"

"No."

"Then why?"

Laphaniel sighed, raking a hand through his already messed up hair. "I did it because I wanted to know what you looked like when you truly smile, when you are not weighed down with guilt or fear...I was curious."

"And?"

"You're breathtaking."

"Oh." I looked down, feeling bare…not because of my lack of clothes, but because it seemed as though someone finally saw me.

His fingers brushed against my lip, soft. Featherlight.

"I'm new at this," I said.

"At kissing in the grass?"

I laughed, feeling as though the world could stop turning and I wouldn't notice. "And the rest."

"There doesn't have to be anything else, if you don't want there to be," he said gently, "I truly didn't bring you here to steal away your innocence."

And I was innocent, untouched…naïve. I had no real frame of reference save for the few movies I had watched. I wasn't counting on the handful of sex education lessons I had at school to be of much use. We had a condom. I could tick that off.

"You did come prepared though, like a good boy scout."

Laphaniel's eyes glinted, not a hint of shame on his face as he shrugged.

Our bodies fit together perfectly, moving in time to our frantic breaths, the thundering sound of our heartbeats. Sweat glistened our skin, dampened our hair as we fucked under the watching trees. He tasted of autumn spice and wild herbs, of liquorice and fire smoke, and beneath that…of me.

I felt unmade. Utterly and completely unmade. I was vulnerable, and fearless, and something other than I was before.

I had too many feelings.

Laphaniel moved off me and I noticed the blood stain on the shirt we had accidently laid upon. He saw it too and reached for his clean shirt and passed it to me. He looked a little lost for words too.

"Did I hurt you?"

I slipped the shirt on, wondering what to do next. My limbs felt too loose. Laphaniel propped himself up against a tree, still gloriously naked. He gave me a crooked grin, and pulled me against him, holding me tight.

It was startling to realise how good it felt…how safe. How like home it was beginning to feel being beside him.

"It hurt and then it didn't," I began, resting my head against his shoulder. "Then it was perfect."

He kissed the top of my head, one hand softly running up and down my arm. His heartbeat drummed in my ear, playing a song only for me.

I allowed my eyes to close, to drift off in his arms. I could trust him…I knew deep in my bones I could trust him, that despite his wickedness, he wouldn't hurt me.

Perhaps, after I found Niven and brought her home, we could discover if there was meant to be more between us.

Trust and friendship.

I liked the sound of that.

CHAPTER FOURTEEN

*L*aphaniel held me in his arms while we watched the
sky slowly fade from late afternoon into early
evening. His fingers entwined with mine, as I
watched the sun sink slowly behind the horizon.

"You have two suns here," I said, gazing up at the twin
sunset.

"Yes," he replied, not looking up. "Our own, and the
shadow of yours."

"Then how come we only see one?"

Laphaniel sat up, pulling me with him so I rested against
his bare shoulder. "Because you don't look hard enough."

I lay against him while he absently trailed his fingers
down my back, watching as the sky darkened. I lifted my own
hand to tuck a strand of dark hair behind his ear, lingering
over the pointed tip. They were as sharp as his cheekbones
and just as inhuman.

"Can you hear my heartbeat?"

His smile was wolfish. "Yes."

"I can't hear yours." I bent my head to listen but could
hear nothing save for the song of the woods.

Laphaniel's finger traced the curve of my ear, then he pulled me close. My head against his chest. I heard it quicken, the steady thump dancing into something more erratic. He placed a kiss on the top of my head, arms tightening around me.

"It sings for you."

Night crept in slowly to snuff out the sunset and set the sky alight with its stars. In the distance, something howled, and I tensed in Laphaniel's hold.

"You're safe here," he said, cupping my chin so I looked at him and not the shadows. "But I can take you back if you want."

I was surrounded by moonlight and stars, the gentle scent of cherry blossom that dangled just above our heads, and lush grass dotted with wildflowers. The nearby stream played out the soundtrack to the night, a personal playlist of music that belonged only to us. It was beautiful...and if it were not for the slow creeping feeling of guilt that had begun to weasel its way back in again, it would have been perfect.

"Can we stay here?" I curled into him closer. "Just for a bit longer?"

"You can stay as long as you like."

The whisper of his words ghosted over my neck, sending my heart jumping behind my ribs. There was something lingering behind those simple words, dripping in tainted promises and painful hope. I didn't dare cling to them, I couldn't...I wouldn't.

God help me.

I closed my eyes as I lay beside him, remembering the way his body felt against mine. The way his heart hammered against his chest, as erratic as mine had been, mimicking it in a song that neither of us really understood. There the press of his hands on my skin, his lips on my neck, my mouth, my breast. A shock of pain, forgotten in an instant. His lips at my ear as he reassured me, whispering words that made my soul sing.

"I still need to find Niven, you know that, right?" My words cut through the quiet. Laphaniel didn't answer straight away, though he continued to run his finger along my arm, his touch igniting my skin.

"I guessed as much."

"What's that supposed to mean?"

I felt him sigh against my neck, the warmth of his breath mixed with the woody scent I would only ever associate with him. "Does it matter?"

"It matters to me," I said, surprised at how true that was.

"Nothing is ever going to be enough for you, is it?"

I wasn't expecting that answer, and it stunned me. I blinked once, twice, feeling his hand slide away from my arm.

"Meaning what?"

Laphaniel shifted beside me, pulling his shirt back, leaving the buttons undone so that it hung loose around his lithe body. "You know you are wasting your life and do nothing about it. You need that feeling of guilt so you can use it as an excuse to exclude yourself. Nothing will ever be good enough for you. I wonder if it would be enough if you did manage to save your sister. Tell me, would you allow yourself to be happy if you had Niven back?"

He turned to look at me, his dark hair ruffled and messy from rolling around on the forest floor. A lump formed in my throat as I turned away.

"I need to find her." I said at last, refusing to answer his question. I reached out and pulled the rumpled shirt over my head, hugging my hands around my body. I had been lying on it and there was a tiny blood stain soaked into one of the corners.

"You keep saying that," Laphaniel said, his tone kind. "But do you want to?"

I closed my eyes and shook my head. Tears trickled down my cheeks as I wished I could just curl back in his arms and forget again.

"You could stay here."

I felt the subtle push in his voice, the one he used when he tried to force me to go back home. It banished away the thoughts of guilt and shame, leaving behind a lightness I craved. It was intoxicating, tempting, and a part of me was willing to give up, give in and forget. A part of me wanted to spend whatever part of forever he had for me, by his side...just like that, until the day inevitably came when he lost interest in me.

"I can't," I said at last. "I'm sorry, Laphaniel, but I can't."

"Why?" His voice took on a haunting lilt that left nothing but a foggy mess in my head.

"I have to..." I squeezed my eyes shut, trying to picture the reason why I couldn't stay. It was like clutching at smoke. "Please...stop..."

The swirl in my head cleared slightly and the heaviness lifted. I took a breath, and let it out again, feeling it shudder as I exhaled.

"I'm here for Niven, okay?" I said more clearly. "Regardless of whether or not I want her, that's my mess to deal with, not yours. She is still my sister, and it's my fault she is here, I want to put that right."

I needed to put it right because the thought of going home without her was unbearable. It was too easy to want to stay, to want to turn my back on the pieces of my family…my home, and pretend I belonged somewhere, anywhere.

I could stay and slowly fade away or I could go home and be invisible. I would fade from Laphaniel's life like a ghost either way.

"Do you really think Niven would have bothered if it was you?" Laphaniel asked.

"I guess we'll never know."

"Forget her, Teya. You would be nothing but a memory to her if things had played out differently."

My head ached; there was a dull throbbing at the back of my skull as I clung on to reason...purpose...anything. Laphaniel moved closer, his hands on my arms as I sunk against his shoulder.

"Please," I pleaded, unable to push myself away from him. Unable to want to...need to. "I need to find...Niven..."

I had to force the words from my lips, just as Laphaniel bent to brush his lips against my mouth. I tasted the sweetness of his breath against the echo of my sister's name, and even to my ears it sounded like a question.

"Stay with me."

There was no force behind his words, and yet it took every scrap of strength I possessed to shake my head, rejecting him.

"Do you want me to let you go?"

Again, there was no force, no gentle nudge, but I couldn't bring myself to move away from him. I opened my mouth to speak, to fight. I wanted to...no, I wanted to want to, which wasn't the same thing at all.

The word I breathed against his ear was not the one I screamed in my head, and as I sank further into Laphaniel's arms, I could hear the echo of the rebellious word scratch at my lips.

"No."

CHAPTER FIFTEEN

In the long days that followed, Laphaniel showed me everything. I saw the waterfalls beyond the woodland pouring over the rocks below, and felt them crash against my skin as I swam in the lake. I watched thunderstorms tear through the skies, ripping apart the calm spring evenings in a roar of noise and light. Under the warm sun, Laphaniel held out my hands so I could watch as sprites alighted on my outstretched fingers. They were tiny and perfect, with their wings as thin as rice paper and as delicate as autumn leaves. With Laphaniel's arms always around me, I saw it all.

It didn't take long to lose track of the days, each one perfect and unique, flowing easily into the warm nights before beginning again with the dawn.

One night, he took my hand and led me deeper into the woods behind his house, showing me clearings filled with white wild flowers. Their petals curled upwards as the moonlight touched them, filling the air with rich perfume that I couldn't breathe in deep enough.

My fingers longed to hold a paintbrush again, to capture

the essence of every wonderful thing around me for all time. I needed to memorise it all because my thoughts were like grains of sand, slipping away before I could blink.

Laphaniel's hands never left me, even when he bent low to pick one of the blooms for me, his free hand lingered whisper-soft on my calf, as if he feared I would run from him. I touched his hand as he slid the stem through my hair, and I watched as his lips twitched into a near smile, though his eyes remained dark.

"Thank you," I said, reaching up to kiss him, but he turned his head, so my lips found his cheek, not his mouth. "It's beautiful."

Laphaniel shrugged, a casual lift of his shoulders that was betrayed by the black look in his eyes. I found myself clinging to his hand tighter, the erratic song of my heartbeat pausing as fear mingled with my delight and longing to be with him. I wanted him to kiss me like he had when he made love to me, but he didn't...he wouldn't, and I couldn't help but wonder if I had somehow disappointed him.

"You're bored of me already."

Laphaniel sighed, reaching up to tuck the wayward strands of hair behind my ear. He pulled me tight against him, the weight of his hands firm against the small of my back. As I nestled close to him, I could hear his heartbeat and I suddenly felt cold. There was a falling sensation in my body that had nothing to do with the closeness of his. It was like walking upstairs and believing there is one more step than there really is, that terrible sensation of displacement as your foot falls through nothing. I squeezed my eyes shut, trying to place the feeling, but I may as well have been grasping at dreams for all the good it did.

"You will be long dead before I grow bored of you, Teya."

I knew his words should have triggered something other than delighted hope, but I found myself grinning at him, my heart soaring once again.

In his arms, I watched the stars blink in the pitch as dark clouds drifted over. They were heavy with the promises of rain, rumbling with the threat of another storm. I looked up as the rain began to fall, soaking my hair as it quickly turned into a downpour. It crashed against the trees, forcing the more delicate blossom to be stripped from the branches and crushed to the floor in a flurry of multicoloured mulch. With a sweep of his hand, Laphaniel brushed away the flowers that had landed on my shoulders, his fingers lingering for a moment against my arms.

"Come home with me," he said, his voice filled with music. "Stay with me."

I untangled myself from him, and he let go reluctantly. I grinned, and his eyes darkened, the silver ring around his pupil the only light behind them. Raindrops dripped from his hair, sliding down his skin to caress his neck, and I envied them.

Laphaniel turned slowly as I moved away, twisting around to face me with his arm outstretched. I held mine out, almost touching his...but as he stepped forwards, I skipped away. I laughed at the look that flashed across his face, turning his beautiful eyes the colour of the storm clouds.

"Are you teasing me?" he asked, amusement warming his voice.

"Yes!" I laughed again, tipping my head back as I swirled with my arms outstretched, catching the raindrops. "Catch me."

I ran giggling through the trees, closely pursued by Laphaniel as he called out to me, his voice merely another shadow in the woods. There was no fear as I ran as fast as I could through the oaks and twisted vines. I wanted him to catch me.

Cold rain hammered down on me, soaking the bare skin on my arms and legs until they were nearly numb and I began to shiver. My legs were stinging from the brambles I had charged through, little trails of blood trickled down and mixed with the rain and I thought for just a moment...that I should stop...to feel something...to feel what? It made no sense to long for anything but the blind relief when Laphaniel's arms found me at last.

"Don't run from me," he said. The storm had calmed behind his eyes so instead they shone like amethysts.

"Are you worried I'll get lost?"

"Lost, fall to your death, eaten."

I smiled shyly. "All of the above?"

"If anyone could achieve all three, I have no doubts it would be you." He glanced down at my legs and narrowed his eyes. "Your legs are bleeding."

"It doesn't hurt," I began, and laughed as he scooped me up into his arms. "You make the pain go away."

"Is that what you want?"

I closed my eyes, leaning against his shoulder, breathing in the wonderful smell of him. "Yes."

"Then I can make it stop, all that pain and frustration. All that fear. I can make it all stop, so you don't need to be afraid of the dark anymore. I can show you eternity and everything in-between. We can watch the sun rise until the end of forever, and you never have to be afraid again."

I clung to him like someone drowning. "I love you."

I heard his breath catch, and waited for him to say something, to repeat those three little words that had simply flown past my lips. I had never uttered them to anyone before, and I truly believed I never would to anyone else.

"You are too willing to give your heart to me, Teya."

"You don't want it?"

Laphaniel sighed, tilting his head so it touched mine, a gentle nuzzle that was as near to a kiss as he would give me.

"I'm afraid of what I might do to it," he whispered, holding me tighter as he began to move silently through the dark woods.

CHAPTER SIXTEEN

*L*aphaniel's hand was warm against my arm, his fingers tight on my skin, ready to pull me back if I got too close to the edge of the lake. He would only allow me to watch from a distance, forbidding me to touch the beautiful creatures as I did the unicorns. From where I stood, I could see them lazing on the rocks as the sunlight shone down on them. Their wet bodies glistened in the morning light, the droplets of water glimmering like gemstones on their naked bodies. I could smell the water that rippled over them, the seaweed that clung to their knotted hair, and the odd tang that seeped from their skin that beckoned me closer.

They watched me, large black eyes unblinking as they whispered amongst themselves. I could see their mouths curve upwards as they smiled at me, their lips tinged blue as if they had spent too long in cold waters.

"Come with us," they coaxed, and if it wasn't for the ever-tightening grip Laphaniel had on me, I would have gone readily. "Come with us, swim with us...drown with us."

My feet ached to follow them, and I pulled against

Laphaniel.

"Oh, come with us, beautiful thing. It's warm down here...oh so very warm."

The bones in my fingers cracked as I wrenched my hand free and tore down the slope to the water's edge, instantly recoiling when the icy waters hit my face. Laphaniel yanked me back hard, sending me sprawling to his feet. He held a rock in his free hand and launched it into the waters. With a gasp of girlish laughter, the mermaids vanished into the lake, somersaulting from the rocks with unnerving grace, leaving barely a ripple.

"Sorry," I mumbled, accepting his outstretched hand. "Doesn't it bother you?"

"What? Their song?"

I nodded, wondering how he could resist it. The alluring lament had seeped into the back of my head, beckoned me forwards, and although I knew to follow it meant death, it didn't matter.

"I can hear what they really sound like. Believe me, you wouldn't be running towards them if you could hear their true song."

"What do they sound like to you?"

"Have you ever heard someone drown before?"

I shook my head, turning around to see one of them bob her head out of the water, her inky hair shimmering in the dark depths. Even from the shelter of the trees, I could hear her sing to me, though this time as my feet inched toward her, I clung to Laphaniel like a frightened child. Her music was as lovely as it was before, but the spell she had woven had been broken.

"What else have you got to show me?" I asked, my grip on his hand relaxing as the welcoming sight of his house came into view.

"What else do you want to see?"

"Everything." I trembled as he ran his fingers down the edge of my cheek and my neckline. "If we really have all of forever, I want to see everything."

"As you wish."

He had me wear a dress the colour of summer. The dew soaked silks of cobwebs were used to stitch together the beautiful hues of sunlight, glistening under the stars as if struck by an August sunrise. My skirts were made from storm clouds, my shoes from summer rain, frozen forever into slippers that tapped out the song of a thunderstorm every time I danced.

With my hair pinned up, loose strands of sun kissed red slipping over my face, I could almost pass for one of the fey...but only when Laphaniel looked at me. He made me feel like I was beautiful, as lovely as all the other fair creatures that joined in our dance. It was like he couldn't care less if they were there or not, as long as I was.

It made my heart soar, ache, race...

Break.

Hundreds of candles flickered in the twilight, placed without care amongst the branches and stumps throughout the forest, sending erratic shadows to join in the throng of the swaying fey. Laphaniel would not permit me to dance with anyone but him, twisting me away from the others when they outstretched their graceful hands to me.

"You are mine," he whispered against me.

"I know." I rested my head on his shoulder, waiting only a moment for those little extra words I wanted from him. I knew that soon I would stop waiting for them all together, content in the knowledge that he wanted to be with me, and had yet to grow bored.

Breathtakingly beautiful men and women begged a dance

from me, but I couldn't bear to move from Laphaniel's arms. We danced until the trees were tinged with the sunrises, watching as the moon faded and daylight took over. We waltzed past midnight and twisted until the light slowly faded again. As we swayed to the third sunset, Laphaniel took me up into his arms, and I fell asleep while he continued to dance with me to the unbroken song of the forest.

I lost count of the sunrises, having watched too many reflected in the waters of the lake to remember them all. The sunsets also rolled into one continuous pattern of night and day, with dawn melting into dusk as I danced until the sun rose again.

I spent every hour of every day with Laphaniel, his arms tight around me as if he was afraid I would turn and leave him. As if it were a possibility that I could leave him.

He watched me as I laughed and danced, and his smile would always creep in a little later, his laugh sounding more forced than mine.

"Do you love me?" I asked, needing to know if he felt as much for me as I did for him.

"I love you, Teya," he whispered back. "As much as you truly and honestly love me."

Laphaniel's words ghosted over me with a meaning that was unfathomable. It was like there was more to what he was telling me...something I was blind to...something beyond the happiness I was embracing.

Perhaps if I looked harder...

...listened to the voice screaming in my head...

...maybe it was too easy to believe he loved me...

...and to forget everything else...

...to watch the sunrises...

...the sunsets...

...forever and ever and ever...

CHAPTER SEVENTEEN

*T*he sunlight trickling through the window woke me, its weak glow seeming to struggle to pierce through the glass and warm me in my bed as it had done before. I curled my legs up, hauling the thick woollen throw around my shoulders, breathing in its earthy and familiar smell. A fire crackled and spat from the far side of the room, and I could smell the pinecones as they caught light and filled the room with warmth.

It wasn't quite perfect.

Laphaniel would always lie beside me until I fell asleep, but every morning I would wake up, and he would be gone. I longed to wake up in his arms, to watch as the light rose over his face, touching his perfect skin making him glow. I wanted to see his eyes as they flickered open, to see what they looked like before he knew I was watching him.

"Teya?"

I glanced up at the sound of my name, pushing back the throw so I could peep out into the darkened room. "Hmmm?"

"Are you awake?"

"I'm not sure if I'm dreaming." I stretched my arms out

over my head, feeling the coolness of the air tingle against my hands. "This just feels like a dream, a weird one."

"Oh?"

"Good weird." I smiled, as I noted the uncertainty in his voice. "One I don't want to wake up from."

I got up, wrapped the throw around myself and wandered over to the window. The sky had since turned an angry purple-grey, lashing down rain so hard that it made the glass sing with every furious drop. Mist coiled around the lake, seeping upwards around the trees, hiding the landscape behind a ghostly veil of smoke and cloud. Inching the window open, I felt the rain splatter against my face. I blinked as the droplets slid from my lashes and ran over my cheeks like icy tears, tasting them as they skimmed over my lips.

"You will catch a cold if you stick your head out of the window in the rain."

I hadn't heard him walk up behind me, so I jumped when he slid his hands around my waist, and melted into him as he pressed his lips to my neck.

"That's an old wives' tale," I replied, tilting my head back so it rested against his chest.

"I'll remind you of that when you fall sick."

"Would you look after me?"

"I thought you said you wouldn't catch a cold."

"No, but I might catch pneumonia."

Laphaniel smiled, reaching over me to shut the window. "Just to be on the safe side."

He turned away, but I caught his hand and gripped it tight. "How long would it take for you to replace me?"

He stopped and ran his thumb along the side of my hand. "Are you thinking of going somewhere?"

"You know what I mean."

"What if I said you were irreplaceable?"

"I would say you were charming me."

I watched with grim satisfaction as his smile faltered. "You are mine, Teya."

"Only for as long as you want me." I took his hands, pressing them against my lips. I closed my eyes. "What am I going to do when you've had enough of me? Will you take me home or leave me in the woods to die?"

"I won't grow bored of you."

"I bet that's what you've said to all the other girls," I said sadly. "My company amuses you at the moment, but it is inevitable that I will become a burden, and you will look for something new."

"Will I?" he said, his voice a warning. "You assume to know my mind better than me then?"

"You've said as much yourself, Laphaniel. You are not human, you enjoy tormenting me. I am nothing to you."

Hurt flickered over his face, and I instantly felt regretful but couldn't deny that I had given him the most fragile part of myself, and I feared for it.

"Why won't you tell me you love me?"

"Teya..."

"Please?" I whispered against him, resting my head on his chest so I could hear his heart thump. The sound was now so familiar, I could sing it in my sleep. "If you want to keep me, say you love me."

Laphaniel pushed back, and my arms fell limp at my sides. I ached for him. "I can't, Teya."

My vision blurred, and hot tears began their trailing descent down my face. I choked on a sob and flung myself on the bed, clutching at the pillow as I wept. I felt my heart break, and with it, all that was left of me began to shatter.

I had nowhere go. No one else to turn to. All I had was

the desperate love I felt for him and it was crumbling, turning to dust and nothingness and I couldn't stop it.

"I know you can't love me," I sobbed. "I completely and utterly belong to you, but you will never be mine."

The bed creaked as he lay beside me, and instinctively I curled up against him. "You do not love me."

"Of course I do!" I said, panicked. My hands curled into his shirt, as if I could stop him from leaving…from pushing me away.

"No, you don't!"

"What's wrong with me?" I asked, my voice raw. "Tell me and I'll change, I can do better, I promise I can. Just tell me what I'm doing wrong."

I couldn't bear it. The words fell from my lips in a torrent of wretchedness and I couldn't stop. I couldn't stop…

"Teya, listen," Laphaniel said, pushing me back. "I can't do this…"

"No!" I begged, grasping at him. "No! I'm sorry, you don't have to love me back. I'm sorry, okay? I won't push you again, I won't. I'll be good, I promise. Please don't send me away…not like Lily…please…please. I'll be good, I'll be a good girl. I can be whatever you want me to be, just don't let me go…"

"Stop!"

With inconceivable swiftness, he was on top of me. He snatched me by the shoulders and dragged me up to face him. His eyes blazed like the fire that spat in the grate. His fingers were harsh on my skin, and his face was a dark fury that wiped any misconceptions of his humanity from my mind. I gasped. His hold loosened, and I fell back against the pillows.

"I frighten you."

A statement, not a question.

"Yes."

"Then why," he implored. "do you think you love me?"

"Because I'm yours...forever."

"Forever?"

I nodded before I turned away, reaching up to touch the branches that swam through his house. They were strangely cold. The flowers, I noticed, no longer bloomed a beautiful pale pink, but had withered and begun to die. The once sweet-smelling petals had browned at the edges, hanging limp from their stems before falling to the floor to join the rest of the fallen. The leaves too had changed. No longer were they a lush green, but a rich union of reds and golds that crumbled as my shaking fingers reached up to touch them.

"Autumn."

My head shot up to look at him, his musical voice echoing around the room, repeating the single word until it finally meant something. A coldness that had nothing to do with the temperature of the room crept up my spine, and my stomach twisted. I swallowed quickly, eyes watering as I forced the bile back down my throat.

"Forever is a long time."

I rose from the bed, letting the throw slide down my body and fall to my feet. I shivered but didn't dare inch towards the fire. I wanted to feel the cold. I wanted it to nudge against my exposed skin, just as it had been doing for the past few weeks. The chill had meant nothing then, but suddenly my world was ending.

Time had fallen around me like confetti.

"How could you?" I gasped, my voice nothing more than a choked whisper. "Why?"

"Because you made it so easy for me."

He started to move closer, but seemed to think better of it and stayed where he was, sitting on the edge of the bed, staring at me.

"You tricked me!" I screamed at him, at last finding my voice. Anger flooded my body, a surge of rage that I clung to in a vain attempt to hold back my grief. "You lied to me."

"I cannot lie to you, Teya. You were all too willing to forget Niven. You would not have stayed unless you wanted to."

Laphaniel stood and stepped towards me. I remained rooted to the spot, glaring at him as my breath hissed through my teeth in seething gasps. "You kept me prisoner here."

"You were never a prisoner."

"You forced your...Glamour on me and made me believe I loved you," I said, disgusted. "I thought I loved you."

Love. I hadn't even known what it felt like. I had clung so desperately to the illusion of it, terrified of it slipping away. I looked at him and wanted to feel nothing but hate…loathing, but the memories of the meadow, the glade, the lake, the forest and the nights where we danced to the sounds of the forest, every memory rose up like a wave until I thought I would drown. Were they real?

Did it matter?

"You could have left at any time." Laphaniel said.

"Would you have let me?"

He hesitated. "I want to think I would have," he said at last, his words chilling.

"I've been here months."

He shrugged, as if it all meant nothing to him and I forced myself to turn away. It was like he was after my soul, as if my heart was not payment enough.

"You have kept me here for months," I repeated, my voice faltering, tears slid down my face.

"Because you did not want to leave," he said, the words gentle. His hand came up to cup my face, tilting it gently so I looked at him.

"You made me forget Niven," I replied. "You made me forget that it was you who stole her away."

"Because you have no hope of getting her back, was it not a relief not to think of her?"

"That's not up to you," I began, trying to halt the world from colliding around me. "You don't get to choose to take that away from me."

Genuine confusion swept over his face. "Why?"

"Because they were my feelings!" My voice rose. "My hate and my fear…"

"You were miserable—"

"Fuck you," I hissed, forcing my face away from his fingers. "What right do you think you have to control me like that? To manipulate me. To make me feel..."

"Happy?" he finished for me.

"Used," I breathed. A shudder ran through my body as I remembered our time in the woods. The feeling of ripped clothes, the scent of him on my skin...his lips on mine as we entwined perfectly beneath the moonlight. "There are words for people like you."

Laphaniel's eyes darkened. "*People* like me?"

"Yes. Men who like to take advantage of vulnerable women. I was vulnerable, Laphaniel, and you knew what you were doing."

"Is that what you think?" he asked, the words quiet. Shocked. "That I raped you?"

Sullying such a perfect memory wounded me more than I thought possible, but I wanted to hurt him. I needed to know I could hurt him.

Laphaniel faltered, uncertain, and for a moment, he looked lost and incredibly young. We stared at each other, working together to destroy a friendship that was built on nothing but lies and magic.

"You knew exactly what you were doing in the woods too, Teya," he began, taking a breath as he stepped closer and forced me back against the wall. "You are so desperate to be wanted…by anyone, that you gave yourself up at the first opportune moment — "

My palm stung as I slapped him hard across his face, and pain bloomed at my cheek when the back of his hand forced my head to the side. My hand flew up, feeling the hotness where he had struck me, and my eyes followed the dribble of red that trailed down his lip.

"Don't follow me."

He said nothing as he wiped at his mouth, smearing his chin with blood, but he moved aside when I ran past. A part of me expected him to grab my arm, but he let me go, his eyes black as he watched me leave.

CHAPTER EIGHTEEN

I tore down the stairs, lunging for the door and praying that he hadn't locked it. I clasped the handle with both hands, heart hammering as I forced it open and fled outside. I didn't look back as I ran, sprinting through the trees as fast as I could with bare feet. Pain shot through my toes and heels as I ran over stones and hard earth, but I felt as if I deserved it all. I ran until I finally tripped and was sent sprawling to my knees into the cold wet mud.

My sob came out like a scream, a cacophony of pain that echoed past my fingers as I tried in vain to muffle the noise. I sobbed until I retched, and finally rested my head on my knees, watching the rain as it slipped from dying leaves onto the mulch below.

I could feel the bruises on my feet from spending too many nights dancing, the warmth of wine against my lips, the sound of the trees as they sang, the weight of Laphaniel's arms around me, his heart beating against mine...all memories that had no right to linger as they did, and I wanted to be rid of them. I wanted them gone, but I ached for them in a way that threatened to tear me apart. I wondered if it would drive me mad in the end.

It had been too easy to forget Niven. She had been pushed from my mind with so little force that my stomach twisted with shame. I should have been able to hold on to her, when I was a child...and as an adult, I should have been able to hold on to her memory. I couldn't bear the thought that perhaps Laphaniel had been right all along, that I was looking for an excuse not to look for Niven. The thought settled heavy and unforgiving in my stomach; why was it so easy to forget about her?

I dragged a hand over my face, wiping furiously at my eyes as I stood up. I took a deep breath and another, until I could breathe without gasping. I looked up and noticed that the way I had come had been completely swallowed up.

Branches and vines were knotted together so tightly it was as if there had never been a path there to begin with. Others crept down, sweeping and curling together, seemingly pushing me forwards. The trees swayed, bending low as if a wind had rushed through them. Branches raked at my face, wooden fingers tinged with autumn raindrops streaked across my cheek, leaving behind a trail of blood and grime. I yelped when the limbs of a young tree tangled in my hair, forcing me back as I struggled to tear free. They came up from the ground, roots breaking the earth to catch my feet as I stumbled on, snatching my hair from my scalp as they pulled me down.

I ran.

Ivy snaked down from the boughs to form a noose around my neck, hitching me up on my tiptoes as creeping vines slid up my leg, coiling up my thigh, crawling higher and higher. I ripped the cursed things from my body, gasping as I freed my neck with a frantic tug at the vine that was choking me. I staggered forwards and shrieked when I tumbled down the sheer edge that had been hidden by the mass of writhing creepers. Ancient laughter followed my descent. I reached out to grab at roots to slow my fall, but as my fingers scrambled for them, they jerked away. I skidded and somersaulted down, each brutal thump forcing the air from my lungs until I was dumped on the floor in a heaving mess. I waited for a few moments until I could breathe again before I stood up, realising I had stumbled upon the lake that Laphaniel had shown me when the summer blossom still bloomed.

It was not as beautiful as I remembered it. Though the waterfalls still crashed down into the perfect blue, and the light still bounced from the ripples caused by the breeze, there was a darkness to it that hadn't been there before. The trees that danced at the edges were bare and stark, the trunks a bleached white as if all the summer sun had faded away. Shadows swam beneath the waters, which had frozen near the banks away from the falls. Ice gathered over the grasses and ferns, bending them low and creeping up over the bank, forcing winter deeper and deeper into the forest.

It was a sinister place, dark and lonely, where the willows seemed to listen to sounds I could not hear. There was a sudden stillness, a bated breath and I tensed.

I saw her standing at the side of the lake gazing into its depths, eyes reflecting the water so for the first time, it seemed they were something other than black. She didn't move but tilted her head to look at me. She smiled, and from where I stood, I could see the glint of her pointed teeth. I stood frozen as Lily stared back, her twisted smile still slashed across her face.

"I've been waiting for you."

Instinctively I stepped back, the sharp branches of the forest behind me stabbing into my skin. There was no way they were letting me back through.

"What do you want?" I called, hearing my trembling echo bound over the crashing waters. Lily's smile widened.

"You..." she replied, her voice soft. Deadly. In an instant she was at my side, caressing my cheek with her bone like fingers. It was so sudden; I didn't even have time to flinch. "Him..."

I tried to wrench my face from her hands, but she held tight, pushing her nails into my skin. She stretched her fingers over my cheeks, so they came horribly close to my eyes. Lily leaned closer to me so she could dart her tongue over my skin, to lap at the droplets of blood she had broken free.

"I never wanted him," I said, knowing how untrue that was.

"Liar." Lily smiled, backing up onto her haunches, her silvery hair gliding over her naked body. "Lying, filthy whore."

"Leave me alone!" I shouted. "Why can't you all just leave me alone? Don't you understand that I don't want him? Why else would I be running around the forest in the freezing bloody rain?"

Lily tilted her head, blinking as if she was only just seeing me. She reached out to run her fingers over the sleeve of the shirt I was wearing. I tensed, hearing the low growl that rumbled in her throat as she fingered the buttons, lingering for a moment with her hand over my heart.

"He loved you?"

I shook my head, barely able to utter the single syllable word without my voice breaking.

"And you do not love him?"

I paused a beat too long. "No."

Lily stared, unblinking as the same twisted smile stretched at her lips. She moved her hands over my shoulders as if to hug me, and I flinched away from her. She grinned and trailed her fingers down my arms, her touch cold.

"I think you are lying to me," she murmured softly, allowing a wicked laugh to swim past her lips. "Oh, how well you lie."

I couldn't move quickly enough before she grabbed my hand and bent it back so it was pressed against my heart. From under my palm, I could hear its quick and terrified thumps.

"I can hear it singing," Lily breathed, twisting my hand further as she bent down to listen. "Can you, Teya?"

"That's fear, you monster," I snapped. "Not love..."

"Oh, but don't they sound so beautiful? A wonderful erratic dance, I could listen to it forever. I could sing to its tune as it begins to break. Can you feel it breaking, little whore?"

"Go to hell."

She pulled back her lips to reveal a mouthful of needles, her eyes an empty oblivion as she laughed at me. Then she lunged, snake-quick and sank her teeth deep into my neck, sucking deep while I screamed.

"You see," she began, pulling away with red lips. "Fear and love sound so familiar that it's terribly easy to mistake one for the other. But when they both play together..." Her fingers began to drum out the song of my heartbeat, her mouth dripping onto my shirt. "Can't you hear it?"

"Please."

"I hear it," Lily hissed, spitting blood. "Though not quite love, is it? There's longing and lust and betrayal. A kiss? More than one? So much more than a kiss? A touch, a sigh, a groan... another…bliss, drops of blood on torn garments."

"He doesn't love me!" I cried, scrabbling away from her, but she just snatched my hand back, baring bloodied teeth. "He never once told me he loved me!"

Lily tilted her head to the left, eyes wide. "Why you?"

"I don't know."

Her voice softened, became tinged with sorrow and despair. It made my head ache and the clouds above us weep. Her hold on my arm slackened. "I would have given him everything."

"He never wanted you," I blurted, as I pulled my fingers from her hand just a fraction too late.

She snapped her hand shut, trapping my fingers inside. With a sickening crack, she twisted my wrist until I felt the bones break. I screamed as hot pain shot up my arm, and I swallowed down the sudden acidic taste in my mouth as black spots danced in front of my eyes.

"Are you going to kill me?"

With a silent grace, Lily knelt beside me and cupped my face in her too cold hands, her fingers brushing lightly over my skin. "Yes."

I was shaking, my voice trembling with both pain and fear. "What makes you think he'll want you after I'm gone?"

"He won't want me, Teya," she said sadly, blinking her black eyes and smiling at me with more than a hint of madness. "But it will be of some comfort to know he cannot have you."

She grabbed me before I could move, wrenching my head back as she dragged me towards the lake by my hair. I cried out as I jarred my hand against the cold ground, desperately trying to fight. She wouldn't let go, keeping her grip on my scalp until her nails broke the skin. I struggled against her as the water's edge grew closer, scrabbling and bucking as she forced my head under water and held me there until I thought my lungs would burst.

I gasped when I surfaced, swallowing icy water as she forced my head under again. It was so cold I couldn't fight back, the shock of the water erasing everything else except for the pain of drowning.

I surfaced again, choking and shivering, my heart screaming in my chest while my mind went blank. With a sharp yank, Lily forced my head back so I was looking at her. I couldn't speak...I hauled in a breath, feeling it tear down my throat in an angry burn.

"You should have stayed away," Lily mused lazily, and I wanted to tell her that I wished so too, but all that came from my mouth was a terrible gurgling.

She pushed me down a final time, but before my face touched the water, I heard the faint sound of singing, and something black burst from the water. It coiled around Lily, great fins powering up to the side of the lake where Lily had begun to scrabble away. I watched in horror as another slick hand crashed out of the water and snatched at her legs before slowly dragging her into the water.

I crawled away, feeling the bones in my wrist grind as I began to heave myself up the bank. I felt the chill of their fingers on my ankle before they touched me.

"Come swim with us," they sang. "Come drown with us."

I scratched at the ground, but they pulled me back. The cold water closed over my ankles, my knees, my chest, until with a last hopeless breath, I went under. I caught a glimpse of Lily as I was pulled down: webbed hands had coiled deeply into her silver hair as they used it as a rope to drag her lifeless body deeper into the waters.

I fought and I struggled. I refused to die quietly. Until the last breath bubbled past my lips, I kept on fighting. The feeling of failure crashed over me before the fear of death. My mother had lost both her daughters and hadn't buried either of them.

Red mist descended, blackness followed.

There was nothing but the soft whisper of my name...

CHAPTER NINETEEN

*T*he blackness was meant to be absolute; that was what I expected...a void that was free of pain, worry and fear. I never really stopped to think what lay beyond that, but I wasn't expecting pain.

Something crushed against my chest, sending my body into a spasm that felt nothing like death. Heat brushed against my lips, again and again and again. I heard my name, a whisper. A curse, then the pain of something crushing me once more.

"Teya?"

Warmth at my lips.

Pain and darkness.

Nothing.

"Damn you!"

More.

Again,

And again...

"Teya, please."

Another breath, another whisper, then more pain as my lungs suddenly constricted and forced black water from my mouth and nose. I couldn't see and I couldn't move, but I felt the cold like a swift bite, and the cool touch of fingers to my neck as someone sought a pulse with a shaky hand.

I heard the soft intake of breath and opened my eyes, panting for air like a hungry junkie. I met his gaze and forced my head away, choking on a sob that scratched at my throat as if it had claws.

I began to shake, my body juddering against his as he wrapped me in a warm dry cloak. He brushed against my hand, and I hissed in pain.

"Why won't you leave me alone?" I asked, my voice a trembling whisper.

"I heard you scream," Laphaniel answered, raking a hand through his sodden hair. "I thought I was too late."

His warm breath was against my ear, the wicked certainty gone from his voice, leaving it raw. I turned away and caught sight of the bobbing body of Lily abandoned near the water's edge, her black eyes huge and unseeing, blue lips bleached white in a permanent twist of horror.

"Oh god," I spluttered, covering my mouth as I vomited up more dark water. Laphaniel rubbed my back until I finished and tightened the cloak around me when I began to shudder. My muscles tensed as they went into spasm.

"I need to get you back."

"No!" I panicked, my throat protesting as I shouted, "No, leave me alone. Please...just go away."

I pushed him away, staggering to my feet, forgetting my broken wrist until Laphaniel used it to pull me back. I screamed, and he dropped my hand as if it had burned him.

"How far do you think you'll get with that?" Laphaniel said, impatience chilling his tone.

"I don't care."

"You're freezing, Teya. You stopped breathing."

I closed my eyes and braced myself against a lone sapling, whose leaves had left its branches to wither and die beneath it. "I'm not going back with you."

"Teya..."

"You'll keep me there forever." I choked on the words before my legs gave way and I slumped to the floor. I held my hands over my face and sobbed on the frigid ground, the ache in my chest breaking me into tiny unfixable pieces.

I flinched when he touched me, but still buried my head into his shoulder as he pulled me close. Laphaniel held me while I cried, his hands cold and his clothes wet, but didn't let go until I had finished hiccupping and could breathe without gasping.

"I'll take you to Luthien."

I looked up at him, searching his face for any deception behind his words, a trap so neatly tucked away that I wouldn't see it until it was far too late. I would find myself in his arms again, unknowingly watching as hundreds of years passed us by.

"If you let me help you, I promise I'll take you to her."

"No." The word dropped from my lips with more conviction than I felt. "Get away from me."

I took a step back, my fingers numb as I tightened his cloak around my shoulders, wishing I didn't need the warmth, but I wasn't stupid enough to hand it back to him. Cradling my hand to my chest, I cringed at the jolt of pain it sent through my arm every time I trembled. With heavy limbs, I stumbled away from the lake and made my way to a little hollow where the wind seemed to have a little less bite. I heard him follow me, so turned to him, gesturing to the ground.

"If you want to help me, light a fire." Anger replaced the

desolate emptiness within me, surging through me with a furious warmth. I clung to it, needing it.

"If we just go back…"

"Ha! No," I snorted, scrubbing a hand over my face. "I'm cold, just do it."

I managed to help gather some wood, piling it up while Laphaniel struggled to get it lit, the flames refusing to engulf the kindling.

"The wood is damp," Laphaniel said, while I watched on with folded arms.

"Maybe this would have been easier in the summer?" I bit back, sitting down on the cold earth, thankful when at last the flames took hold and began to spit against the wood. Laphaniel glared at me but said nothing, his eyes as black as his dripping hair.

The flames spat and crackled, licking at the damp sticks as if finding them wanting. I huddled closer in his cloak, hating the way his scent enveloped me, shrouding me in an illusion of safety. The fire was just enough to ward off the deep chill that bit at me, that had seeped so far down into my bones I wondered if I'd ever feel truly warm again. So slowly, it dried the water from my clothes, melted the ice from my hair…soothed me towards sleep.

"Stay awake!" Laphaniel nudged me and I slapped him away. "Open your eyes."

"Stop telling me what to do," I said, blinking my eyes open anyway, because I really didn't want to die of hypothermia. "And don't touch me, stay over there."

"I want to help."

"I think you've done enough."

"At least let me bind your hand?" He nodded to my wrist which I cradled against me, the pain a shooting ache that was driving me crazy.

"Fine."

With cold fingers he managed to fashion a splint out of a piece of wood and the sleeve from my shirt, tying it so tight I bit through my lip. It held better than I thought it would, the pain easing slightly, but not enough.

"That will need looking at sooner rather than later, else it will mend wrong."

"Do you have a local A and E department around here?" I muttered, backing away again, not liking the way my body had responded to his touch. His eyes flicked to mine, hearing the way my heartbeat quickened. "You backhanded me across the face."

A reminder to myself, not just him.

"You hit me first," he answered. "You drew blood."

I shook my head. "Are we keeping score?"

"No…"

"Because I think I may be winning." I paused. "Or is it losing?"

"I never intended to hurt you." Laphaniel threw another stick on the fire after noticing me shiver.

"Well, you did." I shifted closer to the flames, further away from him. "How did you think this would end?"

Silence slipped over us, cold and uncomfortable. The air around us crackling with so many words left unsaid. Anger pulsed over me and I clung to it tighter still, forcing the hurt…the shame further down. I could hardly breathe around the rage, the desire to just break something almost overwhelming. Grabbing a large log with my unbroken hand, I launched it into the fire. Embers spat everywhere sharing my fury, making Laphaniel jump.

"Be thankful I didn't throw it at your fucking head," I hissed. "Because I wanted to."

"What do you really want, Teya?"

I bristled. "For you to leave me alone!"

He rose to his feet, hesitating, looking like he wanted to say something, before he gritted his teeth and settled on an angry, "Fine!"

Without another word, he turned on his heel and walked away.

I seethed alone by the fire, a hollow emptiness threatening to replace the rage that made me want to scream into the darkness. I wanted to throw more things...I wanted to punch him in the face...I wanted to hate him as much as he deserved to be hated.

Instead, I settled for launching another crumbling, rotting log into the fire, watching as it disintegrated into a burst of sparks. I clung to my anger like a safety blanket, not daring to let it ebb away for fear of what would be left behind.

I shivered again, my wrist throbbing with the movement. I ran my fingers over the splint, at the little knots binding my hand to the wood, and the soft cushion he had made so I didn't rub my skin raw. My throat ached, my thoughts nothing but chaos.

I thought he would come back. Something deep within me simply assumed, after a while, he would return, because he always did. Not for a moment did I start to fear the darkness, believing he was nearby, keeping his distance. I ignored the wandering shadows, because I didn't believe I was alone. I hadn't been alone for a very long time. Not really.

Oh, but I was alone.

I sensed it then...on some primal level, perhaps awoken by the time I had spent among monsters.

I knew.

Fear swamped me in a sudden wave, a suffocating terror that wiped out everything else.

"Laphaniel?" I called out, my voice echoing too loudly. "Laphaniel, are you there? Because this isn't funny."

I hated calling for him...needing him, but nothing answered save for the sound of my own voice bouncing off the looming trees. A cold, horrible realization hit me, gutting me. He had left.

"You faerie bastard. Are you trying to teach me a lesson? That I need you? You really are despicable."

Hovering close to the fire, I peered into the shadows. I took a breath... another, swallowing down the dread that threatened to overwhelm me.

I took a step into the darkness, the way barely lit by the moonlight trickling down through the striped branches. Venturing out of the hollow I had found, I pulled myself up over the rocks, gritting my teeth against the cold.

My fingers found and slid over something wet and sticky, and when I pulled my hand up to the feeble moonlight, my hands were coated with blood.

"Laphaniel?" I hissed his name, unable to tear my gaze away from the crimson streaking down the stone.

There was a trail of red, splatters of blood leading through the trees. I had no doubts it was his, and that something terrible had happened.

Every nerve in my body was alight as I crept through the shadows, and I froze at every sound, every crunch of leaves, every distant cry that filled the woods with the sound of something else dying.

I fought against the urge to turn and run, at the fear that threatened to engulf me...I fought against the basic human nature to save my own skin. If something had managed to sneak up on Laphaniel, what chance did I have?

The low rumble of voices stopped me instantly, and I crouched behind a circle of jagged rocks to avoid being seen, my heart threatening to leap from my throat. I cringed against the rock, closing my eyes briefly at the horror before me.

Six bulbous creatures sat around a fire, huge long heads bent low as they snarled at one another. Thick, curling horns glowed red hot as the flames reached up to lick at them. The remains of wings slouched against the ground, great jutting bone with the barest scraps of flesh hanging between, and as their wings twitched, they thumped their long, long tails.

Something monstrous hung over the fire, held up by thick sticks that had been rammed through the meat. Its hide had blackened, no longer the deep moss-green of the others surrounding it.

I flinched at the sudden shriek of laughter, the sounds of ripping flesh drowning everything else out, sickened by the wet slobbering that followed.

"It's tough," the beast spat, taking another bite, fat slithering down its mouth to dangle at its chin. "But it tastes good."

My stomach clenched, fear a blinding force that made everything cold.

"Wait until you taste the new one," another growled, slicing a strip of meat with a curling black talon. "Wait for the baneshood to wear off, then I'll cut his throat."

I backed up, my stomach twisting and rolling with the smell of whatever…whoever they were eating. I looked away and spotted Laphaniel, and that sick feeling turned to dread.

They held him in a cage made of bones, rotten meat still clinging to the yellowing cartilage. His head rested against the grotesque bars, blood seeping from above his brow to pool over his face. I crept over to him, keeping low, staying in the shadows and never once taking my eyes off the creatures around the fire.

"Shh," I whispered when he stirred, his eyes blinking back at me. "I'm going to get you out... Somehow."

Gingerly, he moved a hand to the base of his skull, grimacing when his fingers came away red. "You need to get out of here."

His words were slow, deliberate, as if thinking straight was too hard a task. He groaned and his eyes shuttered closed.

"Have they poisoned you? Look at me!" I hissed the words, fighting panic as I pressed against the bars, cringing as my words echoed. Laphaniel flinched, but the monsters didn't turn.

"I think so..." he gestured to a discarded dart, the tip broken. "Pulled that from my neck. Teya, I can barely feel my legs... Everything's spinning... Please... Go."

"They're going to slit your throat." I breathed, searching the hideous cage for any signs of weakness, my hands coming back sticky. "What are they?"

"Trolls," he said, voice soft. "They're clever and fast." He swallowed, his face ghost white. "Leave me."

"Which one has the key?"

"I don't...I don't know," he murmured, blood dripped from his head onto the ragged bones holding him.

"Okay," I said, my fury dissolving into a frantic need to get him out. "I'm not leaving you, I'll be back as soon as I can."

"Teya, wait!" He made a feeble attempt to grab me through the bars, his fingers brushing over my wrist, causing a spasm of pain to shoot up my arm.

I shook my head, determined. "You wouldn't have left me."

"Don't..."

I reached for him, giving his hand what I hoped was a

reassuring squeeze. "I'm going to make sure I can point out the irony of this later."

He made to say something, but his eyes rolled back instead, and he slumped down with a horrible gagging noise at his lips. I shoved him onto his side just as a thin dribble of bile bubbled from his mouth.

"I'm coming back," I said firmly, running a hand over the back of his head, my fingers stopping over the sizeable bump on the back of his skull. "Trust me."

Steeling myself, I backed away from Laphaniel and crept closer to the trolls. I kept to the shadows, crawling behind rocks that covered the ground until I could feel the heat of the fire on my face. I looked back only once, but Laphaniel was motionless in his macabre cage, hurt and helpless.

In that clearing, it didn't matter what had happened between us, the words that had been said, the wrongs done. I was going to get him out or die trying.

I could smell them, the reek of sweat and filth drifted from their bodies in a foul smog. The meat they cooked over the flames gave off a greasy odour, like overdone pork and I had to fight not to lose the contents of my stomach.

Their laughter shook the ground, wicked and cruel, their great tails thumping back and forth as they shoved each other. Claws raked over scaled flesh, spilling black blood that caused the fire to hiss and spit as it dropped down.

"Do that again and I'll spit and eat you!" snarled one, forked tongue lashing out to lick at his wound. "I'll skin you before I skin the boy-elf!"

"Ha! I'd like to see you try," replied the other, bearing its teeth, huge and monstrous in its wide jaw. "What are you waiting for then, you little runt? I'd carve your skin off before you could blink, I would…"

I pressed my hands over my mouth when the smaller troll

lashed out with surprising speed, slashing a handful of claws across the other's throat in a spray of blood. It splattered on my face, hot and foul, stinging my eyes.

Blinded, I cowered in my hiding place, hands still at my mouth as roars erupted from around the firepit. I dared a glance, wiping at my eyes, my heart a jackhammer in my chest. They hurled themselves at the body, barely waiting for the flames to lick at it before tearing it to pieces. They ripped at it with a fervour, sending the scent of blood and ravished flesh into the air, turning the mist around them red.

Shards of rock dug into my hand as I gripped it hard, but I caught sight of what I was looking for and barely acknowledged the stinging pain. Hanging from a rough belt around the waist on one of the trolls, was the key.

They were lost within a frenzied bloodlust, seemingly blinded to anything but the fresh carcass in front of them. I took a breath. Another. Desperately forcing my body to move when every nerve, every instinct was screaming at me to run…to leave Laphaniel and live.

With a strangled cry I pitched forward, keeping low, not daring to think what would happen if it all went wrong. If I would be swallowed whole…or skinned alive…or watch as Laphaniel was first…

My fingers curled around the crude handle of the key. I it snapped off its binding with barely a tug, and for a moment I simply had it in my hand. It was made of bone, foul and old, with fragments of mummified flesh wrapped around the smooth handle.

I backed away slowly, gripping it tight to my chest while the trolls continued their frenzy, digging into the carcass until there was nothing left. I took three steps before I was thrown to my knees, a blinding pain shooting up my spine where one of the tails had whipped back. I rolled and froze, sucking in breaths as I lay winded out in the open.

I couldn't move, couldn't force enough air into my lungs to do anything but gasp like a landed fish. The tail came down again, cleaving earth just shy of my head, and again. I forced my body into a ball, muffling my cries as it whipped into my shoulder.

They didn't turn away from their feast, drunk on blood-lust…consumed by it. I sucked in another breath and crawled, clinging to the key as I dragged myself forwards, feeling the warmth of blood seep over my back.

With the sounds of snarls and snapping of bone behind me I struggled to get the key into the lock, my hands shaking uncontrollably as panic flooded me. My hands were slick, my eyes burning with black blood, sweat, and tears.

I dropped the key…

Thick mud instantly swallowed it up and I fell to my knees, digging through the sludge, my fingers brushing over fragments of bone and skulls that were all useless. A broken cry slipped past my lips, and behind the rotten bones Laphaniel stirred, wide eyes meeting mine.

"It's gone…I'm sorry, I'm sorry."

"Run," he hissed, giving me a weak push. "Teya, go!"

I slipped back, my hand brushing over something solid and large when I landed, and I dragged the key up with a barely concealed yelp of relief. Shoving it into the lock, I twisted hard, nearly weeping at the sound of the lock releasing.

"You need to move!" I flung open the door to yank him out, slipping down beside him as he sank to his knees. "Get up."

I hauled him to his feet, taking most of his weight as he swayed, his knees buckling. He took a staggering breath as he moved his feet, watching them closely as if he weren't sure they were touching the floor or not.

"Move faster," I urged, practically dragging him. "Please."

The roars behind us changed, a rage seeping in that raised the hairs on the back of my neck. The fury shook the trees around us, and I dared a quick look back as five huge beasts turned their heads as one, ruined wings snapping in rage behind them

"Go!" I shoved Laphaniel and grabbed at his shirt before he pitched forwards, screaming at him when the trolls leapt to their haunches.

He moved faster, sweat trickling over his face as he forced himself onward, his hand a vice against mine as we fought for the trees.

The floor beneath my feet vanished as I was swept up by my ankle. A screech tore from my lips as I dangled above a gaping mouth. Vile breath hit my face, the remnants of flesh still hanging from its yellow teeth. A long tongue shot out, trailing thick drool over my body as it laughed. It unhinged its jaws in a grotesque scraping of bone, lowering me down into its maw so I could see the back of its throat.

With a sudden, guttural scream, it hauled me back, claws retracting so I plummeted to the floor to crash against Laphaniel. He dragged me up, stumbling into me before shoving me to the side as another claw raked where I had just been standing. Thick black blood was smeared over his mouth, dripping down his chin.

I snatched at Laphaniel's hand as the trolls lunged at us, their great size making them clumsy, and it made me realise there was a reason they poisoned their victims…they weren't elegant hunters…quick, yes…but they lacked the haunting gracefulness of the other fey I had encountered.

We made it to the trees, though barely. But the roars of fury didn't stop. The trees creaked and groaned as the creatures followed us through, branches snapping beneath their clawed feet.

"You bit one?"

Laphaniel nodded, and I jerked as he stopped walking. His hand went to his stomach before he doubled over and vomited up a mouthful of black gunk. "I wouldn't recommend it."

"Are you okay?" I asked.

He wiped his mouth on his sleeve. "Better now…"

"Hey, don't slow down," I urged. Laphaniel staggered.

"I think…"

"What?"

"I'm going to pass out…"

"Laphaniel? Don't! Keep walking!"

A bellow of fury echoed behind us just as Laphaniel slumped against me, forcing me down too. I dragged him into the undergrowth, while the thunderous sound of angry trolls reverberated through the trees. I shoved Laphaniel down a sharp incline before sliding behind him.

I pressed close to him, my head against the dirt as the trolls passed us by, their bellows sending every creature nearby running in terror. Something else screamed, high and helpless, and far too close to us. There was the sound of bones crunching, and the screams fell silent.

"You're going to have to walk," I said, shaking him awake with my good hand. Pain throbbed over my shoulder and down my back, my shirt clinging to my sticky skin. "Please, I can't carry you."

"Give me a minute," he murmured, pushing himself up again. He closed his eyes as he stood, bracing himself against a tree until he stood steady.

"We don't have a minute," I said, wrapping my arm around his waist and taking most of his weight again. "Come on."

He half stumbled, and I half dragged him onwards, my feet crunching over dried bits of wood that lay scattered around the ground. I nearly tripped, taking Laphaniel with me, my feet catching along what looked like a small stone wall. It crumbled, but I managed to keep upright,

"Hey!" a sudden voice shouted. "Do I come to your house and stomp all over it?"

I jumped, looking for the source of the voice, finding myself looking down upon a hunched old man with a brown weathered face and snow-white beard trailing right down to his knees.

"You smell like troll," he said, coming closer to give us a sniff. "But you're not trolls, are you?"

"No…we're being hunted, my friend has been poisoned," I began, tensing as he continued to smell us, his long, pointed ears twitching through his white hair. "They're still close."

The man stepped back, huge black eyes going wide as he scanned the trees, ears pricking up. "Poor dears, you must come in."

I glanced at Laphaniel, who was looking at the strange, withered man with what looked like relief on his face.

"You live close by?" he asked, to which the man gave an impatient snort.

"Since you've just trampled my flower garden, I would say so! My poor dahlias!"

"I'm sorry…" I began, but the man shook his head, dismissing my apology.

"No matter that, girl. It will be utterly destroyed if those trolls come this way, and I cannot tend to my garden if I'm nothing but bones. Come, come, quickly now."

With no other choice, we followed the little man up his winding path, ducking low to enter his home that stood nestled between two knotted oaks.

"My name is Aurelius," the old man said, opening the twisted branches that made his front door. "You are safe with me, my dears."

CHAPTER TWENTY

*A*urelius had us follow him deep into his home, the dirt floor beneath our feet sloping slightly as we walked the winding passageway, leading us deeper underground. Torches flickered on the walls, casting a warm glow around the burrow, and scattered over the ground were worn, muddy rugs in various stages of decomposition.

We ended up in a large circular room, with tiny alcoves carved into the walls where dripping candle stubs twinkled cheerfully. Cluttered bookshelves strained with the weight of volumes, globes and compasses. Above us, strung up over the vaulted ceiling, were thousands of golden hourglasses, spyglasses and crystal orbs that held swirling black smoke. They clattered against each other as we walked in, the sands within the glasses pooling back and forth, back and forth as if time had no meaning…which in Faerie, I guessed it didn't.

"Please sit." Aurelius gestured to a plump, worn sofa which we both sank into gratefully. "I'll fetch some tea. Trolls! Hateful bastards, utterly hateful! Ate my wife, would you believe?" He wandered off into a back room, igniting more candles as he went, shaking his head to himself.

"Are we really safe here?" I asked and Laphaniel nodded, leaning heavily against me.

"He's a hobgoblin," he mumbled. He rubbed a hand over his face, fighting to keep his eyes open. "They love helping people, usually whether they want it or not."

"So not everything around here wants to kill and torment?"

He gave a little smile. "It's best to be cautious."

Aurelius came back carrying a tray laden with dainty teacups and a steaming teapot; a little flowery plate had been piled with golden biscuits. He placed the tray onto a wooden table, and hopped up into an armchair, reaching over to pour three cups of yellowish tea into the pretty china.

The tea was strange, bitter and gritty, but as soon as I swallowed, I felt myself stop trembling, a wondrous calm seeping back into my body.

"Better?" Aurelius smiled, passing me a sugar loaded biscuit.

"Yes, thank you," I replied, taking it politely. I nibbled the edges, my stomach not quite ready for food. Laphaniel declined the offer with a quick shake of his head, his tea slopping over the edge of his cup as he slumped against me.

"Give me that." I took it away from him. "Before you burn yourself."

"You'll need to sleep it off, boy," the hobgoblin said gently, gesturing to a small bed in the corner, piled high with thick patchwork quilts. "All the tea in the world won't make you feel better. Get some rest before you fall asleep on that poor girl's shoulder."

Laphaniel didn't protest, which surprised me, and got up from the sofa without a word to stumble to the bed. He didn't even climb under the covers but passed out cold on top of them.

"He'll be fine," Aurelius said, sensing my concern. He wandered over to the bed, tugging one of the colourful blankets over Laphaniel. "The trolls won't risk poisoning the whole body, else they can't eat them. It's just enough to stop them fighting back."

"He doesn't look like he'll be fighting anyone for a while," I said, taking another biscuit. The hobgoblin smiled, little pointed teeth glinting in the low light. "I'm sorry about your wife."

"She was one of the good ones." He closed his eyes. "A rare gem, she would have liked helping you. She always had a soft spot for young lovers."

My cheeks heated. "We're not together…"

"Oh, right you are," he said, giving me a wink. "Well, shall we do something about that wrist of yours? Looks painful."

"It is."

Aurelius narrowed his pitch-black eyes, face darkening. "He didn't do it, did he?"

"No!" I answered. "No. He saved my life actually, more than once. He did hold me against my will, and I can't forgive that…but he's here now, helping me."

I wanted to stop. I should have stopped, but the hobgoblin was looking at me with such understanding, his large black eyes patient and kind. There was a quiet reassurance resonating from him that I was in desperate need of, and I just couldn't hold back the words that poured from my mouth.

"It's all so confusing, because he infuriates me, he frightens me. I want to scream at him to leave me alone, but I don't want to be on my own anymore. He keeps the nightmares away, but he is the reason I have them. I should be running for the hills, but I can't seem to let him go." I took a breath, and it caught. "The fact that he is the closest friend I have ever had makes me so sad I could just…"

I couldn't finish, couldn't do anything except lean forwards and allow my body to shake with sobs. The weight of everything was simply too much, the shock of barely escaping the trolls breaking through a dam I hadn't realised I had put up. There was a soft thump as Aurelius hopped from his armchair and gently patted my shoulder until I composed myself.

"Sorry," I mumbled, wiping my eyes and pouring myself another cup of tea, spooning three sugar cubes into it.

"Have you told your friend of these feelings?" he asked and handed me a spotted handkerchief.

"God, no," I replied, dabbing my eyes on the cloth. "We just yell at each other a lot, but it seems to work for us, so don't worry."

"Indeed," he said, taking the handkerchief back and looking at it strangely before glancing back at me. "I don't suppose, if you wouldn't mind…could I keep this? Human tears are worth a pretty penny around here."

"Have it as payment for helping us."

"No, no, no, no!" he squeaked, holding his hands up, looking suddenly panicked. "The help is free, I want nothing…no…what would Mabel think of me? Keep the tears…"

"No, take them," I said, folding his hands over the fabric. "With our thanks."

"Not as payment."

"No, because I don't need them, and I want you to have them."

"Right you are." He smiled, giving a sigh of relief. "Your hand, girl. Let me fix that now."

The hobgoblin wandered back out into the other room, which I guessed was a kitchen of sorts. After a few minutes he trotted back in, carrying a colourful box covered with intricate carvings of woodland animals and flowers.

"Any other injuries, before I fix this?" he asked.

"I got whipped by one of the tails," I said, wincing when he lifted my shirt and tutted.

"I'll clean these first. They'll heal on their own, but you will have scars." He rummaged in his box and pulled out a jar of sticky looking wax. It smelt strongly of herbs and something sharp that I couldn't name, leaving behind a pleasant warming sensation as he slathered it over my skin. "Now give me your hand."

He held out his hand for mine, wrinkly, warm fingers closing over my wrist, and I winced as he pressed down on the break. With a slow nod, he unwound Laphaniel's makeshift splint, placing it with care on the arm of the sofa. A whimper escaped my lips before I could swallow it back down, tears stinging at the edges of my eyes.

"It's definitely broken."

"I guessed as much," I gritted back.

Aurelius hummed while he worked, rooting around his box to find strange bottles of glowing liquid, uncorking them to slather over my hand. Blue, then yellow, then finally a sickly green that for some reason turned all the others a vibrant purple. They burned as he rubbed them into my skin, almost unbearable, and I had to fight not to tug my hand back. Slowly, the feeling faded, bringing instead an odd numbness that tingled up my arm, erasing all pain. I sighed, and the room around me wavered.

"What…" I tried to speak, but suddenly, simply talking took too much effort. The numbness spread over my shoulder, down my back…to everything else.

"It won't be broken when you wake," the hobgoblin said, his voice sounding very far away.

I had the sensation of something binding my wrist, but it was like it was happening to someone else. My head was a swirl of fog, light and heavy at the same time.

Dull panic crept in at the edges of my mind, a strange feeling settling at the base of my stomach as the world around me dimmed and swirled. I stood, stumbling against the table, willing the world to be still. "Laphaniel?"

"Shh, girl." Something caught my elbow. "He's right here. Lie down. Plenty of room for two."

My head hit something soft, and warmth enveloped me as a heaviness settled over my body. A thick quilt was tucked in tight, a gentle hand running over the top of my head before patting it softly.

I sighed and turned, rolling against the solid lump beside me, a familiar scent of spice invading my senses before sleep dragged me under.

I dreamt of sun-drenched glades, my feet moving to the song the wind sang, never once growing tired. I spun with my head thrown back as my laughter echoed madly around me. I twirled and twirled and twirled until the glorious world around me was spinning as madly as my dance. Strong hands held me at my waist, lifting me up, his own wonderful laughter joining mine.

"I love you."

I forced my eyes open, blinking away the sleep that wanted to pull me back under. The few candles that remained lit barely illuminated the bed, leaving the burrow in a cosy darkness. Light glinted off the hourglasses dangling above, and I noticed the sand within them had stilled, as if they too slept.

Laphaniel shifted beside me, his nose touching mine, the warmth of his mumbled words still tickling against my cheek. His eyes were closed, breaths coming out deep and slow. One arm was tight over me, holding me close. His heart thumped a steady beat against my chest, and I realised I was holding him back, my arm locked firmly around his body.

"Are you awake?" I whispered, my own words sounding strange in my ears, falling heavy from my tongue. I blinked again to try and clear my head, but my thoughts remained muddled, and I wondered if I had dreamt his words. "Laphaniel?"

He barely moved, but his hands tightened around me, slowly tempting me back down in the comforting warmth of sleep.

"Do you love me?" I whispered, unable to keep my eyes open any longer. He sighed against me, stretching his long legs out in the too small bed and buried his head against my neck. A soft snore brushed over my skin, then a few jumbled words, barely coherent.

"More than anything."

A heavy slumber settled over me, leaving his words nothing more than an echo in my swirling mind. I fell asleep in a dreamless dark, not moving until morning.

There were no windows in Aurelius' burrow, so I could only guess it was dawn because when I stirred again more candles flickered with life, bathing the room in a welcoming light. The hourglasses had awoken, too, the glittering sands flowing back and forth as the globes beside them span.

I opened my eyes just as Laphaniel opened his, his irises shining lilac in the soft glow. We were still tangled together, my arms wrapped around his body, his legs around mine. His face a breath away from my own.

For a moment neither of us moved, we just stared at each other, remaining wrapped up in each other beneath a sweet-smelling quilt. I broke away first, looking away as I slowly withdrew my hands from him, his sleepy words repeating over and over in my head.

"Wait." His hand tightened on mine, his voice soft.

I turned my head, breath catching at the way he looked at me...as if there was no one else in the world. My heart quickened at the thought of what he might say, and then he kissed me.

And I kissed him back, every worry, every doubt fading away as I gave in and let myself go. They were soft, gentle kisses, slow and careful...patient. Wonderful.

I pulled back, and he hesitated, desire and hunger and something else blazing within his eyes. His hand came up against my face, bringing my forehead to his, fingers reaching into the tangles of my hair.

"I love you," he breathed, and I closed my eyes at the words, something deep within my soul crying out for his. "I don't know what that means for you...I'm not asking you to forgive what I've done, I just needed you to know before we reach Luthien."

"Is this another trick?" I asked, remembering his arms around me as we danced under the trees, the weight of blossoms in my hair as spring rained down upon us. I remembered the dull ache in my chest when he rejected me under the singing oaks... and how different that had felt. "Because if it is, it's cruel."

What was stirring deep inside me wasn't numb and dizzy and drunk on Glamour. It wasn't a whispered promise, a veiled dream, but raw emotion that threatened to claw at my heart...and quite likely my soul.

"I'm not trying to hurt you," he said, drawing back. "I don't expect you to say it back, it's just that somewhere... after everything, I realised I don't want to be without you."

Stupid, unwanted tears slipped down my cheeks, and he

brushed them away, his fingers leaving behind a warmth I found myself longing for. I shook my head and brushed him off.

"Until you grow bored."

He dropped his hand, fiddling with a stray piece of thread that had unravelled from the quilt instead.

"You're not denying it," I whispered. "Even if it takes a hundred years...when all that is left of me is madness and bloodied feet, you'll grow tired and walk away."

"I wouldn't..."

I swallowed against the lump in my throat, the ache in my chest. "I don't believe you."

He nodded and untangled himself from the blankets, not saying a word as he left me on the bed, but there was nowhere he could go. He sank down on the sofa, raking a hand through his messy hair, looking up sharply when Aurelius skipped in.

"Ah! You're both awake, just in time for breakfast." He set a large tray onto the table and clapped his hands in delight, grinning. "I watched you two all night, is that strange?"

I forced a smile onto my face. "A little."

"Your auras could light this room, so bright, so... tangled." He nodded, pouring green tea into matching teacups. "I could scarcely see where one began and the other ended, I would love to bottle it up... I won't of course, but oh, it would be divine!"

He wagged a finger at me before passing Laphaniel a cup and a huge plate of bacon. "You and your fibs, little human. Not lovers, eh? Something else entirely then, like my Mabel and me."

He handed me a plate and a cup of tea, his black eyes

suddenly sad. He caught me staring and quickly wiped at his cheeks, where a stray teardrop had trickled down.

"She was my Mabel," he said, and he didn't need to say anything else.

"Thank you for all your help, Aurelius." I said, closing my wonderfully healed hand over his gnarled one. "I won't forget this."

He tapped my hand. "You'll be leaving soon I am guessing? I've packed you a bag. There's not much, but it'll see you right for a few days at least. Where is it you're off to?"

"To Luthien, to bargain for her sister back," Laphaniel said from the sofa, placing his empty plate back onto the tray. Aurelius stiffened, ears going flat as he stared at me.

"Foolish!" he said, baring his teeth. "Gods above, girl!"

"I…"

The hobgoblin whirled and smacked Laphaniel hard around the head. "You should know better, boy!"

"Oh, don't you start," Laphaniel snapped, rubbing his head. "She is the most pig-headed creature I have ever met. In the short time I have known her, I have bargained my dreams away, fled for my life, been almost drowned by mermaids and very nearly eaten by trolls. If I keep saying no to her, I'm going to end up dead."

"Love will make you do all sorts of strange things," the hobgoblin said, resting his chin on steepled fingers. "But that beautiful witch will have your head."

"We'll see."

"You didn't tell me the mermaids tried to drag you under too," I said, my voice quiet.

"Did you think they gave you up after I asked them nicely?"

"No…"

"You need to stop running off into the woods," he said,

and I could tell he was still hurting at the increased distance between us, a void I wasn't sure we could fix.

"You sulked off into the woods and nearly had your throat cut," I said bristling, for I was in no mood to be told off.

"You asked me to leave, I was giving you some space to think! I was barely ten feet away before I was struck, and I wasn't listening…I wasn't paying attention because all I could think of was you." He raked a frustrated hand through his hair.

His words raked over the rawness in my chest, seeking to pierce at my heart and I was powerless against them…against him and I hated it.

I hated it.

I hated that I didn't hate him.

"I have nothing to give you," I breathed, feeling helpless. Slowly he made his way back to the bed, crouching low to take my hands in his. I didn't pull away, needing him to hold onto me for a moment. Just a moment.

"Please don't believe that."

I laughed, and it was a dark and bitter sound. "You've said it countless times before, I'm just a worthless girl who's going to end up dead."

He flinched. "I have never said you are worthless."

I took my hand back. "No, but you've made sure I thought it."

I glanced over at Aurelius, who was pretending to dust his books, ears twitching while he listened to every word we said. He caught my eye and gave a sheepish smile.

I placed my untouched food and tea back onto the tray, hoping I didn't offend our host, and stood up, backing away from Laphaniel when he rose beside me.

"I can't do this right now."

"I just wanted to keep you safe," Laphaniel began, his

words making me pause. "I never intended to hurt you. There is this fire inside you that is the brightest thing I have ever seen, and there are so many monsters that want to snuff it out. You are fearless and reckless...and yes, stupid! Because you don't listen, and you think you know better when you don't! You punish yourself for something you had no control over, again and again and again, thinking you are undeserving of any scrap of happiness because you were left behind. I want to make you happy, and I have done it all wrong...but I don't know what to do. I wanted you to stay, so I made you, and I hate myself for it." He took a breath, looking lost. "I love you, Teya. More than I can bear."

The words were on the tip of my tongue, three little words that my heart was screaming out to say. I swallowed them back, keeping my gaze on Laphaniel, expecting perhaps a glimmer of hurt to flicker over his face...but there was nothing. He truly hadn't expected me to say it back.

I did love him though, an all-consuming love that threatened to burn me up from the inside, and I feared it would destroy me. I ached for him, my heart a frenzied mess whenever I was close to him. He invaded every one of my senses where he had no place to be, and it was as wonderful as it was terrifying.

I just wasn't ready to give him that sort of power over me; they were my feelings, and he had hurt me in a way no one should ever be hurt.

"We should be getting back on the road soon," I said, and Aurelius nodded as he handed a pack over to Laphaniel. He took it without another word, his revelation hanging heavy between us.

"Promise me you'll stay off the paths after dark," the hobgoblin said, handing me another pack, stuffed to the brim with food. "Go in an easterly direction from here, don't follow through to the Lonely Lakes: It's kelpie mating season, and you don't want to be disturbing them when they're rutting."

"We'll be passing through the Eerie, if we go the other way," Laphaniel said, shouldering his pack. "The covens will be there."

Aurelius nodded, stroking his long beard. "Yes, yes, but they will be busy selling the stock they have, they likely won't be looking for more."

I glanced at Laphaniel, not wanting to walk through a bunch of witches. "Is there another way?"

"You can loop right around to the bottom of the White Mountains, but it will take a few weeks to get there," Aurelius replied, crouching low to fumble around in a cupboard. "You'll need a lot more supplies, give me a moment."

"We are not going through the mountains," Laphaniel said, wearily. "We'll take the Eerie, I would rather face a few hags than a herd of Kelpies."

"Wise choice," Aurelius nodded. "Yes, good, good. Will that be everything then, lovers who are not?"

"I think so, thank you so much," I said, kneeling so I could wrap my arms around the little man. He patted my back with a gnarled hand, smelling of earth and damp.

The hobgoblin smiled as I drew back, his yellow teeth crooked in his wide mouth. "Then I have nothing left to give you but my blessing. Good luck to you both."

He shook Laphaniel's hand as he passed, both little hands gripping Laphaniel's larger one, whispering something to him that I couldn't hear. Laphaniel shrugged, a subtle lift of his shoulder as he flicked a look at me, and the hobgoblin smacked him again.

"Take care of each other," he said as a final parting, leaning against his door frame as we ducked beneath the twisted branches and back out into his ruined garden. He caught sight of his flowerbeds and winced. "My poor dahlias."

Beside me Laphaniel held out his hand, his fingers folding over mine when I reached for him. We didn't say anything, but walked side by side through the giant oaks that loomed over the hobgoblin's house, and followed the path that would lead us through the Eerie.

CHAPTER TWENTY-ONE

*T*he road to the Eerie was thankfully uneventful, though the long winding paths we walked for hours became increasingly uncomfortable as we both refused to talk about what had gone on between us at Aurelius' house. We didn't talk about before either, the months I spent with him in his home, enchanted and blissfully ignorant. I couldn't even begin to talk about it…the betrayal that burned within me…the hurt…the shame, the disgraceful way my body still yearned for the feeling of wild abandon that sparked through me.

We talked about anything else, meaningless conversations that at first were stilted and awkward, but slowly flowed smoothly as we started to learn more about each other. I told Laphaniel of the last Christmas we had shared as a family, before Niven was taken. How it had rained so hard, the village flooded and there had been a power cut. We cooked Christmas dinner on the camping stove, surrounded by candles, and it was wonderful. Niven and me both received Furbies as gifts and I had loved my little pink one. Niven never took hers out of the box.

"What's a Furby?" Laphaniel asked, helping me over a wide crevice that he had simply leapt across like a gazelle.

"It's a weird, soft toy that sings at you," I replied. "They're a bit creepy really, maybe I'll get you one someday."

"I'll hold you to that." He smiled back.

Laphaniel filled the gaps with snippets of his life, how he had found his house as a crumbling ruin and had rebuilt it, preferring to be away from politics of his court. He had shrugged his shoulders when I mentioned his relationship with Lily, explaining how he had found her in his kitchen one day and she had something he wanted.

"Which was?" I pressed, knowing he wouldn't answer.

"Nothing that concerns you."

"Did you let her bite you?" I asked, remembering the sharp pain of her teeth in my neck…the way she had sucked deeply.

"Yes."

"Why? What did you get in return?

He looked at me like I was stupid. "I got to sleep with her, Teya."

And just like that, we descended into painful silence again.

I heard the Eerie before I saw it, the cackle of laughter, the shouts of sellers, of fortune tellers, the fragments of spells…the echoes of screams. The smell hit me next, a sharp incense that rose from deep within the Eerie, heady and intoxicating. It burned at my eyes and stung my throat, sending my thoughts into a whirlwind, until Laphaniel nudged me.

"Hold your sleeve to your nose," he said. "Try to take smaller breaths."

"It doesn't seem to be affecting you." I replied, pressing the fabric to my face, inhaling the scent of Laphaniel instead, which made my head muddled for completely different reasons.

"It's not meant to." He stopped walking, turning me to face him, his hand tight on my shoulder. "Do I have to tell you not to touch anything?"

I glared at him through my sleeve. "No."

The trees thinned out as we entered the Eerie, and it was magnificent.

As far as I could see, black tents rippled in the wind, all bearing battered flags with different insignias emblazoned upon them. Some tents looked ancient and tattered, stitched with pieces of black cloth to hold them together. Some were shiny, pristine and glittering, perfect shadows against the tall skinny trees that wove in and out of the tents.

Animals prowled the labyrinthine walkways, slinky black cats and fat rats sprinted past our feet. Huge wolves with blinding white coats padded behind, eyes shining with intelligence as they glanced at us, lips lifting to reveal unkind teeth. Tall, shining horses waited with patience in front of many of the tents, hooves covered in thick hair, black eyes bored and cruel.

Above us, witches circled on broomsticks, soaring against the wind, filling the air with a cacophony of screeches and fragments of song. I stared up in wonder, mouth open as they were joined by great winged serpents, their scales glittering bright blue against the morning sky. I saw saddles, reins…the flowing cobalt cloaks of the witches that rode them.

"The Eerie is a meeting place of all the covens in Faerie," Laphaniel explained, a smile warming his face as he took in my wonder. "They meet at the brink of winter, when everything begins to die down. It's a chance to exchange wares, to settle old feuds and establish the hierarchy. The lower covens pay a tribute to the Witch Queen; on rare occasions someone will make a claim for her throne and these grounds will become a bloodbath."

"Will we meet the Witch Queen?" I asked breathlessly, my head still tilted towards the sky, mouth open.

"Absolutely not," Laphaniel said quickly. "I want to be out of here without drawing much attention to us. We need to look like we're interested in buying though, they won't like it if they find out we're using their sacred ground as a short-cut."

"Will we be buying anything?"

"It might be sensible, just a charm, or a trinket."

We moved through the tents, the cloying incense twirling around my legs in a purple smoke, clinging to my clothes until I reeked of it. Witches of all shapes and sizes watched us as we passed by, some ancient and crooked, reminding me of Slimy-Soo and making me recoil. Others were beautiful, though their smiles were not. Some were covered in feathers, avian heads clicking in my direction as I passed their tents.

"A boon, little love!" one shrieked, feathers rustling as she swivelled her head, a clawed hand shooting out to grab at my arm. "A wish for just one of your fingers!"

Laphaniel pulled me back. "I need her with all her fingers."

"Pity, I could eat them all up, I could," the witch replied, huge owl-like eyes blinking at me as Laphaniel dragged me by.

"Are we going to buy anything without me losing a body part?" I asked, rubbing my shoulder where the witch's claws had sunk in.

"Depends, is there any you'd be willing to lose?"

"Ha, ha," I muttered, stopping by a table weighed down with jars and jars of swirling, glittering goo. I watched it move from behind the glass, greens and blues melting into blacks and purples, so it looked like a moving oil-spill.

"Would she like one?" another crone asked Laphaniel, her furry ears peeking out from beneath her wild hair. She didn't look at me, assuming I belonged to Laphaniel, like a pet. The thought sickened me, but I didn't want to draw more attention to myself than I had to. "She can pick it up if she's careful."

I lifted one up, the glass strangely cold against my fingers, colours inside swirling erratically at my touch. Laphaniel watched me carefully, and I wondered if he was worried I would drop it, or stunned that I hadn't mouthed off to the witch.

"I harvested the souls myself," the crone said proudly, silver whiskers twitching. "Wisps make the most beautiful Lumious, don't you think? It takes a thousand for each bottle, crushed down beneath the full moon and left to dry for a phase and a half. So much work."

She finally turned to me, her pupils glowing green against the shadows of her tent, and with a fuzzy hand she reached out to pat the top of my head. "So pretty, I'm guessing whoever sold you got a decent price? Look at you! Look at these cheeks!"

I winced when she pinched my face, her grin wide enough to show off her pointed canines. "He paid two vials of blood and a month of dreams for me."

"It was more than a month's worth," Laphaniel added, tapping the crone's hand away from my face.

"What a bargain, little boy," she mused, trailing a sharp fingernail down my nose. "She is exquisite."

"I know," he said, rousing up something inside me. "How much for the Lumious?"

"I'm looking for the dreams of a virgin, any chance…"

She trailed off as she saw my face redden and pouted. "Well, these are not for you then, little whore."

She plucked the jar from my hands, placing it back among the others before I even had the chance to feel insulted.

"Have a sweetie instead!"

I didn't have time to react before she had shoved something hard and tart into my mouth, and I had to force myself not to swallow it and choke. It tasted of lemons and was surprisingly nice. I just hoped it wouldn't turn me into a frog.

"It's a sherbet, you'll be fine," Laphaniel said, leading me away from the woman. "Did you actually want one of them?"

I shrugged, feeling awful. "I did a little bit."

He laughed, pulling me close while the other witches began to eye me hungrily as we wove our way around the dark pathways. They held out their bottles and bones and swirling nightmares, all shouting their prices to Laphaniel. A fragment of my soul, my left eye, my right hand.

No one spoke directly to me, and I played my part of dutiful little pet, hating myself for it. There was nothing unusual about us; to the surrounding witches I was simply a spoilt plaything, one that had yet to be broken and replaced.

Some of them cooed over me, petting my hair while saying how lucky Laphaniel was to have me. Some gave me treats, small vials of silvery tears, a packet of rainbow sweets that apparently made my eyes change colour for a while. I swallowed the sweets, along with the scrap of pride I had, and decided to have a little fun.

Two old hags took a lock of Laphaniel's hair, for a bottle of thick green wine that tasted of dirt and aniseed. They cackled as they handed it over, sneering at me when Laphaniel took it from my hands and stowed it in his pack.

I gave up three drops of blood for a mug of frothing hot chocolate, knowing I would never again taste something as divine. We sat for a while to rest, perched beside each other on a bench carved from the rotted trunk of a tree. I shared my drink begrudgingly, gazing up to the slowly darkening sky to watch the witches glide effortlessly between the hazy clouds.

We followed through the maze, passing a few other fey who ducked in and out of tents, swapping ragged humans for shining gems without a backward glance. Other noises drifted from behind some, doorways knotted tight…the sighs and moans and cries drifting through the seams. A different type of smoke trailed from the swaying tents, overly sweet and floral. I peeked between a gap, my eyes falling onto writhing bodies that paid me no heed. Their eyes were glazed over, mouths slack…some sprawled limply over the huge pillows, unmoving. Laphaniel gripped my hand tight and dragged me onward without a word.

I stopped and pulled away at one glistening tent, the fabric seemingly made from the shadows themselves. It swirled and danced with the breeze, speckled throughout the pitch with thousands and thousands of twinkling stars. I reached a hand out to the furry creature perched upon a branch, my fingers stopping just shy of it. A glittering thread tethered it down, tied tight enough to leave a welt on its scaled leg.

It looked like a cross between a monkey and a parrot, long, curling tail swishing back and forth, the tip covered in bright red and yellow feathers. I opened my mouth to speak, but Laphaniel cut me off, grabbing my hand and hauling me away before the squat little witch could name her price.

"Stop it!" he hissed, and I jumped at his tone.

"Obviously I know we can't have the flying monkey!" I snapped back. "It's completely impractical right now. I was just curious, I've never seen one before."

"No, stop acting like that," he said, dropping my hand.

"Like what?" I asked, knowing exactly what he was talking about. "We can't walk around like equals, can we?"

"You're enjoying yourself," he accused, and I lifted a brow, refusing to be shamed.

"So what?" I folded my arms, creating a barrier between us. "I'm making the best of a shitty situation. I like getting presents, I like keeping all my body parts. It's even nice to be ignored. So, I'm sorry you're feeling uncomfortable, but if they think I'm different, if they think I'm special…what will they do?"

He blew out a breath. "They won't like it."

"Will they try to snatch me away?" He nodded, and fear bloomed in my stomach. "Until we leave this place, you own me okay? I'm your dutiful little pet that you overpaid for."

I tried for a smile, but couldn't quite manage, remembering the feeling of being tied to a table leg, sick and dying…my body and soul all up for sale. Laphaniel stepped closer, a careful hand coming up against my arm.

"I would have paid whatever she demanded."

With a shaking hand I reached into my bag of sweets and popped one into my mouth. Strawberry and candyfloss exploded against my tongue, making my entire mouth tingle. Laphaniel dropped his hand.

"What colour?"

He rolled his eyes. "Pink."

I ate another. "Now what?"

"Purple."

I smiled, a real one. "Just like yours."

I stowed my sweets back into my pack with care among the other trinkets I had collected, and fumbled over the straps as I felt Laphaniel's gaze upon me.

"This is a horrible place," I said. "It's breathtaking, and impossible and brilliant, but it's terrifying. Don't believe for a moment I don't realise how dangerous this place is. I've seen what they're selling amongst the wishes and candies. I've seen the bags of baby bones, the still beating hearts and the children for sale. I've not been blind to it, and I know they won't have someone like you to rescue them. I am terrified of getting snatched, and you not being able to buy me back."

"I won't let that happen."

"I don't want to need saving," I said, weary. "I don't want to need you."

I had hurt him, I could see it in his face.

"This isn't what I wanted," I continued, watching a pair of black rats that ran by us. "I didn't come here for this...for you. It's always been for Niven. What would she think? If she knew? It's unforgivable."

So gently, he pulled me against him, barely holding me, giving me the option of pulling away if I wanted to. Deep down, I knew Niven would have never wandered into the woods to look for me; it was a simple fact I had always known. There would have been no guilt driving her to even think of it. Though it did not pass my notice that it was guilt driving my quest, and not a love for the girl that had been snatched away. I was just clinging to a hope my sister was enough to pull what was left of my family together, so I could move on.

"Would you feel different if it wasn't me who took her?" he asked, and I just knew it was a question he didn't want to know the answer to.

"But it was," I said, because there was no point in going over what ifs. "I wouldn't have met you if you hadn't taken her. You wouldn't have walked away from Luthien, you wouldn't have found me in the woods. I wouldn't have..."

I didn't finish, I just let the words hang there, heavy with everything left unsaid between us.

He sighed against me, his arms tightening, drawing me close and I let him. "Is there anything I can do to make this better?"

I rested my head on his chest, closing my eyes against the screams and cries and jeers of the Eerie. Just being in his arms made it better, but I wasn't going to tell him that, not yet. "You could buy me the flying monkey."

His laugh huffed against the top of my head, and some of the tension surrounding us lifted, settling into a quiet comfort.

As the sun began to sink below the tree line, the Eerie changed. The tents all seemed to dissolve into the new black, and the witches all began to stare at me with a renewed hunger, no longer content with selling trinkets for a scrap of blood.

Screams rang out over the shadows, sharp and quick. Laphaniel tightened his grip on my hand as we quickened our steps. Above us, the high-pitched screeches of the serpents pierced the sky, cawing at the sun as it gave way to night. The riders sang high upon their bright steeds, cloaks whipping behind them in a flash of brilliant blue. The riders on brooms joined the chorus, balancing on tiptoes as they soared in loops against an indigo sky. Words to a wild song were screamed into the wind, laughter falling to the earth to stir the witches below.

Something grabbed me out of the darkness, a cold hand snatching me from Laphaniel so quickly, my shoulder clicked.

"A heartstring," sang a voice at my ear, the words soft and lovely. "For one heartstring, I will carve this one up and use her skin for a book. I can make her scream for you with every page you turn."

Pain bloomed at my side as something sharp and cold slid

against my ribs, and I gasped, the sound choking in my throat.

"What will I do with a screaming book?" Laphaniel said, not quite hiding the alarm in his voice. "Will a book clean my home? Cook my meals? Satisfy my needs?"

There was a laugh at my cheek, a twist at my side. "Suit yourself."

Laphaniel caught me as I was shoved back, my arm throbbing where slender fingers had dug in. Warmth trickled down my side. I searched for the witch who had grabbed me, but there was nothing there.

"Come on," Laphaniel said. "Stay close."

I stumbled forwards, gritting my teeth as pain launched up around my ribs. I bent over with a gasp. "She…she stabbed me."

In an instant, I was on the ground, Laphaniel gently lowering my head before he pulled my shirt up, his eyes bright with concern. His hand brushed over the wound, coming back red.

"It's okay," he said. "I'm going to need to stitch this up, but not here. Listen to me, I'm not going to let anything happen to you."

"I want to get out of here," I said, panic settling in. "I don't want to be here anymore, Laphaniel."

As gently as he could he prised my fingers from his hands, ripping a chunk off his shirt and balling it up. He pressed the wad hard against my side and I hissed.

"We need to get out of here," I said, struggling upright, ignoring the pain that sliced down my ribs. "Come on. Please…"

"Hey," he cut in, voice firm as he gave me a quick shake. "You've just outwitted a group of trolls, you saved my life. This is nothing, okay? I won't let them take you, I swear it."

I nodded, gritting my teeth, his words not doing enough to quell the frantic dread that was rushing through my body. The thought of being locked away in one of the pitch-black tents...kept alive in the darkness while bits of me were harvested up...

"I'm going to pick you up, because I don't trust you enough at the moment not to run off," Laphaniel said, rolling me against his chest as he stood. He guided my hand to the bloodied rag at my side. "Hold onto that."

I clung to him as he moved, flinching as every step he took brought with it a new wave of pain. I noticed the shadows begin to move, becoming solid as we brushed past. They materialised from the black, eyes gleaming, teeth bared. Laphaniel tensed, holding me close.

"What a burden you carry," one rasped, forked tongue lashing against her lips. "Let me relieve you of such disappointment."

"I can cure the meat for you!" another grinned, her cracked lips parting to reveal broken teeth. "Boil it in blood and salt it good."

"Her soul! A human child for her soul!"

"The marrow from her bones!"

They screamed their demands, closing in against us as Laphaniel backed away, unable to sweet-talk us out of the mess we were in. He shifted me in his arms and ran.

He sprinted through the labyrinth of tents, clinging to me so tightly I could hardly breathe. The cackles and jeers and the baying for blood followed behind.

Laphaniel's heartbeat crashed against my ear, his breaths panting, but he didn't slow. He didn't stumble, he just kept going. He didn't dare stop running until the echoes of the taunts dimmed, their laughter sounding far away. He clung to me, resting back against a tree as he looked frantically around.

"Are we lost?"

He tilted his head, listening. "I don't know where we are, hush a moment."

While waiting for him to find his bearings, I glanced down at my side and lifted the cloth slightly so red bloomed over my fingers.

"Keep pressing against it!" he snapped, then softened when he took in my wide-eyed look. "It's this way. Hold on."

He started to run again, not hesitating on which turns to make, which of the identical pathways to take, and if perhaps I wasn't in so much pain, I would have marvelled at it.

A boom reverberated around the Eerie, shaking its foundations, causing Laphaniel to skid to a halt. Another boom sounded, tearing up the night, then another and another and another. Boom. Boom. Boom. Boom. Boom.

It rattled the skies, louder than the crash of thunder, then it stilled. I heard Laphaniel swear above me, the curse the only sound against the sudden quiet. Then there was the sounding of drums, wild and primal. Feral.

"What is it?" I whispered.

"The Witch Queen," Laphaniel whispered. "She's calling the covens."

"I think now would be a good time to slip away then…" I trailed off, loss of blood creating a sudden weariness that threatened to swallow me.

"Stay awake," he hissed, "Keep your eyes open! We need to leave quick…I'm going to steal a horse."

"That seems like a really stupid idea," I muttered, forcing my eyes to stay open. "We'll be spotted."

"Not while the covens are distracted, but if they descend into a revel, I won't be able to get you out."

"But…"

"Shh!" His hand came up tight against my mouth and he slipped back against one of the tents, just as an enormous shadow loomed overhead. It swooped down, its pale underbelly brushing against the pitched roofs. Great wings stretched wide, sending everything in its path crashing down as it beat them gracefully to the pounding of drums. Its head hung low, nostrils flaring as it scented the grass, its scales shining a perfect midnight.

The rider held her hands to the sky, head bent back in a cry of ecstasy. Red dripped across her stunning face, her mess of black hair trailing back along with her tattered cloak. A scream tore from her throat and the beast rose upwards with a screech of its own. Laphaniel darted to the side, narrowly missing the razor-sharp talons hooked on its wing tips.

It shredded the tent like tissue paper.

"We're leaving. Now."

Laphaniel kept stealing glances up at the sky, even though they had quietened. Even the drums had died down, and a tense, bated silence slipped over the Eerie. With the witches' attention focused elsewhere, he walked right up to one of the massive black horses that roamed the pathways. He held a hand out, and its ears flicked back, eyeing the two of us with distrust.

"Safe passage from the Eerie in exchange for your freedom," Laphaniel murmured, his voice low and quiet. The horse snorted, stomping at the ground.

"A pint of blood."

The horse took a step forward, obsidian eyes flashing.

"Two." Laphaniel glanced around, his voice growing frantic.

Great hooves pounded the ground, tearing up chunks of earth.

"Three?" he asked, and the beast threw its head back, letting out a low whinny that was too loud against the quiet of the Eerie. "You'll have to collect payment when we've reached a safe place, understand?"

It lunged at Laphaniel, a furious hiss slipping from its mouth, revealing pointed teeth. Laphaniel spun with me still in his arms, wincing as teeth scraped along his shoulder.

"I can't ride if I'm barely conscious, can I?" he hissed. "I'll pay when we're away from here. It's safer for everyone."

For too long, the horse did nothing but stare, but then without a sound it lowered itself to the ground, its eyes never leaving us. Laphaniel helped me on, keeping an arm around me as he climbed on behind.

"Three pints of blood is a crazy amount to lose," I said, clutching a handful of the beast's mane, hoping it didn't mind.

"We'll camp somewhere for the night, I'll be fine," Laphaniel replied. "Just worry about yourself for now. The Night-Mare will take us as far away as we can get, Night-Mares are fast. Just stay awake, okay?"

The horse rose with a fluid grace, rearing up with a cry of its own and with the thundering roar of drums behind us, we flew through the Eerie as if we had wings.

CHAPTER TWENTY-TWO

I lay on the cold ground, sharp stones digging into my back as I stared at the dripping rocks above me. The small cave we stumbled across was cold and damp, but far enough away from the Eerie that all I could hear was the faint echo of drums. The wild beat sped up in tempo, a frenzied song filled with chaos and discord. I knew the revel had begun. We had managed to get out by the skin of our teeth.

Sick and dizzy, I watched Laphaniel as he placed candle stubs around the nooks in the cave walls, banishing back some of the darkness with a subtle flick of his fingers. My hand was sticky with the blood seeping through the cloth at my side, the wound stiff and sore.

"I'm going to clean and stitch this," he said, crouching beside me, reaching into his pack to pull out the bottle of green wine he had swapped for a lock of hair. "This is going to sting."

He poured the liquid over my side, and I gritted my teeth as it burned. "Would you save me some of that? I could do with a drink."

He passed the bottle to me with a wry smile, and I took a large swallow, grimacing at the sour taste. With quick hands, he washed the blood away, then drew a needle and thread from a leather pouch tucked into the pack.

"Well, at least the hobgoblin was good at guessing what supplies we might need." Laphaniel stroked the hair back from my face while I stared at the needle in horror. With a flick, flame danced at his fingertips, and he held the needle over it until the end burned red.

"If you poke me with that, I'm going to be sick," I said, turning away.

"I'll be as gentle as I can."

I squeezed my eyes shut as he deftly sewed me back together, biting my lip every time he slid the needle into my skin, cringing when he pulled it tight. It didn't hurt as much as I thought it would, and for the few minutes it took him to finish, he didn't stop talking to me. He told me the compasses at Aurelius' house were made to map the entire world of Faerie, that they were worth more than an entire dragon's hoard. That merchants had set off to find the end of the world and had never come back, because the world had no end.

"How do you know they didn't just fall off?" I asked and accepted his help to sit up, my breath catching as the world tilted slightly.

"Maybe one day, I'll take a look myself and find out," he replied, keeping an arm around me. "Are you okay?"

"Just shaky, I'm fine," I said, forcing a smile. He wasn't convinced, and very gently guided my head between my legs, ordering me to take deep breaths. I did as I was told, simply because I didn't want to faint on him.

"Eat something." Laphaniel handed me a couple of the sugary biscuits Aurelius had packed for us.

"You're going to need some of these soon," I told him,

and rested my head back against the cave wall, my breathing steadier, my hands less shaky. I ate one of the biscuits and immediately felt better, I bit into another and the light-headedness faded. "What is the horse going to do with three pints of blood?"

"Drink it."

"Oh."

"She's called Angmar by the way," he said, and I blinked in surprise.

"Since when can you talk to animals?"

He laughed, reaching out to tuck a strand of hair from my face, before hesitating and pulling away. "She might have told you, if you listened. You once thought the wind couldn't sing, or the trees couldn't dance. The Night-Mare is taking us as far as she dares, no doubt trying to get as far away from the Eerie as possible."

I shifted against the rock, drawing my knees up to my chest as I peered out of the cave, at the massive black horse tossing her head with displeasure, no doubt impatient at waiting for her meal. Her inky mane flew around her sleek shoulders like a living shadow, her eyes unfathomable and hungry.

"Why didn't she just leave?" I asked, breaking away from the Night-Mare's penetrating stare.

"The witches enchant them, so they can't, not until they're sold off," Laphaniel answered, unscrewing the lid off a jar of familiar smelling wax, coating my newly stitched wound with the herby gunk. "Night-Mares are incredibly proud creatures though, and will never undersell themselves beneath what they believe they are worth, even if it means losing their freedom."

"That's really foolish…"

"Shh, she'll hear you," Laphaniel said, tentatively lifting

the edge of my battered shirt, which looked as if it were being held together by dirt and blood. "May I take a look?"

I nodded, and he pulled it up over my back as I leant forward. I winced; Laphaniel sucked in a breath.

"That bad?"

"These are really going to scar," he breathed, more to himself than to me. "You've got black bruises all down your back."

His fingers trailed over my shoulder and down my spine, rubbing salve against the wounds I couldn't see, and could no longer really feel. I tensed at his touch, the feel of his hand over my bare skin, the way it lingered over the welts. I heard his breath catch, then he slid my shirt back down and rose to his feet.

"I won't be long," he murmured, making towards Angmar, who bowed her head slightly at him, waiting. "Try to get some rest."

I dozed on the cold ground, my mind too full to truly fall asleep. Too full of aches and pains, with the ever-present fear of darkness, and of course of Laphaniel, who constantly haunted my dreams.

Cold and hungry, I opened my eyes, my hand coming up to rest against the blanket covering me. I sat up, lifting my head from the pack that had been placed carefully beneath my head in a makeshift pillow. A fire crackled just outside, giving off barely enough heat to ward off the chill. The candles still wavered within the rock face, banishing away much of the dark.

Laphaniel rested against the other side of the cave, his head on his knees, a half-nibbled biscuit lying beside his feet. I got up, keeping the blanket tight around my shoulders, and wandered close to him. Sitting down beside him, I noticed the bite mark on his wrist, a raised circle of puncture marks that had already bruised his skin. I took his hand in mine to take a closer look, and he jumped.

"Did I wake you?" I asked, as he folded his fingers over mine, squeezing gently before letting go.

"No, I wasn't sleeping," he said, shaking his head before wincing. "She was quite hungry."

"Are you okay?"

"Hmmm," he murmured, and scrubbed a hand over his face. "I'm fine."

"Are you going to faint?" I teased.

He snorted.

"No."

"Throw up? I gave blood once because mum made me. I threw up on the nurse and then fainted, I never went back. Do you want me to stop talking?"

He was quiet for a moment, head resting on the rock, eyes closed. "No, I like it."

"When I talk nonsense to you?"

He smiled, a tired quirk of his lips. "I just like it when you talk. I like the sound of your voice, I like the stories you tell."

"Laphaniel?"

"Hmm?"

"Can I sleep here?" I asked, and he drew me close without a word. He fell asleep long before I did, fingers sliding against my back as his head lolled forwards. I lay with my head on his chest, listening to the sound of his heartbeat, telling myself it was okay, that I could be happy, smiling as I started to believe it. Even the feel of his clothes on my skin had become a comfort I craved, his scent something that could evoke a smile, his warmth a security I never found anywhere else. And that was okay.

I fell asleep somewhere near dawn, the blackness of night

just beginning to lift as I closed my eyes. The sun had barely risen when I opened them again, finding myself too restless to sleep, too filled with all the things I wanted to say and do. Too filled with everything. Uncurling myself from Laphaniel, I wandered to the mouth of the cave, where the Night-Mare fixed me with a knowing stare, which felt as if she were mocking me.

Leaning against the cool rock, I stared out into the early morning, at the hint of frost that sparkled on the lush mounds that surrounded us. Crisp leaves scattered the ground, curling up as the chill began to seep in, pushing the warmth further and further back. It was a bitter reminder that spring was far behind us, and the months I had lost would never be mine again.

I didn't hear him walk up and he startled me, breaking me away from my thoughts as he passed me a bowl filled with dry fruit.

"How much further?" I asked, popping an apricot into my mouth.

"Another day's ride," Laphaniel said, standing beside me to watch as the double sunrise crawled higher. "Maybe two, depends if we run into more trouble."

I rubbed my arms, stepping closer to the fire to keep warm, absently throwing more sticks into the flames, making it hiss. "I know you don't understand why I'm doing this, why I need to, but I just wanted to say thank you for agreeing to help me."

He nodded, taking a bite of an apple and swallowing. "Just promise me that when we get there you will keep your mouth shut and your temper in check."

I opened my mouth to argue, but quickly closed it again at the look he shot me. "I promise."

He said nothing for a moment, his shoulders tense, not

looking at me. I tossed a handful of raisins into my mouth, not really enjoying them, feeling the weight of unsaid words heavy in the air.

"Are you going to talk to me?" I asked. "Or are you going to go all moody and silent?"

"Will you be willing to find a replacement?" he enquired, tossing his barely touched apple into the bushes.

"What?"

"For Niven," Laphaniel said, and I went cold. "We still need a queen, and if Luthien agrees to free Niven, we still need someone to take her place. Whose child will it be next?"

I hadn't even given it a thought...saving Niven had always been my goal. I never thought of the price I might have to pay. Could I really swap her for another girl? Someone else's daughter...sister? My hands trembled at the thought; a sickness creeping against my stomach as I fervently shook my head. I couldn't...wouldn't force that on someone else.

"I'll find someone," Laphaniel said softly, finally turning to face me. "Forget I said anything."

"No."

"I've done it before. You won't even need to know who it is."

"No!"

"Perhaps an orphan? Someone no one will miss."

"I said no. I will not force that misery on someone else, do you understand?" I snapped, horrified at the ease in which he was willing to snatch up someone else's child.

"I understand, Teya," he said. "I have done it for years, and you cannot imagine the guilt that eats at me. Do you not wonder why I am not with my court? Why I live out here away from them? I cannot stand the screaming; even when they stop, they haunt my dreams...even Niven." He took a breath, and my heart ached for him. "If you choose to go to Luthien and strike a deal, I will find Niven's replacement. I will not put that on you, you have suffered enough."

I hadn't given too much thought as to why he lived alone with only Lily for company. I remembered the night Niven had been taken as if it were yesterday, the dancing and the magic...he had taken her with a smile. Was it forced? A mask to hide the remorse beneath? I could only hope so.

"I could take her place."

He turned to me in one graceful move, the little candles dotted around the cave suddenly snuffing out. The fire dimmed and spluttered. I could sense the swirl of Glamour creep around my body, lifting against my hair, causing the bowls and cups on the ground to rattle. Barely contained rage washed against me as Laphaniel snarled, all colour gone from his eyes.

"You'll take her place?" he said, and I winced. "You'll take her place?"

His fury made the cave sway, and I reached for the rock to steady myself. "Laphaniel, stop."

"You think I am going to take you to Luthien, so you can hand yourself over? That you mean so little to me? After what I have told you, you want me to put you in that castle?"

"I just..."

"Are you completely insane?" A deep guttural snarl escaped his throat. "What the hell is wrong with you?"

I stood up, wiping at the sudden wetness beneath my nose as it began to bleed, though he didn't notice. "Laphaniel..."

"Sit down."

I sat with a bump, glowering up at him, my head pounding. "Will you calm down? You're hurting me."

"I don't have to take you anywhere," he said, the words soft and quiet, a wonderful lullaby. I closed my eyes and heard him exhale. The fury surrounding me died down, and the ache in my head subsided. "I could still make you stay."

"I would never forgive you."

He dragged a hand through his hair, his breath coming out in a shaking gasp. "I will not make you live in your nightmares, Teya."

"You can't control everything I do!" I snapped, standing up to grab his shoulder, forcing him to look at me. "You don't get to do that when you lose your temper, do you understand? You need to talk to me, like a normal person."

He blew an exasperated breath through his teeth. "You don't listen to a word I say."

"I have been listening," I said, closing the gap between us. "To everything, but I am never going to just obey you, Laphaniel. By now you should know that. I don't think you'd want me to either, right? I'm not going to offer myself up to Luthien, I promise. We'll think of something."

He tensed, his eyes still so, so black. "You'll think of something, will you? Or will I have to? You are going in blind, Teya. You're just human…"

"Just human?"

"Breakable." He hissed the word, gesturing to the wound at my side, his hand coming over my wrist, fingers lingering over the newly mended bone.

"I'm not made of glass, Laphaniel," I began, but he shook his head, cutting me off.

"No. You're flesh and blood, but do not underestimate the ways you can be broken until there is nothing left to put back together. Don't you dare throw around a flippant remark on how you'll find a way. Because it is utterly foolish, and it's going to get you killed."

I stared at him, unable to find any words to say as his own echoed over me, filled not with anger…but with fear.

"I didn't mean it like that," I said at last. "I'm sorry."

He made an unconvinced noise before drawing me close, his chin resting on top of my head, and I marvelled at how comfortably I fit against him.

"I'm...sorry too," he said, the words faltering. "For all of it."

I wasn't ready to forgive him — unsure if I ever could— but I wanted him, I wanted to be close to him...and despite everything, I trusted him. "I know."

"Can I take a look at your wound?" he asked after a few minutes of silence, moving away to lift my shirt as I nodded, his fingers gentle on my skin. He brushed over the edges of the stitches, along the side of my ribs, tracing my skin with soft delicate strokes that awoke every part of me.

"It's pretty neat," I breathed, running my own hand over the tiny, one-inch slash. "It looks so small."

"Small, but deep," Laphaniel said, not moving his hand away. "You're lucky it missed anything vital."

"I never want to see another witch as long as I live," I declared, sliding my shirt down, Laphaniel's lingering gaze not going unnoticed.

"I don't want to lose you, Teya," he whispered.

It would have been too easy to lean in a little closer, to let everything I felt for him slip past my defences. "At the end of all this, I don't want you to go."

"I don't know what I want to do," I replied, taking a breath. "I don't know if going back is an option to me anymore...even if I manage to save Niven, I can't just go back and play happy families. I just want to make my mum happy."

"And you think Niven will do that?"

I shrugged, not sure what I thought any more. "I don't know what else to do. I can't go back to that house filled with the people we've lost. I have to believe Niven will be enough, or there's no point."

"Then what?" he coaxed gently, a thread of hope lifting his voice.

"I'll never forget this place. I'll never forget about you." I folded my arms, turning my head as the suns finally poured over the treetops, bathing the forest with a hazy light. "Maybe…when everything has settled down…when I know Mum will be okay, perhaps then you'll show me everything you once promised. Without the Glamour. Just us. I think I'd like to see that."

"Okay," he replied, his voice soft. "I'll travel to the ends of the world with you, Teya, and whatever lies beyond."

At the mouth of the cave, Angmar tossed her head, lip curled to reveal her sharp teeth. She gouged the earth with shining hooves, impatience snorting through flared nostrils.

"I think she wants to move on," Laphaniel said, not moving away from me. "Are you okay to ride?"

I stretched, feeling the stitches in my side pull and I winced as it stung. "I'll be fine. What about you?"

"Fully recovered."

My eyebrows rose. "That quick? After losing so much blood?"

He nodded, shouldering our packs. "It would have been quicker if I hadn't been poisoned the day before."

We finished packing our supplies and I walked over to Angmar who continued to glare at me with impassive eyes. Cautiously I held out a hand, placing it gently between her ears, her sleek coat cold beneath my touch. She hissed low, teeth glinting.

"I just wanted to thank you," I said to her, not flinching away. "Because I was taken by a witch too, and I know how it feels. I was nearly snatched away again, but you saved me…

us. You don't belong to Laphaniel, you know that, right? You're free to go, you belong to no one."

The Night-Mare blinked, hiding her teeth as she snorted, ears lifting slightly when she turned her head.

"I don't think she's planning to eat you now." Laphaniel smiled, lifting me onto her back. "I would consider that a win."

With a graceful leap, he jumped on behind me, his arms coming around to hold me tight. I reached forward to take a handful of Angmar's mane again.

With no warning, she rose up, a wild cry screaming from her mouth before she tore forward. I could do nothing more than clamp my legs tight around her and pray I didn't fall off, the wind snatching away my own screech of alarm.

CHAPTER TWENTY-THREE

he forest whipped past in a whirl of autumn
colour, the recently fallen leaves swept upwards
by the sheer force of Angmar's beating hooves. Laphaniel's
hands held me tight around my waist while I clung to the
Night-Mare's mane, fearing I was going to be flung from her
back. My legs screamed with the effort of gripping on, my
back flared as she launched herself over fallen branches,
brooks and two wide, fast flowing rivers.

The closeness of Laphaniel was little comfort as we rode
on and on and on, and the only thing keeping me from
sobbing in pain was the slowly darkening sky. Laphaniel had
promised we would stop at nightfall, and never before had I
longed so much for a sunset.

Angmar slowed when the sun dipped below the trees,
temporarily setting the sky alight before twilight ghosted in,
shadowing the skies with its hues of indigo and ink. She led
us to a small clearing, a lush meadow that still bloomed with
late wildflowers, their delicate petals flourishing with steely
determination.

Laphaniel leapt down from Angmar's back, showing no

sign the ride had caused him any discomfort, and reached for me. My legs buckled as soon as I touched the ground, and I would have sunk to the floor if he hadn't caught me. He helped me to sit, and I stretched out my legs with a groan, wondering if I would ever be able to stand again.

"Here," he said, wrapping a blanket around me. "Are you hungry?"

I nodded, and he handed me a strip of dried meat and a piece of fruit. The meat was salty and tough, but I gnawed on it anyway, and it did the job of pushing my hunger away. I watched while he gathered sticks for a small fire, lighting them with just a wave of his hand.

"Have some of this." He took a swallow of the green wine before passing it to me. Angmar wandered to the nearby stream and drank deeply. "Just don't drink too much."

"It tastes like swamp water," I said, making a face as the thick liquid burned down my throat. "You keep it."

He smiled, taking the bottle back and taking another few sips, and I wondered how he could stomach it. He pulled a knife from his pack and tucked it neatly into his belt. He leant forward and rested his elbows on his knees.

"Should I be worried what's out there?" I asked, not liking how exposed we were. He turned to me, the bottle dangling from his fingertips, his gaze sparking something deep within my stomach.

"Would you like me to list everything that wishes to devour you?" he said, a wicked smirk lifting the edge of his lip. "Because there's likely selkies, phookas, wisps, just to name a few, not to mention the…"

"What about you?" I asked, and he blinked, his smirk faltering. Uncertainty etched across his lovely face, fuelling the desire I could no longer keep at bay. I no longer wanted to. "What do you want to do to me?"

"Umm…"

I grinned as he continued to stare at me, looking so unsure…all traces of the cold, graceful fey I knew him to be, gone. Before I could lose my nerve, before I could over-think, I leant closer, brushing my lips against his.

The closeness of him erased the aches and fatigue that had begun to weigh me down, his tentative hands on me pushed back the fear of what lay ahead. He stole away my breath with his answering kiss, his moan soft against my lip.

"Are you sure…"

"Stop talking," I whispered, pressing a finger to his mouth as his eyes shuttered closed.

His hands gripped my hair, his mouth trailing kisses along my neck before finding my mouth again. Teeth grazed over my lip in a kiss that sent all coherent thoughts from my head. The fire beside us spluttered, flames spitting, roaring and hissing as Laphaniel pulled me into his lap, his heartbeat crashing in time to mine.

"Sorry," he gasped and drew back to catch his breath, his hand lingering beneath my shirt as he fought to keep control of the magic swirling around us.

The fire calmed slightly, and he bent to place a gentle kiss against my forehead, hands reaching up to hold me close. I kissed him back with my legs wrapped around his waist, completely done with holding back, of finding reasons why I shouldn't love him. I could list them all, and it would take a while. But there was a reason why they didn't matter that trumped them all.

He made me happy.

I didn't look away from him as I unbuttoned his shirt, teasing it off so I could trace the smooth lines of his stomach, lingering over the dark hair that circled his bellybutton. He squirmed slightly under my touch, and I couldn't help the smile that bloomed at my mouth.

"You're ticklish?"

I could taste his laugh against my lips as I kissed him again, lifting my arms over my head so he could remove my shirt, his gentle hands working to remove the rest of my clothes, until there was not a scrap between us. Laphaniel shifted so he was on top of me, his mouth on mine, moving slowly against the sound of the roaring fire and whispering trees.

"I love you," I whispered in his ear. "More than anything."

He swore against me, my name slipping from his lips like a curse. I drew him close, his heartbeat a drum against my chest.

I fell asleep cradled against him, barely feeling him move away to pull his clothes on so he could keep watch. I didn't know how long I had been asleep before I was woken by a hand over my mouth, and someone hushing me softly.

I opened my eyes, and the lingering shadows of my bad dream clung to me like tendrils of mist, slowly dissipating as I gripped onto Laphaniel. He kept his hand to my lips, silencing my screams that still echoed around the meadow, tempting anything that might have been listening.

I couldn't remember it, only recalling the sound of laughter, the weight of darkness, and a sense of loss that I had never encountered before.

I hadn't realised I had been screaming, or why.

"I was gone less than a minute." Laphaniel cradled my head against his chest, hands running up and down my back. "I thought you were being ripped apart. What on earth were you dreaming about?"

"I don't know," I said, taking a breath. "It was different from the others, nothing happened, but it just felt...awful."

I shivered and fumbled for my discarded clothes lying in a heap beside me, dragging on the shirt and trousers while Laphaniel hovered, failing to hide the concern behind his tired smile.

"It was only a dream," I said.

"You haven't had a nightmare for months."

I hadn't really dwelled upon the absence of my nightmares, simply enjoying the freedom and weightlessness of the dreams I had while close to Laphaniel. It seemed my subconscious felt safe with him. "I haven't had a nightmare since I've been with you, in your house, in your bed."

He sighed against me, his fingers playing with strands of my hair, coiling them so they curled by my face. "I think you forget I am the reason you have nightmares to begin with."

"I haven't forgotten."

He paused. "Do I still frighten you?"

"No," I replied. "But now you have both my heart and soul, and I'm unsure what you will do to them."

"I will keep them safe, if you promise to take care of mine."

I smiled, closing my eyes as I drifted back to sleep in his arms, feeling them tighten around me while he kept watch, staying close so the nightmares couldn't find me.

We rose with the stars still glittering in the far away skies, chasing each other through the pitch, almost taunting me to wish upon one. I didn't dare.

I took his hand as he helped me back onto Angmar, feeling his fingers trail over my back and linger on my hip. It was a swift touch, a reminder of what I was to him, and I treasured it. With a swift jump he was behind me, and once again we took flight through the forest, following a trail only the Night-Mare seemed to know.

I could smell the sweat on her coat, feel it cling to my legs as I sweated with her, not used to the hours of relentless riding. We didn't stop for a rest, and I had to wonder why Laphaniel didn't want to stall our journey. He could have made it last days and I wouldn't have questioned it. Instead, he hurried Angmar on at an unforgivable pace, his hands tight around me, silent.

He wasn't giving me a chance to change my mind, knowing it would carve a wedge between us eventually, and destroy something that was only barely beginning. We reached a clearing after what seemed like a lifetime of riding, and Angmar suddenly stopped. She shook her neck, obviously distressed, snorting as she pounded the ground, and I had to cling to her to stop from falling.

"What's the matter?" I asked, stroking her coat. "What is it, girl?"

"Hush, Teya," Laphaniel hissed behind me, dismounting from Angmar before hauling me off and shoving me behind him. "Go!"

With a quick smack from Laphaniel, the Night-Mare reared up and bolted, not needing much encouragement to flee back into the woods. I didn't miss the fear in her eyes, the deep black rolling back to show just the whites. There was foam at her mouth, her entire body tense with panic.

"Laphaniel..." I gasped as something sharp whipped past my face. There was an instant stinging sensation before I felt the warmth of blood seep down my cheek.

"Keep still," Laphaniel said, his hand against my chest. "They want you to run."

A whooshing noise shot out from the shadows of the distant trees, and I tensed as Laphaniel clung to me, both of us staring at the arrow that landed a breath away from my feet.

I raised my hand to my cheek, feeling the sting of the graze against my fingers. I swallowed thickly at the thought of the arrow sliding against my face, the aim so impossibly precise that it had only nicked me. I didn't think for a moment that it had merely missed.

"Let her go," called a voice to my left. "I want to see how far she gets before I shoot her down."

"No," another voice replied, just as musical, just as deadly. "Let her join us for a while."

They stepped from the trees and walked towards us, six otherworldly figures that watched me with cruel eyes and wicked smiles. Laphaniel tensed, keeping a hand on my arm, his grip painful.

"Are you done with your Unseelie whore then?" sneered one of the faeries. Her hair trailed to her waist in waves, the colour of winter moonlight. "I wouldn't have thought you could choose lower, and yet look."

She gestured to me, her lovely face distorted into a sneer, her blue eyes blazing with malice.

"The girl belongs to me," Laphaniel said. "I have paid for her, and she is mine."

"But you have brought her onto our lands," accused a faerie with close cropped brown hair and eyes like sunrises. "Allow us to have our fun, and perhaps we shall let her live."

With a quick bark of laughter, the pale haired fey grabbed me, her laugh hissing in my ear while she twisted her fingers through my hair.

"Nefina!" Laphaniel cried out, making no move to help me. I wondered how he knew her. "Please."

"Please, what?" the faerie asked, her voice a terrible

whisper against my cheek. "Why should I let her go, after you ruined me?"

Oh god...

"Your ruin was not my doing," Laphaniel replied. "Let her go!"

Nefina twisted my head so I looked at her, her nails sharp. "He will abandon you too, little thing," she said, almost sadly. "He does nothing but leave a trail of wretched hearts. Tell me, what happened to his harpy when you showed up?"

I stared at her, my mouth opening, though no sound came out until she shook me so violently, I felt my teeth rattle. "He made her leave," I choked.

"And what will happen when he grows tired of you, little thing?"

"He...he won't..." My words didn't even convince me, and the surrounding fey sneered, filling the clearing with their miserable laughter.

"You believe you are good enough for him?" asked a willowy girl, her hand still aiming her bow at me. "When he had the Queen of Seelie in his bed?"

"Almost-queen," I bit back, and gasped as a fist collided with the side of my face, sending me sprawling to the floor.

"Disrespectful maggot," she snapped. "I could tear your heart out."

"Wait, Alyssa," said the dark haired fey as he stepped forward, his boot coming close to my fingers as he trod down, scraping my fingertips. "What do you think we should do, Nefina? After all, Laphaniel is your kin."

Nefina raised her hand, and as one, the faeries raised their bows, pointing their arrows straight at me. All bravery I pretended to feel fled, and I cowered at their feet.

"I just want to see Luthien."

Nefina snapped her head to me, and in a graceful swoop

of her white skirts, she was at my side, so close to my face that I could smell the lilac scent coming from her skin.

"Why would you want to do that, little maggot?" Her eyes narrowed in a mirage of concern. "Do you like getting hurt? Do you wish for death?"

"No..."

"How many times has my brother hurt you? Do you still bear bruises? Or do you just wash the blood from your skin? You entertain him now; just think of what he will do when you start to bore him, what he has done to countless girls far prettier than you."

"That is enough, Nefina," Laphaniel growled as I pulled away from her, glancing at the fey surrounding us. Some were grinning, others crouched low with wings unfurled, all of them baring their teeth as they waited.

"It will never be enough," she spat, leaving me to imagine what Laphaniel had done to make her hate him so.

"Shall I shoot her, Nefina?" Alyssa prompted, a terrible smile on her full lips. "I can hit her straight through one of those wonderful green eyes without spilling a drop of blood."

"No, take her to Luthien; perhaps it will give me some respite." Nefina did not look at me but at Laphaniel, and something passed between them. Regret possibly. "What did you think would happen to me when you left?"

Laphaniel said nothing, not a word to defend himself, or me, and I couldn't help the feeling of cold abandonment. I tried to catch his gaze and he turned to me briefly, his eyes hard.

"To Luthien then," called the dark haired faerie, placing his hand on Nefina's shoulder before crouching to face me. "Are you awfully brave, little maggot? Or simply exceedingly stupid?"

"I don't know," I said honestly, looking down. "Perhaps both."

He laughed, placing a warm hand against my face. His nails were sharp. "Stupidly brave will still see you dead, foolish thing that you are."

I was beginning to believe it; watching Laphaniel standing with his brethren, I understood how much he belonged there. He could be as cold and ruthless as they were. He was their equal in beauty and wickedness. He could be cruel just as quickly as he could be lovely. I was starting to believe how foolish I was to think I could keep him.

"Put her out, Alyssa."

The words barely registered before the willowy faerie lunged at me, smacking the back of my head with her bow in a burst of white stars. The world went too bright for a moment as pain exploded through my skull with a sickening velocity. Blackness descended, silencing the gasp that tried to escape my mouth until it was nothing but a wet gurgle.

CHAPTER TWENTY-FOUR

I woke with a sickening headache, remaining completely still until the world around me stopped spinning. There was a metallic taste in my mouth, and I had to take several deep breaths to stop myself from vomiting.

"Speak so brazenly to Luthien, and she will paint the walls with you."

I turned my head, the chill of damp grass brushing against my cheek, soothing the pounding in my skull. Laphaniel sat beside me, knees drawn up to his chest, his gaze fixed ahead. I noticed his knife had been plunged in the earth, buried to the hilt in front of him.

"You just stood by and let them torment me," I said, closing my eyes as a wave of betrayal threatened to suffocate me.

"Yes, I did," Laphaniel stated coldly, grabbing the blade from the dirt as he rose to his feet. "But you should not mistake submission for indifference."

"You never said you had a sister." I pushed myself to my feet as I fought to keep up with him.

"You never asked me."

I tried to think of something to say. "She seems charming."

"She's not."

"Laphaniel..."

He spun on his heel, his eyes dark. "Do you understand that I cannot keep you safe here? The archers will have your heart simply because they can— Nefina will break you because you are mine, and because she can."

"And Luthien?"

He closed his eyes, hiding the black. "I wish I could have stopped you coming here, Teya."

I took the hand he outstretched to me, watching as the heavy clouds parted in places allowing sunlight to trickle over the angry bruise of sky.

"I think I have something to offer Luthien," I said as he took a breath.

"What?"

"I'm not going to bargain my life away," I said quickly. "I won't do that. We'll replace Niven with someone else, and maybe Luthien will accept a few years of my life as payment?"

He stared at me, and I braced myself for the retort I just knew was itching at his lips. "How many are you willing to give up?" he gritted out instead.

I shrugged, not really knowing how many would be sufficient...what price would Luthien put on Niven's head? What did I truly think she was worth?

"I've been thinking about it since the Eerie: anything can be bought with blood and souls and the swapping of years. You bargain with lives and heartache. I didn't think I had anything I could offer, but I could afford to lose the last few years of my life. Perhaps ten?"

"You wouldn't know how long your natural lifespan

could be," Laphaniel pointed out. "A decade is a long time for a human, Teya…to lose so many years…"

"We always want more than we ever get," I answered. "Perhaps I am destined to live until I am a hundred with you, that will mean I get ninety years before payment is taken. That's a huge chunk of forever, enough time to see the end of the world and everything beyond it."

He touched his forehead against mine, his body tense. "I don't like it. I don't want to give Luthien any part of you."

"It's all I have to give her," I said, kissing him gently.

He led me out of the clearing and down the hillside in silence, gripping my hand as the looming shadow of Luthien's home bore down upon us. The consequences of all my choices suddenly weighed around me like a millstone.

The mansion boasted four twisted towers, their pointed roofs tiled with green stained glass. I counted eight floors, with hundreds of windows that gleamed as if the rays of a thousand suns danced off them. Flowers exploded over the pristine stone, even as winter crept in, edging the surrounding trees with frost. It was beautiful and unsettling, perfection with a sinister shadow, and it was then I realised how much I didn't want to go in.

Fey sprawled across the lush green lawns in front of the mansion, some with their mouths open so they could catch the raindrops. They barely glanced up when we passed them, but they noticed us all the same with a flash of teeth or flicker of wing. Lazy smiles crept over lovely faces as they watched us walk by, and I had to wonder if they could hear my heart screaming.

"Keep walking," Laphaniel whispered, and led me down stone steps that were flanked by two lifelike carvings of horses, frozen forever to rear up out of the stonework.

My head turned at the sound of musical peals of laughter.

I barely felt Laphaniel's grip on my hand as he tried to pull me on.

"Keep walking," he repeated.

The unmistakable swirl of Glamour snaked around the hedgerows, teasing against me in tainted promises. I tensed, shaking the sudden fog from my mind. I gripped Laphaniel tighter.

"Someone's laughing." I fought against the urge to follow the sound. I pinched myself hard, forcing my heavy feet away from the intoxicating sound. "Come on, before my disobedient feet wander off without me."

"You're getting good at that."

"I've had a fair amount of practice fighting off Glamour," I said, noting the look of surprise on his face and tugged on his hand.

"I guess you have," he replied dryly.

"Laphaniel!" A voice called out, making me jump as Laphaniel spun around, his hand coming up quickly around me. "I heard whispers it was you, but you know what dryads are like, insufferable gossips. Yet look, here you are!"

A lithe faerie strode towards us, eyes as red as his hair. His lips were stretched to a wide smile, revealing pointed incisors.

"William." Laphaniel acknowledged the fey with a quick nod of his head, his arm tight around me. "We're not stopping, this is a fleeting visit."

William's eyes flashed, darting to me. "Oh, I insist you join me, and tell me more about that exquisite thing hanging from your arm. Come, come!"

He snatched at me, twirling me into his arms, and I was thankful that Laphaniel released me because I really didn't want my shoulder dislocated.

"I'm not allowed to eat anything, sir," I began, averting

my eyes away in a show of meekness. "He would be very cross at me if he had to carry me home."

William cupped my chin and tilted my head up so I faced him, his irises dancing like flames. "So well trained, so polite. Come and sit with me, girl. Laphaniel, keep a tight hold on this one, else someone will snatch her away."

"Noted," Laphaniel replied, rolling his eyes when I winked at him.

We walked around a maze of ornamental walls covered in flowering vines, stopping at a picnic laid out beneath a canopy of rich silks and velvets.

Wine stained the blankets on the ground, pouring from the cracks in a broken glass held up by a young boy. Blood welled between his fingers, though he didn't seem to notice as it oozed down his hand to spill amongst the wine. Glamour flowed around the silks like incense, I could smell the desperation clinging to it, a tang of something that had never been present within Laphaniel's home.

There were three of them sitting around the stained blanket, all human. They were pale and drawn, torn edges of their clothes revealing a collage of bruises, and yet they were still smiling. I shuddered at the looks on their faces, the vacant dullness of their eyes and wondered how long they had been there. How long had it been since they had stopped fighting the Glamour that was holding them?

William gestured with clawed hands to the food in front of him, sitting down to wrap an arm around a waif of a girl who leant heavily against him, her eyes drooping. There were teeth marks on her neck, down her arms, and over the small swell of her breasts.

"Sit, girl," he said, curling his lip around pointed teeth. "Don't disgrace your master."

"I would prefer to stay at his side, sir," I said. "I have an awful habit of wandering off."

"Ah," William nodded. "You need to beat that out of her, Laphaniel, quell that defiance, it may be alluring now but it'll cause no end of problems. I am happy to show you how I force submission into my own pets. Do it right, and you'll only need to do it once."

Laphaniel said nothing, his hand squeezing mine, as maybe for the first time he was lost for words. William's eyes darkened, the flames within flaring a strange blue.

"I would never run from him again," I said quickly, lifting my shirt to reveal the red mark on my side, not needing to embellish the fear in my voice. "Never again."

William tilted his head, sharp nails trailing along the wound. "That's incredibly close to the parts she needs to live, Laphaniel. It's brutal and it gets the message across, but it is wasteful."

"I do not need your advice, William, thank you," Laphaniel said, barely veiled fury radiating from him.

I felt him tug at me, but I couldn't tear my eyes off the small group, my eyes resting on something William was holding in his free hand. He caught me looking, his grin widening as I felt the familiar weight of Glamour snake around me, like a noose.

"Do you want this?" William asked, his voice lilting as it filled my head with a malicious lullaby that made me forget everything else. He shifted so the girl resting against him slid to the floor. "I only have the one."

Two pairs of eyes snapped towards me, human teeth bared as they crouched low, readying themselves to fight me for what we all suddenly wanted more than anything. The girl was drooling, her gaze flicking from the apple to me, and I realised my lips were wet too.

William tossed the apple, and my body lunged for it. I needed it like I needed air to breathe, craving it more than anything I had ever wanted before. The need for it consumed me, and it would have destroyed me if Laphaniel hadn't thrown himself at my body, using his entire weight to pin me down.

I kicked and bit at him, feeling the bones in my arms crack as I grappled for the fruit, screeching in his ear to let me go. His fingers scraped at my skin as he held me down, snatching at my hair to keep me still. His voice was a whisper against the madness in my head.

"Listen to me," he breathed, the words a song. "You don't want it, you know you don't."

"It's mine!" I snarled, my mouth snapping against his fingers. "You can't have it!"

His hand tightened on my hair. "It is only an apple, remember? Nothing more."

Something on a primal level recognised the cadence of his tone, the different weight of magic that swirled my mind, and didn't shy from it. The fight left me, my head cleared and I could do nothing but watch with a fading anguish as the dead-eyed girl clutched at the apple, her face a picture of sheer rapture.

The human boy lunged at her, grabbing at her hair and twisting it around his hand so he could use it to smack her head against the hard ground, again and again and again. He didn't stop until she stopped moving. She hadn't even let go of the apple, and still clutched it with bone white fingers.

The boy dropped her wetly to the floor, prising her fingers open to retrieve his prize, not seeming to care that the shining green apple was dripping red as he bit into it. When he had finished... only when he had finished did he begin to cry.

Though whether it was for the girl, or because he had finished the apple, I never found out.

William stood, scooping up the waifish girl who clung to him, whimpering. "You should never have brought her here," he said, shaking his head before he walked away, leaving the weeping boy behind.

I choked on a sob, unable to move from where I lay on the ground. Laphaniel held me there while I watched blood seep from the broken girl and trickle down the paving to pool close to my hands. A small moan pushed past my lips, and Laphaniel dragged me up, his arms tight around my waist since my legs refused to hold me.

"You used to do that," I said, my voice cracking as I slowly broke.

"Yes," he answered, and I could no longer bear to have his hands on me.

"I let you do that to me...I let you torment me..."

"I no longer enjoy tormenting you, Teya."

Cold sweat broke out against my face and my vision wavered. "I'm going to be sick."

I threw up where I stood, and Laphaniel grabbed at my hair, dragging it away from my face.

"You know what I am, what I have done and what I am capable of. You once thought I was a monster, but you chose to stay in the end, with me. I will not apologise for being cruel, Teya, not when it is my nature to be so." He paused and took a breath. "I love you, but I don't know if that's going to be enough for you."

"I don't think I can do this right now," I forced out, straightening up and wiping my mouth with my sleeve.

"Then when, Teya? You worry that I'll grow bored of you, but perhaps one day you'll decide you no longer want to wake up beside someone like me."

"Just leave it, please?"

"As you wish."

"My head is a mess, Laphaniel, okay? You've thrown my world upside down and I've had barely enough time to think, let alone know if I am okay with it." I sucked in a shaking breath and shoved the heels of my hands against my eyes to stop the tears that threatened. "No...do you know what? I don't care what you did, who you've hurt, because I know damn well I am just thankful that you took Niven, so I could find you, and it sickens me! I am a monster, Laphaniel. I have torn my family apart, and I cannot fix it and god knows I have tried. I don't want Niven back because I love my sister, I want her back so I can move on and live, and now I just wish I had listened to you and stayed away because there is nothing I can do to make this right. It's too late."

"Why are you saying that now?" he countered, his voice hopeless. "You can't just turn around and change your mind now...back in the cave, if I had asked you to stay what would you have said?"

"I don't know!"

"Teya!"

"I probably would have said yes," I hissed through gritted teeth. "Does that make you feel better? If you had asked me to stay with you in the cave, I think I would have chosen to abandon my family and all I believe in to be with you."

"Damn you," he snarled, looking away. "You can't turn back now. Luthien knows you are here, and she will be waiting for you. I will beg for your life if I have to, but dwelling on what could have been is helping no one."

"It feels good finally getting it off my chest," I muttered.

"I despair of you," he replied bitterly, and took my hand to walk away from the stone maze and away from the garden.

Laphaniel led me up to the great doors of Luthien's

mansion, stepping over the various fey that lounged on the steps. They all curled their legs up for Laphaniel, but as I stepped by, they kicked them out again, barring my way.

"Adorable," one said, curling long fingers around my calf as she leant towards me. "Isn't she, darling?"

"Simply divine," laughed another, not looking up from the book she was reading. "Remember to scream loudly in there, dear one, so that we can hear you."

I clutched at Laphaniel's hand like a lifeline, my heart thudding against my ribcage. He pushed open the doors and I followed him in, wincing when they slammed shut behind us.

I wondered if I would ever see the outside again.

Laphaniel bent his head low to whisper in my ear, his voice coming out rushed and desperate, scaring me witless. "Do not stray from me, do not touch the food, keep your eyes low, and for the love of all things keep your mouth shut."

My footsteps tapped noisily on the polished floor, the dozens of mirrors bouncing my terrified reflection back infinitely. When I stopped walking, the musical chatter filling the cavernous room silenced instantly, as all the occupants turned and stared at me.

There must have been more than a hundred fey settled in velvet armchairs, or sprawled over giant cushions, entwined in each other's arms. Some were sitting at tables, cards in hands as they gambled over souls. They flew around the delicate chandeliers, the size of fireflies, and they crept out of the fireplace at the end of the room, smiling as the flames licked at their bodies.

It didn't matter that the room was crowded with faeries, as my eyes were only drawn to the heartbreakingly beautiful woman at the end of the room. No one else mattered. Unlike all the others, she was smiling at me, though I truly wished she wasn't.

Luthien's deep brown eyes stared at me with an unnerving familiarity, her lips set in a cruel smile that lit up her face with beauty and horror. She stood up, her silver gown flowing around her body like mist, the neckline plunging so low I could see the white of her breast. The unease in the room was tangible, I could almost hear the fey holding their breath in anticipation. They all watched their mistress, who only had eyes for me. I felt Laphaniel's hand on my shoulder, and I took the hint and sank to my knees.

Luthien stepped towards us, her arms outstretched to embrace Laphaniel, who kept completely still as she pressed her lips to his cheek.

"Welcome home," she said, dark eyes flicking to me. "I see you have brought a friend. Pretty little thing, isn't she?"

Luthien crouched down beside me, her fingers against my cheeks, trailing along the tear tracks on my skin. I stiffened when she leant closer, her tongue darting out to lick my cheek as her grip on my face tightened.

"I know you," she said softly, a whisper meant only for me. "I have tasted these tears before. It is your sister who haunts our castle, is it not?"

I nodded.

"Would that make you a little princess then?" Luthien continued, her voice daring me to answer, but I couldn't summon the courage to say anything. "Perhaps we should bow to you?"

Luthien's fingers coiled in my hair, her fingernails digging against my scalp before she dragged me to my feet. She held me so I stood on tiptoes, forcing me to circle with her so she could show me off to her court. They sneered as we turned, dipping their heads in a shameful parody of a bow.

"Tell me your name," Luthien demanded, releasing my hair so I crashed to the floor.

"Teya," I choked out, keeping my face low.

"How long has it been, Teya?"

"Ten years."

I glanced up as Luthien swept past me in a ripple of silks, her smile as cold as her eyes. "Only ten? How fares your family, little Teya?"

"You left behind nothing but suicide and madness," I breathed, and flinched as she caught my face in her hands, forcing me to look up at her.

"You forgot courage," Luthien sang, her lips against my cheek. "I do admire courage, Teya."

"Do you admire it enough to grant me a wish?" I asked, my heart a violent crash against my chest.

She cocked her head, dark hair splaying across her bare shoulders. "A wish?"

"Just one."

She raised one finger, pushing it against my lips. "Does your heart know what you truly want?"

"I want...."

"Shhhh," she whispered, so close to me that her words were for me alone. "You came here to ask for your sister back, no? Ask yourself what you really want, little girl."

"I just want Niven back," I said, my words faltering and pathetic, and I knew she could taste the lies upon my lips.

"And what will you give me?"

I fought to keep her gaze, my offer falling meaningless from my mouth. "Ten years of my life."

"To do with as I please?" Her question was a caress, suffocating.

I closed my eyes. "Yes."

She rose with a boneless grace, leaving me on the ground with the twisted hope that perhaps she was willing to help me after all. That hope dwindled and died the moment she spun around to face Laphaniel and struck him so hard I heard something crack.

"How dare you bring your whore to me!" she cried, and outside the skies darkened and thunder purred in the distance. The surrounding fey cowered, each one making themselves smaller to avoid Luthien's wrath.

"I still belong to this court," Laphaniel replied calmly, speaking around the blood in his mouth. "It is my right to call upon you for your favour."

"You left."

"But I was not banished. You can choose to grant Teya's request or refuse it, but she belongs to me, she is not yours to break, Luthien."

"You dare come to me, after all these years and beseech my help?" Luthien asked, splaying out her fingers so the candlelight flickered and waned. "For a human girl?"

"Yes."

"Solitude has changed you," she said, longing creeping into her voice. I watched as she softly wiped at the blood dribbling from Laphaniel's lip.

"Time has not changed you," Laphaniel replied, closing his eyes as she touched him, her hand lingering against his cheek until I had to force myself to look away.

"Tonight, we hold the Full Moon Ball. Join us in our revelry as once you did so long ago. I will consider what you ask after that," Luthien ordered, allowing her red tipped fingers to drop. "Oonagh! Dress this wretched thing, she is filthy, and she reeks."

Laughter shattered through the unease of the court, and before I could seek out Laphaniel, a woman dressed in blue silks dragged me from the halls.

CHAPTER TWENTY-FIVE

*I*f you do not wish me to break your arm, then stop struggling," Oonagh hissed, giving me a sharp tug as I strained my head to search for Laphaniel.

I couldn't see him anywhere, but I remembered his orders for me to stick beside him. I didn't know what I was supposed to do if we were separated.

The faerie marched me from the halls, winding around corridors and up spiralling staircases that gleamed even in the absence of sunlight. Tapestries lined the walls, depicting pictures of enchanting maidens and bloodstained knights. Golden thread glittered throughout as strands of luminous hair, stitched to tumble over naked shoulders. Darker scarlet pooled around the embroidered bodies of fallen warriors, corpses sewn with fine detail amongst the appliquéd flowers and silken vines. Red seemed to be a dominant colour.

Oonagh guided me past the tapestries and portraits, her hand on my arm cold, though her grip was far gentler than Luthien's had been. She was the only faerie that hadn't bruised me.

Like all the other fey, she was stunning. Her silver hair trailed down over her hips, tied loosely at the nape of her pale neck, and when she turned to me, I noticed her eyes were the colour of crystal, pale and breath-taking.

"You will need to bathe first, I think," Oonagh said, her nose wrinkling at the smell of me. She opened a door, gesturing for me to enter. "Don't sit on anything until you are clean."

I stood in the middle of the room, watching while Oonagh swooped around lighting the candles with a flick of her fingers. Balancing on tiptoes, she turned to me, her elegant fingers coaxing more flames to light in a chandelier that was dripping in black jewels.

We had entered a bedroom that was nothing like Laphaniel's rustic woodland room, and as wonderful as it was, I missed the simplicity. Black wallpaper lined every wall, shining with jewelled butterflies and creeping vines blooming with flowers. Huge serpents were painted against the black, green scales glimmering with real emeralds, their wings stretching out as a canopy for the bed that eclipsed the room.

I walked over to the enormous four-post bed, trailing my hands over the carvings etched into the woodwork. Tiny animals were carved up the posts one on top of the other, tails and claws wrapped around each other, so it looked as if they alone were holding the bed up. It would have been enchanting and whimsical, if not for the looks of horror and agony cut into their faces.

"You are a quiet little thing, aren't you?" Oonagh said behind me, making me jump, and I flinched as she smacked my hand away. "I told you not to touch anything."

"Sorry."

"Hmmm." Her eyes narrowed at me. "Where is your fight, girl? Where is your spirit?"

"Gone with my hope, I think."

Oonagh's lips curled back as she grinned, her entire face lighting up. "No, it's here."

She pressed her hands to my chest, splaying out her fingers as she cocked her head to listen, and I tensed.

"I can hear it screaming within your heartbeats. You are stronger than you would have us believe; he would not have chosen you otherwise." Her smile faded, and she reached up to cup my cheek, her touch so gentle I wanted to weep.

"I thought I was strong enough to do this, now I'm not so sure."

"It's a little late to change your mind," Oonagh said softly.

"So I've been told."

"It is dangerous to meddle in the lives of fey, Teya. Mortals seldom escape unscathed."

I sighed and absently reached towards the soft silk of the bed sheets. I caught myself before my dirty hands soiled it. "Are you warning me against Luthien or Laphaniel?"

She smiled, her lips lifted, but her eyes remained sad. "I fear for the both of you. I fear you and he are going to tear each other apart."

"Laphaniel wouldn't hurt me," I said, bristling at her words. Oonagh tilted her head, fixing me with a knowing stare as her fingers came up to brush the hair from my face.

"Never underestimate the fragility of a human heart, Teya."

"I would never hurt him, either." I pulled away from her touch.

"Oh, but you already have, you just do not realise how much."

Her words hit me like a physical blow, but my mind went to Laphaniel, always Laphaniel.

"I don't even know where he is," I admitted painfully, because suddenly it felt crazy not to have him beside me. I needed him and he needed me.

Oonagh turned and gestured for me to follow. "Yes, you do."

She led me into a grand bathroom that glittered with the green and blue mosaics on the walls. I closed my eyes, my heart aching at the thought of Laphaniel with Luthien.

"Is he safe with her?"

"No one is safe with Luthien."

Oonagh turned the taps on and filled the bath with scented water, steam rising from the brass. She filled it to the top, smiling to herself as the water lapped at the sides and poured down over the golden floor. The moment it splashed against the tiles, the mosaics on the walls began to shimmer and move, flowing into mermaids that swam over the walls.

"It's beautiful," I gasped and watched as they flipped over the ceiling and trailed down over the floor, darting past my feet. I flinched before realising they were only paintings and were not going to drown me.

"There is more to this world than darkness." Oonagh reached up to unbutton my shirt.

"Hey! I can do that."

"If you wish."

"Could I have some privacy?"

"No." Oonagh shook her head. "I have orders to have you cleaned. Undress now or I'll tear your clothes off."

I stared at her, confused by her behaviour towards me, the soft touches, the gentle smiles followed by the subtle threats of violence. She wasn't as cold as the other fey I had met, but there was still a wicked glint to her iridescent eyes that made me heed her warning. Covering myself as best as I could, I took my clothes off, lowering my eyes to the floor as I huddled naked in the middle of the room.

"Stop that!" she snapped, and I jumped. "What have you to be shameful of? Keep that pretty head of yours held high, Teya. You will not survive us with your head cowed."

"I don't know what I am going to do," I said desperately before I climbed into the deep bath.

Oonagh passed me a washcloth and got to work on my hair, lathering it up with a divine scented shampoo. I relaxed under her touch, her fingers kneading against my scalp. "Why would he bring you here?"

"He told me to go home; he tried to make me..." My voice cracked as I scrubbed the filth from my body. "He opened his home to me, but I wouldn't listen."

"Oh." The fey took back the cloth, running it over my back, scrubbing away the flakes of dried blood. "You foolish girl."

"I know."

"We all have regrets in life, Teya. Don't let it consume you."

I nodded, feeling as if it already had. Forcing a smile, I accepted the towel Oonagh offered me and stepped out of the bath, watching with a strange sadness as the mermaids stopped swimming and disappeared back into the mosaics on the walls.

Back in the bedroom, Oonagh turned to pull a dress from a mannequin and held it up for me to step into. She hesitated, narrowing her pale eyes before placing the gown back and indicating I should stay wrapped in the towel.

"Have you eaten yet?" she asked. "I won't have crumbs on that silk."

I shook my head. "Laphaniel told me not to eat anything."

"Wise words," Oonagh said, gesturing for me to sit on a plush velvet chair. "But it is foolish to enter a ball on an empty stomach."

She clapped her hands sharply, and two rake-thin faeries flittered into the room, pale pink hair floating around their heads like candyfloss. They sniffed at me as they passed, magenta eyes blinking as rapidly as their transparent wings behind them.

"Bring a platter of food," Oonagh demanded, barely glancing up. "Now, if you please."

"Poisoned or not?" one said, her voice high and childlike.

Oonagh sighed. "I would think not."

"I won't eat anything they bring up," I said, as the pink faeries drifted away. Oonagh lifted an eyebrow, not looking up from the glittering hairpins she was sorting through.

"You will do as you are told."

"And if I don't?"

She turned, a crackle of angry Glamour sparking around the room, though her face remained stoic and calm. "Would you like to find out?"

I shook my head, curling my legs up in the chair, resting my head against the soft velvet. Oonagh said nothing as she fiddled with pearls and bracelets, holding them up to the light before tossing them back into a drawer without care. She held up two huge diamonds, scowling as she noted that my ears weren't pierced. I sincerely hoped she wasn't going to offer to pierce them for me.

The buzzing pink faeries returned with a silver platter of food and a jug of steaming silver liquid that filled the room with the delicate scent of fresh rain. They leant close and placed it upon a table, pressing their faces into my hair to breathe deeply.

"Get out," Oonagh snapped, shooing the faeries away

with a wave of her hands. She poured two cups of the shining drink into goblets. "Eat and drink, Teya, we have much work to do."

There was no point in arguing with her, so I took a tentative sip of my drink, gulping it down as the gentle bubbles burst upon my tongue. I picked at the strange cured meats, enjoying the odd sweetness. The grapes were fat and juicy, the cheese crumbly and strong, the bread still warm from the oven.

"Better?" Oonagh plucked a piece of cheese from my plate and popped it into her mouth. "When was the last time you had food like that?"

"When Laphaniel cooked for me," I answered, longing for that rustic kitchen with the worn table and tatty chair.

"The boy can cook?" Oonagh smiled. "I did wonder. I couldn't imagine he would let that foul demon prepare his meals."

"Lily is dead," I blurted.

"Oh, thank goodness," she said. "Now, let's get you dressed."

The green silk glided over my body as if made for me alone, a shimmering mass of sheer fabric that fell to my feet in waves. The flowing sleeves billowed over my arms, held in place with golden thread tied to my fingers. Oonagh ordered me to grip the bedpost while she fastened the corset, yanking on the stays until my cleavage was on show.

"I can't breathe."

"If you can talk, you can still breathe," she retorted, and pulled tighter. "It fits better than Laphaniel's clothing, does it not?"

I nodded, taking small breaths, already missing the feel of his shirt against my skin, the scent of him close to me. The irrevocable love I felt for him was threatening to overwhelm me; it had already changed me absolutely into someone I could scarcely recognise. There was an ever-growing part of me that wanted to be overwhelmed by it, to drown in it.

"It nearly broke you to refuse him, didn't it, Teya?" Oonagh said, her voice soft as she smoothed out the layers of fabric.

"How long have you known Laphaniel?" I asked, avoiding her question, but feeling it pinch at my heart all the same.

"Long enough to call him a friend. I have missed him."

"Were you two ever..." I couldn't bring myself to finish the question, and jumped slightly at Oonagh's quick bark of laughter.

"Lovers? Oh, my goodness no! The thought of it. Believe me, Teya, Laphaniel is not my type at all."

"Did Luthien love him?"

"She still does," Oonagh replied, twisting my hair off my face and fastening it with an ornate pin, curling loose tendrils to frame my face. "I am sorry, but Luthien will not allow you to leave here with him."

"He told me he was going to rule beside her. He was to be your King."

Oonagh smiled sadly. "That was a long time ago."

"I can't compete with a Queen, Oonagh."

Oonagh's strange eyes met mine as she fastened a velvet choker around my neck, an emerald dangling to sit against my breast. "Laphaniel walked away from Luthien, do not forget that. He chose to be with you. I fear she will not be able to compete with you."

"What am I going to do?"

"I have no idea, but right at this moment, you will attend the Full Moon Ball with your head held high, and after that, your fate will be decided." She paused. "Was she worth it?"

I knew she meant Niven, and I glared at her, furious that she had the nerve to ask the question I could not bear to ask myself.

"I thought not," she breathed, her hand closing around mine as she led me from the room and down the corridors to where the distant thrum of drums began to play.

CHAPTER TWENTY-SIX

*T*he music drifted around the ballroom like a cloud of hypnotic smoke, causing those who heard it to sway and bend as if pulled by invisible strings. Thousands of candles shone from golden chandeliers, their light streaking through the dripping crystal to paint rainbows on the floor.

Dancers glided over the polished marble, twisting together with elegant steps that no human could ever hope to accomplish. There was barely a breath between them, lips and hands locked together so it looked more like lovemaking.

I backed against a wall, overwhelmed by the wildness of it all. The rich scents of perfumes and sweets, cakes and breads and meats floated across the ballroom, making my head spin. I closed my eyes as my head hummed with the wild beating of the drums and the lulling pipes that were tempting my feet to move. I didn't dare. I knew that if I stepped foot on the dance floor, I would be swept away with the others, and who knew what would become of me after?

I turned to gaze out of the window where the gardens were lit by the moonlight, and found myself watching a couple kiss upon the dew-soaked lawn. The girl tipped her head back, mouth open as her skirt lifted. Hands wandered over her breasts, curling against her golden hair, until finally the man lowered himself over her, a sigh at his lips.

"Enjoying the show?"

I started, blushing furiously. My heart was thumping and my breaths were little gasps. My face burned at my longing for Laphaniel.

"You look lost," said the fey, his bronze eyes as wicked as his grin. "Can I offer you a drink?"

He offered me a goblet, his lips lifting to reveal sharp incisors. I glanced at the cup and then to the short horns that peeked out from his curling blond hair. I shook my head.

"I'm not supposed to drink that."

He sat beside me, stretching his long legs in front of him. "Do you always do everything you are supposed to do?"

"I wouldn't be here if I did."

He laughed, his eyes glinting, his lips stained red. I could smell the sweetness of the wine on his breath, the ripeness of the berries, the tang of something dark and forbidden, the undertones of broken promises.

"It will be more fun if you join in," he said, swirling the wine in his glass. "Did you know we can smell the fear coming off you? It will only be a matter of time before it overexcites someone. You don't want to get hurt, do you?"

I went to move away, though there was nowhere I could really go. "I'm waiting for Laphaniel, leave me alone."

"You are alone," the faerie cooed. "I was just being friendly. My name is Gabriel."

He took my hand even though I hadn't offered it, pressing his lips against my skin.

"Angelic," I replied, the echo of his kiss lingering at my hand.

"Do you think?" His teeth glinted in the low light, tips of pointed canines peeking through his lips.

"I think you'd sooner damn me." I pulled my hand back.

"And what fun we would have. Allow me just the one dance? You cannot spend your first Faerie Ball merely watching."

Gabriel offered me his hand, strange amber eyes peering out from behind his curls, a smile dancing at his lips, just hinting at the devil that was lurking beneath his charming mask. Laphaniel was still nowhere in sight, and the golden haired faerie was right...it wouldn't be long before something else noticed I was alone and unguarded.

I placed my hand in Gabriel's and his fingers closed over mine. I swallowed hard. He swept me over to the dance floor with a devilish smile, his bronze eyes alight. With quick fingers he plucked a goblet of wine held up by a passing faerie and tipped the golden liquid into his mouth. He grinned and pulled me closer, his mouth pressing against mine, and he poured the wine from his lips to my own.

Warmth burst against my throat and bloomed at the pit of my stomach, tiny, sweet bubbles bursting at my nose and mouth. Gabriel deepened his kiss and my body tingled with the mouthful of wine. One hand snaked around my waist while the other caught my fist as I went to thump him.

He spun me around with expert hands, his smile never faltering. He caught me again to lift me off my feet to the pounding of the music around us. I glared at him, my own traitorous lips breaking into a smile. I gave in, throwing my head back with a laugh, and danced with him.

"See? Now you're having fun." He laughed with me, gliding around the floor with dizzying speed. Faces all blurred together as I spun with him, some wore masks and others not, revealing long muzzles and pointed teeth that snapped at me if I brushed too close.

I spotted Oonagh standing in one corner, her silver hair wild around her bare shoulders. She lost herself in the arms of a girl with butterfly wings and paid no attention to me. I lost her again when Gabriel waltzed me across the room until my feet were bleeding.

"Stop!" I gasped. "Stop, please."

With a theatrical bow he stopped beside a golden table, gesturing for me to sit on one of the plump velvet seats dotted around the cavernous room. I tried to catch my breath, feeling my chest strain against the restraints of my corset. I kicked my shoes off, not needing to look to know my blood had stained them red.

"You cannot say you did not enjoy that."

"It was certainly an experience I won't be forgetting for a while," I replied, already wanting to throw myself back into the music, although my body was begging me to rest. "Thank you for looking out for me."

"Thank you for the kiss," he grinned with a wink, and I rolled my eyes.

"You're welcome, but don't think you'll be getting any more."

"Worried your lover will get jealous?" Gabriel said, licking his lips. "Or worried you'll fall helplessly in love with me?"

I snorted, leaning over to massage my sore feet, even as they continued to tap to the sound of the wild music. "Perhaps both, likely neither."

He grinned as I smirked up at him, his hand resting on the wall above me, his bright eyes drifting to the writhing mass of bodies, itching to get back into the fray.

"What are these?" I asked, spotting the rows of minuscule

bottles lined up neatly on the table near me. I picked one up and watched the contents swirl in my hand, glittering gold and red.

"Those are Goodnight Kisses," Gabriel said. "Party favours."

"What do they do?"

Gabriel's smile faded and he plucked the vial from my hand, turning it up towards the candlelight until the liquid turned black as if eaten up by shadows. "They put the drinker into a deep sleep until the sun rises. It is tasteless and undetectable when slipped into wine."

"For what purpose?"

"Can you truly not think of any?" Gabriel answered, his smile dark. I shuddered, not wanting to dwell on what the fey would do with someone unable to fight back.

"You really are just monsters," I said, disgusted, as he closed my fingers over the vial with a wicked grin.

"Yes, we are. Never forget that," he whispered, leaning in so his words ghosted over my cheek, his breath warm and sweet. "Keep hold of those kisses, you never know when they may come in useful."

"Have you ever used them?" I blurted out, uncomfortable with his closeness but unable to move away from him.

He laughed again, soft and gentle and wonderful, his fingers coming up to pull the pin from my hair, so it tumbled in waves over my shoulders. "Do I look as if I have to force someone to my bed?"

"No," I replied. "I bet they tumble over you like skittles."

His laugh was a filthy chuckle, one that screamed of wild nights and abandoned morals and I didn't doubt he could charm the stars from the skies if he wanted them.

"Oonagh spent an age doing my hair." I gestured to the

pin he twirled in his fingers. "She's going to be pissed you've ruined it."

"Ah," he grabbed at my hair, twisting it tightly before poking my head with the pin. "How do you get it to stay up?"

I laughed, shoving him away. "I have no idea. Leave it alone before you impale me. I won't tell her it was you."

"You have my unwavering gratitude, Teya," Gabriel said, holding a hand to his heart before reaching out to me. "One more dance?"

My own smile matched his as he pulled me close to rejoin the untamed swirl of fey. He twirled me with expert hands, lifting me up so my gown spun in a whirl of ripped silk and glittering beads. His hand was at my hip, the other entwined with mine as he kept a firm hold upon me, keeping me close. I spun until I felt sick, the writhing world around me nothing but a blur of flashing colour and crazy noise...but I didn't care, the ball had an insatiable grip upon me, and I allowed it to engulf me.

I cried out as I crashed to the floor, sprawling across the marble when suddenly Gabriel's hand was torn from mine and he staggered backwards. Blood bloomed against his mouth, yet the frenzied beat of music played on, and the fey continued to dance. Violence it seemed, was all part of the ball.

I jumped up just as Laphaniel raised his fist to lash out again, and caught his arm before he could swing.

"Wait!" I yelled at him. "Stop! What the hell are you doing?"

"What do you think you are doing?" he snarled, turning to me, his eyes black, fury radiating from him.

Gabriel stood, wiping the blood from his face with his sleeve. He placed a hand on my shoulder, forcing me to back away from Laphaniel. "She was enjoying herself. You left her alone," Gabriel began, teeth flashing. "You are lucky I came across her or who knows what would have happened."

Laphaniel shot forwards, grabbing Gabriel by the throat before smacking him hard against the wall. I screamed at him. The candles above us guttered out, responding to his anger. The dancing fey close to us turned to watch, amusement settling over their graceful faces.

"Don't you touch her!" Laphaniel hissed, his voice low and deadly. "She belongs to me."

"I kept them away from her," Gabriel spluttered, scrambling at the tight grip around his throat. "She is sober and untouched, my friend...more than I can say for you."

"I never asked for your help."

"Stop it!" I grabbed at Laphaniel's hand, but with a sweep of Glamour, he sent me to the floor. My knees hit the marble and I gasped with the sudden sharp pain, fighting against the weight of the angry, desperate Glamour that was pressing me down.

"You never ask anyone for help," Gabriel croaked. "Look at the state you are in, look at the mess you have created by bringing her here."

Laphaniel released his hold on Gabriel's neck so he slumped to the floor, bruises already forming around his throat. I rushed forwards to help him, but Laphaniel snatched at my arm, hauling me up and away from Gabriel.

"Leave her alone," he spat, his words slurring as Gabriel looked at him with a mixture of fury and pity.

"What did you bargain for her?" Gabriel asked, his voice hoarse. I shot a look at Laphaniel, watching something pass over his face...regret...shame...disgust. He met my gaze and turned away.

Gabriel pushed himself to his feet, the marks around his neck already fading. "Take him somewhere to sober up."

I nodded and watched him wander into the dance, the mass of bodies swallowing him up into the frenzy he seemed to enjoy so much.

"You're drunk," I snapped, utterly furious. "Just look at you!"

Laphaniel stared at me, his head tilting to the side, a wicked quirk at his lips as if silently daring me to carry on.

"What happened?" I asked.

He blinked, and some of the darkness lifted from him so he simply looked pale and miserable. "What happened?" he breathed, stepping closer to me. "You happened."

His words came out thick and heavy, and beneath the smell of strong liquor, he smelled of her. Looking closer I could see marks on his arms, scratches and faint bruises and when I thought my heart couldn't take any more, I noticed his shirt was buttoned up wrong.

"We need to talk." I swallowed the lump in my throat, wondering what he had done to bargain for me. "Right now."

We left the ballroom, and I was aware of the glinting eyes that watched us from the mass of dancers. I ignored them, taking Laphaniel's hand and led him back to the room Oonagh had shown me.

Laphaniel didn't speak as we walked, his silence pounding at me in a fog of pain and fury and despair. At his sides, his knuckles were white where he clenched them tight, his face shut off to me, turning him back to the cold stranger I had met that night in the woods.

We reached the room and I made to take his hand again, but he grabbed me instead, kicking at the door so it swung open with a shriek. I barely had time to gasp before he pinned me to him, his mouth hard against mine. His hand wound up into my hair, tugging tightly so I couldn't move away. I moaned softly as he backed me against the wall, the candle-light exploding, sending us into darkness.

They ignited again and spluttered out, flashing between life and shadow as any control Laphaniel had over his Glamour...his emotions, failed him completely. His kisses screamed to me, and for just a moment, I gave into them, allowing his hands to tear at the stays of my corset, as his mouth moved to my neck, his teeth biting down at the soft flesh just above my breasts.

"Laphaniel...stop..." My head spun, a part of me wanting once again to get lost within him, that part of me wondering why I had ever fought to find my way out. "Stop."

His eyes met mine and they were bottomless, an abyss without end. He pulled away and sank down on the bed, and finally the candlelight around the room stopped flickering.

"What happened with Luthien?"

"I asked her to let you go," he said, his voice hollow.

"And she said no," I said, and it wasn't a question. Laphaniel nodded as I settled down beside him. A thousand questions flashed through my mind, but only one pushed past my lips, dangling with uncertainty, sharp with jealousy. "Did she kiss you?"

"Yes."

I tensed. "Did you kiss her back?"

Laphaniel turned to face me. "Yes."

My eyes followed the marks on his arms, the fingerprint bruises and I felt sick. "Did you sleep with her?"

Laphaniel shook his head slowly, as if he were unsure, his hands reaching up to adjust the collar of his shirt. I noticed that there was blood on his neck.

"Did she..."

"Don't!" he snapped, rising to his feet and away from me,

crashing against a bookshelf as he stumbled. "She said no, Teya. Nothing else matters."

"It matters to me if she's had her hands all over you."

"Why? You had your... little hands all over Gabriel tonight," he slurred. "It...it looks as if we both wound up in someone else's arms... though you by far seemed to be having more fun."

"If you think I'm having fun, Laphaniel, then you really don't know me at all," I replied, irritated, tired and terrified of what lay ahead for us. For a moment I stared at the jewelled wings of the serpents overhead, wishing I could tear them down and use them to fly far away.

"You forced me to bring you here."

"Well, at least we can establish this is all my own fault," I bit back. "Thank you."

"I tried to make you stay away from here," he said, words overlapping each other.

"You tried to force me to stay with you, Laphaniel. Maybe..."

"Maybe what?" he said, eyes flashing. "Are you blaming me now?"

I growled, the noise scratching against my throat. "I think we both did pretty well screwing this up."

I moved towards the door, unable to stay in the same room as him without falling apart. I needed some air, space away from the frantic tempers and the sheer hopelessness of everything.

Quicker than I would have thought was possible in his state, he grabbed at my arm and pulled me back, his hand tight against me.

"You are not leaving this room without me," Laphaniel said softly, a warning giving his words an edge. "Do you understand?"

"Why, are you going to hit me again if I disobey you?" I hissed.

He dropped his hand instantly, and I regretted the words the moment they fell from my mouth. Laphaniel backed away, his face anguished.

"I didn't mean..."

"Why don't you just go? Gabriel seems keen on your company."

I swallowed, but as much as I wanted to, I couldn't take back the words I had spat at him.

"I'm just going to get some air. I won't go far," I said softly, pushing down the bitterness I felt. "Why don't you try and get some sleep, and maybe we could talk some more later?"

"I tried so hard to fix this," Laphaniel said.

"I know." I gave a small smile before I turned away, reaching for the door. I hesitated, torn between needing space from him and needing to be with him. "This isn't your fault."

"Yes, it is."

I barely heard the words as I closed the door behind me, and I wondered how long we could carry on with so much blame and guilt between us. I feared that it would push everything else out, everything that really mattered. Our love was new, a fledgling beating against so much darkness and hopelessness. I didn't know if it was strong enough to endure what lay ahead. I only had a fool's hope that it would.

CHAPTER TWENTY-SEVEN

I had only wandered down the hallway a short way when the sound of my name made me pause, the word floating on the tip of music, sung only for me.

"Teya."

My blood froze, fear rising inside me at the poisonous whisper singing my name.

"Teya."

I spun around, but there was nothing there. Not even the candles flickered in their holders.

"Teya, little lost thing." A breath at my ear. I tensed, feeling a hand curl around mine. "May I have a word?"

Luthien stepped out of the shadows, an enchantress in black silk. Her unfathomable eyes met mine, a half smile caressing her lips. My soul cringed before her.

"What is it?" My voice was a quivering mess.

"I do not converse in corridors, Teya," Luthien sighed, her hand still on mine. "Find me within the hour, and then we can talk. We have much to discuss, you and I."

The chilling touch of her fingers melted away and she disappeared as quickly as she had come, leaving behind fear and a strange longing I couldn't place. I could not fathom what she had to discuss with me and could only guess that she hoped to torment me more. It would have been tempting to crawl back into Laphaniel's arms, but although Luthien had sounded courteous, I was certain her request was a thinly veiled demand. What happened to those who disobeyed the Almost-Queen of Seelie?

With heavy dread, I realised I didn't know where Luthien's drawing room was, and in a mansion as enormous as hers, it could take days to wander the labyrinth of corridors and stairs, and still never find her. Letting out a growl of frustration, I tore down the hall with my skirts in my hands, seeking out someone...anyone who would show me the way. I was hoping to find Oonagh, or even Gabriel, but as I found my way back to the great hall with its frantic pulse of music and dancers, I found neither.

I did find Nefina.

"It is not safe to run around this house, little thing. You may get eaten."

"And wouldn't you just love to see that," I snapped, and clutched at my side where a stitch was forming. Nefina curled her lip, her blue eyes darkening as she stepped closer to me.

"Oh, I would," she purred. "More than you know."

"I've done nothing to you."

"You bring happiness to my brother, little thing, when he deserves none."

Around us the dance had fallen into complete disorder; any illusion of civility had broken down as the drums thumped out their primal beat. Bodies sprawled on the floor, a tangle of torn silk, naked limbs and gasping mouths. Laughter filled the room, heavy and drunk and fearless. Mouths devoured, and hands caressed, the table of Goodnight Kisses standing empty. I shuddered.

"Don't drink anything," Nefina said, leaning back against the wall, her silvery gown flowing down past her feet as she turned to watch the madness.

"Careful," I muttered, "I may start to think you care."

She smiled, a quirk of her full lips and nothing more. "I would love to see you suffer, Teya, but not like that. Never like that."

A fey with a fox-like face swooped by and took up Nefina's hands, his mouth open in a strange grin, showing two rows of finely pointed teeth. He made to pull her back into the fray, and I saw that the front of her gown was torn, red marks marring down between her breasts.

"Wait, please..."

"For what, little thing?"

"Tell me where I can find Luthien."

Nefina stopped, her hands still in the claws of the fox-fey, her pale skin beginning to flush as he tried to drag her away.

"Luthien will destroy you, do you know that?"

"Yes."

"She'll be on her balcony. Follow the hallway with the fireflies in the stained glass."

She turned to me just as she was disappearing into the chaos, her eyes bright with mischief. "Take your time with her, little thing; allow me to have this night without her taunts and games. Let her punish you for Laphaniel's shortcomings and not me."

I wanted to ask her what she meant, but she vanished amongst the writhing bodies, and I was left on my own.

I turned away from the ball and towards a twisting staircase, its golden handrails embedded with rubies. I cried out as my hand touched one, the jagged points slicing at my palm. Blood swelled against my skin and dropped onto the jewels. I watched as it dribbled down the gold, snaking over the rubies to pool over colourless gems. They absorbed the blood the moment it touched them, standing out like cut glass until, like the others, they glimmered scarlet. Shaking my head, I realised they were not rubies at all, but pieces of broken mirror. It was unfathomable how much blood had spilled in Luthien's home so that it seeped from the very fixings of her mansion.

I found my way up to the balcony with little difficulty, making sure I kept my hands to myself. I walked past the windows with the fireflies, hardly surprised when I discovered that they were real insects trapped within the glass, their flickering lights casting desperate shadows over the otherwise dark hallway. I paused at the doorway and reached out to touch the door that held not fireflies, but roses in full bloom within the pristine glass. I was careful where I placed my hand, not wanting to impale myself on the sharp thorns that pierced through the doors.

The scent of wisteria hit me as I stepped out onto the stone balcony, its mauve flowers trailing up over the surrounding columns. In the distance, I could hear music from the Ball: a hypnotic melody mingling seamlessly with the faint sounds of screaming, all blending together to create an orchestra of pain and abandonment.

"Do you know why I called you here tonight, Teya?" Luthien asked, reclining against a pile of plump cushions. Her black gown pooled around her feet like spilled ink, the neckline slashed down to her navel. I cringed at the thought of her being so close to Laphaniel.

Her dark eyes met mine, cold and cunning. Her lips turned up into a cruel smile as she reached for the wine glass beside her and drained its contents without turning away from me. I noticed the empty bottles around her, another glass upturned on the little jewelled table, empty.

"You want to bargain with me," I said, breathless, as her smile bloomed, and it was as dreadful as it was lovely. I tore my eyes away from her and settled on the daybed set in the centre of the balcony, its sheer white drapes floating in the wind like ghosts. The sheets were dishevelled, spots of blood soaking into the silk.

"How do you know I do not wish to kill you?"

"Because you would want an audience for that. You would make Laphaniel watch."

"Clever girl," Luthien said, beckoning me closer. "I will give you what you came for."

She watched me carefully, noting how I cringed at her words. She knew...as much as I had known all along, that it was something I no longer wanted.

"You'll let me leave?" I said, relief sighing from my body.

"Yes."

Luthien waited patiently for my next words, anticipation lighting up her elfin features, almost softening them.

"But you won't let Laphaniel leave with me, will you?"

Luthien shook her head, spilling the soft waves of her hair over her shoulders. "I offer you Niven's freedom and the chance to take her place."

I swallowed, a coldness taking over my body as I sunk to my knees at the thought of exchanging one prison for another. Luthien sat, triumph erasing any softness from her face and revealing the monster that dwelled beneath.

"What about Laphaniel?" I asked, desperate.

"I offer you solitude and your life, nothing more."

My chest tightened, splinters threatening to pierce my soul. "And if I refuse?"

Luthien rose to her feet in a swirl of midnight and sank beside me to take my face in her hands, forcing me to look at her. She caressed my cheek, her fingers chilling against my skin, her words a deathly whisper against my ear.

"I will kill him, and you, my little lost thing, will mourn beside me for all eternity."

"You wouldn't..." I gasped.

"Oh, but I would," she said gently, her head touching mine. "In a heartbeat."

"If you force me into this decision…"

"I'm not forcing you to do anything, child. I am giving you exactly what you set out for. I'm simply not accepting your paltry offer of a few years. What use have I for them?"

"He will hate you," I said, a sob forcing its way out of my body.

"I would rather own his hate, bear his sorrow and his wrath, than allow you to have his love."

Luthien snatched her hand away as if she couldn't stand to touch me a moment longer, and it left me to wonder if all love ended in madness.

"What did he offer you?" I asked, tears running down my face. "What did you refuse him as he bartered for my freedom?"

Luthien tilted her head, her own eyes shining as she reached to pluck a teardrop from my cheek. "He offered up his soul for you." She placed her finger to her lips, closing her eyes, tasting my grief and despair. "I nearly took it just to spite you."

I felt the longing deep inside my chest become an ache. "I will give you anything," I begged, "if you allow us to leave."

"Anything?" Luthien smiled and hope bloomed within me. "Would you give your sister's life for your freedom, for his?"

"Yes," I said it without hesitation. I realised in that

moment that I would leave Niven with Luthien again if it meant I could have Laphaniel.

"I don't want anything from you, Teya." Luthien said, turning her back to me. "You will leave at midnight, alone. Say your goodbyes to him, then go to that accursed castle and rot. Niven is waiting."

"No...please..."

With a swirl of black, she spun and clutched at my temples. I screamed as darkness pressed against me, the feel of cobwebs swept across my skin, and the damp of mould glistened against my clothes. I choked on stifled air, feeling the ghostly weight of a crown settle against my brow.

"I have chosen you as the next Queen of Seelie, Teya Jenkins," Luthien snarled, her eyes an abyss. "May your reign be long and lonely."

I stumbled forwards as she released me, clasping my hands to my mouth to stop the scream that clawed at my throat. Luthien hovered beside me, the black silks rippling like shadows.

"You have got what you came for, lost thing," she stated, already melting into the darkness. "Love is never forever, remember that. Not for mortals and not for fey— it is fleeting and swift and merciless."

She left as the weight of my new destiny settled like irons around me, and it took everything I had to get to my feet and stumble back out into the hallway. The fireflies trapped within the glass buzzed incessantly, their lights a frantic flash in the darkness as I fell against the wall, a sob breaking from my lips.

Knowing my choices had just ripped us apart, I made my way back to Laphaniel, wondering what I was going to say to him. How could I put into words that I had destroyed everything because I simply refused to listen to him?

I didn't know how to say goodbye to him.

He was sitting on the bed when I pushed open the door, glancing up at me with relief on his face. I tried to smile, but it died on my lips.

"Please don't cry." Laphaniel moved to my side in an instant and folded me in his arms. I was thankful to find he wasn't swaying any more. "I'll find a way to fix this."

I took his hand, squeezing his fingers, allowing the little lie to slip past my lips. "I know."

"I won't let her hurt you, Teya," he said, his hand coming up to wipe the tears trailing over my cheeks. With a soft sigh, he curled his hand around mine, lifting my arm to gently spin me away before pulling me back again. My feet moved obediently, dancing the steps they knew by heart. "I didn't get to dance with you tonight."

"I know, I missed you." I leaned against his shoulder as he led me in a dance with no music.

"You look really beautiful," he murmured, fingers trailing over the ripped and stained silk.

I touched my head to his, breathing him in. "I really could do with a drink."

"Shall I open a bottle?"

A laugh bubbled up past the despair. "I think you've had enough."

"I can't do anything tonight, Teya. I don't know how to make this right, but depleting some of Luthien's vintage liquor seems a fairly good start."

I smiled, hiding the pain beneath. "I'm not arguing."

Laphaniel grabbed a bottle of wine from a selection in a carved, elaborate cabinet and snatched up two glasses before moving back to the bed. I took the bottle from him, noting the chill of the glass against my skin, feeling it settle in my veins.

The wine was thick and blood red, filling the air between us with overripe fruit.

"You were going to give up your soul for me," I said, draining my first glass, feeling it coat my tongue and burn my throat. I poured myself another and topped up Laphaniel's glass when he wasn't looking.

"It still wasn't enough."

I reached for him. "What would she have done with it?"

"Take it to pieces and make it worthless."

"Oh, Laphaniel." I couldn't bear the thought of Luthien's hateful hands on Laphaniel's soul...on his body...breaking something that no longer belonged to her.

"It's yours." He watched with a wry smile as I refilled my glass again. "My soul and my heart are yours now, Teya. Always."

"Always," I murmured, taking a large sip of the cloying wine.

"Are you trying to catch me up?" he said, leaning close to kiss me. His lips were stained red. He tasted of wine and misery, and I wondered if I tasted any different.

"Oh, I think we would need a lot more alcohol." I took another sip wishing I could drown my sorrows as he had done. "You've had a pretty big head start."

"I don't know how to make this right," Laphaniel admitted, long fingers running down the edge of his glass. "I keep hoping I'll find an answer, but there's nothing."

"It's not your job to keep me safe," I replied, needing to feel him close to me. "This is not your fault."

"I should never have brought you here."

"Don't..."

"I should have made you stay," he murmured, leaning heavily against me. "I should have tried harder."

"I should have let you."

"I would...I would have made you so happy."

I nodded, unable to speak, watching as he emptied his glass. The darkness in his eyes lifted slightly.

"My head's spinning..." he said thickly, trying and failing to lift his head from my shoulder.

"Because you're drunk." Anguish strangled my voice so the words came out raw, and broken.

"No...I..." The glass slipped from his fingers, landing in the space between us. Dribbles of wine stained the bed. "Teya..."

"I love you," I said, as his eyes drifted closed. "More than you know."

"What...have you done?" he said, his words nothing more than a breath as his body went limp against mine.

"Laphaniel?" I shook him gently, but he didn't stir. His head lolled from my shoulder to rest against my chest, lips parted as he breathed deeply. I held him there listening to the softness of his breathing, staring down at the empty vial of Goodnight Kisses on the nightstand. Gabriel had been right after all, it had come in useful.

I lowered Laphaniel onto the pillows and stroked the inky hair away from his face. A part of me wanted him to wake up and stop me from leaving, to scoop me into his arms and flee into the darkness together. But that would mean death, I had no doubts about that, and sleeping would always be better than death.

I whispered my goodbye, my soul crying out for his and walked away. By morning, I would be long gone.

CHAPTER TWENTY-EIGHT

*N*ot a soul stopped me from leaving, and with the chimes of midnight echoing behind me, I fled the mansion, running over frost-tipped grass that soaked through the already ruined silk of my shoes. I ran past entwined bodies sprawled over the cold ground, their gasping breaths misting from parted lips as they paid me no heed. Discarded bottles were strewn around the winding pathways, upturned goblets lying shattered amongst the prone forms of intoxicated fey.

I fled through the gardens, back into the woods, with no idea where I was supposed to go. In a moment of utter madness, I closed my eyes and spun in a circle, choosing my direction purely by chance. It was stupid and thoughtless, but I wasn't thinking, and the emptiness within my chest was making me feel reckless. The forest could swallow me up for all I cared...better that than a lifetime haunting some forgotten castle.

Midnight bloomed dark, despite the moon that hung fat and silver. The eerie light filtered through the treetops, catching the tips of frozen dewdrops so everything around me glittered. My breath fogged in front of me, the late autumn chill biting through the thin layers of silk that made up my gown. Fear settled around me like a physical presence, a familiar weight of despair that fit against me like a cloak. I fought to stay calm, to soothe the panic I could feel heating my blood.

It had been a while since the dark had frightened me as it did then; every threat, every monster I'd faced had brought with it a feeling of terror I hadn't thought possible...but I hadn't faced them alone...I was never alone. With an instinct that nearly broke me, I reached out my hand, but the comfort I sought was no longer there.

A howl tore through the stillness, shattering the quiet with a scream of hunger and fury. Another followed, feral...the sounds of nightmares, of dark shadows lingering within whispered tales, of archaic beasts without thought or mercy.

My breath caught in my throat, my body readying itself as I decided whether to run or stay. I stood frozen, struggling to get a decent breath in around my corset, and I silently cursed Oonagh for strapping me into the damned thing. Howls chorused together in a wild sonnet, their song a promise of blood and teeth and death.

I chose to run.

I bloodied my knees tumbling down slopes and over roots, and clawed my way back up while I fought to keep the bellows of the wolves behind me. My dress caught around my legs, slowing me down, the gauzy fabric snagging on thorns to tug me back. I couldn't catch my breath, the corset was too tight, the boning digging painfully against my ribs. I fought to reach the stays at my back, tearing the silk but not the rigid casing crushing me. Stars burst before my eyes, my breaths an agony as my lungs screamed.

My vision wavered and I closed my eyes, reaching to

steady myself. I took a breath, sucking down a meagre amount of air that refused to clear the blackness settling over me. I slid to my knees, sprawling forwards as I desperately clung to consciousness. My head whacked the trunk of a tree, and I passed out.

Warmth misted over my legs, stirring me. The humid exhalation of breath on my cheek brought me back, as whatever it was sniffed my legs and turned its focus on my face. It snarled, teeth grazing over my skin. I froze. Yellow eyes met mine, black lips drawn back over a muzzle that was longer than my forearm, thick globs of drool oozing over its panting tongue.

I stretched my hand out along the ground, not breaking my gaze away while I fumbled for anything I could use as a weapon. My fingers found a crooked branch, damp with rot and moss...nearly useless. I swung it as hard as I could, but the wolf snapped and broke it easily with its powerful jaw, sending splinters flying. It gave me just enough time to get my legs working. I scrambled up, spinning on my heel to face the creature, and kicked it hard, taking it by surprise. I managed to knock the wind out of it with a well-placed kick to the ribs, but I bought myself only seconds.

Frantic, I dragged up one of the rocks it had fallen on, gasping at the weight before dropping it onto its skull. Blood sprayed over my face as it yelped, but I held the rock up again and brought it quickly down until it stopped thrashing.

I wanted to scream, but I held my bloodied hands over my mouth instead, my trembling fingers muffling the sounds of my panic. The howls rose up again, and with a defeated sob, I took off once more into the darkness.

Clutching my cramping side, I fell to my knees and pressed myself as close to the base of an old tree as I could get, cringing against the cold wood while I fought for breath.

It came out in painful gasps I couldn't quiet, and I couldn't stop the cry that slipped through my lips when I heard snapping branches behind me.

I shrank back against the tree, drawing my knees up to my chest, and tried to disappear. I trembled against the bark, my body aching as I tensed, readying myself for the onslaught of wolves that were going to pull me apart. I couldn't help but wonder if perhaps that had been Luthien's plan all along, to feed me to the dogs, knowing there was no way I could escape them and free Niven.

There was a silence...a nothingness that stilled the trees and filled the darkness, a waiting hush that pulled at every instinct. I crawled forwards, forcing myself to stand as I searched deep down to find the strength to flee again. A tiny cry slipped from my mouth, echoing loudly, as if I had shouted. I froze...waited...one foot in front of the other. It was too dark.

Too quiet.

My breath a cloud of fog in front of me, my heart a drum.

I couldn't hear the wolves...just the sound of my own panic. It was a pounding in my ears, a rush of breath past my lips, a blinding knowledge that I wasn't fast enough.

I would never be fast enough.

Something snapped behind me. Before I could think, before I could move, it had grabbed me, clamping a hand over my mouth to shove the scream straight back down my throat.

"You crazy bitch," a voice hissed in my ear. My knees gave out at the sound, my hands digging against him as his arm came around tight to hold me up. "You drugged me? What the hell do you think you were doing?"

He spun me around to face him, his hand still over my mouth. There was no colour to his eyes, just deep and utter blackness. His hair was a wild mess around his face, his cloak snapping like a furious shadow behind him. He looked as wild and untamed as the wolves. I struggled against his hold, and he dropped his hand.

"How are you awake?" I asked, my voice quiet and lost. His lip curled, and he was literally shaking he was so furious.

"Oonagh found me," he gritted out, as if that was answer enough.

I shook my head, a new panic settling over me. If Luthien found him with me... "You're not supposed to be here."

"Would you rather I was still tucked up in bed sleeping soundly?" he said, his voice low and dangerous. "Would you rather be out here alone?"

"Yes," I breathed, my heart aching at the pain that washed over his face, tingeing the blackness of his irises with a bright purple. "She said she would kill you."

"You did this to keep me safe?" he asked, incredulous, as if the very idea was unthinkable.

"It was the only thing I could do, I can't lose you!"

"So you take off without even a goodbye?" he snapped, clinging to his anger, thinking I couldn't see how much I had hurt him.

"I did say goodbye." I reached for him, but he flinched away. "It was the hardest thing I have ever had to do, but it was what I had to do, Laphaniel."

He narrowed his eyes at me, still not closing the distance between us. "What did she make you bargain?"

"It doesn't matter, it's done now."

"Tell me," he demanded, but I couldn't meet his eyes. "Teya!"

"This is how it was supposed to be all along," I choked. "This is what I came for..."

"You didn't..." he spluttered, and I could see the moment

understanding hit him. He took a step back as if I had physically struck him. "Please tell me you didn't offer to take Niven's place."

"I did." I held my head up with a determination I didn't feel. "And I would do it again if it meant keeping you safe."

"No," he breathed, finally stepping closer so I could fall against him. "I won't let you do that."

"It's already done," I said. "There's no going back now."

He closed his eyes, shuttering the anguish burning within them away. "I'm not worth throwing your life away for, Teya."

I placed a hand on his cheek. "I have made my choice."

"It's a castle of nightmares." He folded his hand over mine. "Its shadows bleed darkness, it is a forsaken place, Teya."

"I wasn't expecting it to be the Bahamas," I replied, and pressed my lips against his in a brief, desperate kiss.

We both tensed as the wolves screamed again, the noise sucking away any shred of hope I was still holding onto.

"We need to run," Laphaniel urged, pushing me forwards. "Now...go!"

"This seems to be a common theme with us, doesn't it?" I said, as my feet slid against the frost-soaked ground.

"And you were worried I'd grow bored of you." He clutched my hand, his eyes focused on the surrounding darkness. "This way!"

I scrambled up with my hand clamped in his, my fear mingling with the sheer relief I felt at having him back at my side. I couldn't dwell on what that could mean for him, what wrath Luthien would bring down upon us when she found out he had helped me.

Laphaniel's legs were much longer than mine were, so it wasn't long before he was practically dragging me behind him, his fingers unrelenting on mine as we tore through the woods. My legs tangled in the silk of my skirt and I stumbled, dragging Laphaniel down with me as we skidded over a rocky slope. We tumbled together, my skull rattling when it hit the ground. I tasted blood on my lips as the back of Laphaniel's head struck mine.

"Are you hurt?" he asked, dragging me back up, a steady dribble of blood trailing down his face.

"I don't think so," I answered, and reached to lift the hair from his face, taking in the gash above his left eyebrow. "Are you okay? That looks pretty nasty."

"I hit my head on the way down, don't worry, I'll live."

I glanced up to where we had just fallen from. The wolves stared back, edging around the rocks to source a safer way down. Smaller rocks skidded down the incline, low snarls rumbling deep within their chests as they began to circle us.

Laphaniel's hand gripped my arm, tugging me away. I stared at the hungry dogs that pawed against the rocks, working as a pack to find a way down to us. From where I stood, I could feel the warmth of their breath, smell the tang of blood on their lips. They were far bigger than normal wolves, a mass of matted fur and slitted eyes, reeking of death and screaming like nightmares. They were everything I had feared was hiding beneath my bed as a child.

"Move slowly," Laphaniel whispered, pulling me back. "Don't look away...just keep walking backwards."

"Laphaniel..."

One of the wolves had found a way down, lips pulled back over a mouthful of teeth as long as my fingers. It inched closer, feet splayed slightly on the uneven ground, hackles raised. The others joined it, slowly…creeping down as if they had all the time in the world. They lifted their noses in the air to scent blood, heads snapping at the air as they watched us, yellow eyes blazing with hunger while thick saliva pooled around their mouths.

Laphaniel raised his hand to his head, his palm coming back red since the wound to his forehead continued to bleed freely. It was driving the pack crazy, stirring up their bloodlust.

"Run!" Laphaniel urged, all but yanking my arm from its socket when he hauled me onwards, and, with the beasts howling at our heels, we fled.

My feet pounded over the ground and my heart hammered in my chest. Everything in my body was shrieking, and I knew it was only blind fear that was stopping it from collapsing. I didn't dare look back. I didn't need to. I could hear the wet snapping jaws as they hunted us.

Laphaniel's hold on my hand was relentless as he wove in and out of the trees, skidding down slopes and through brambles that tangled around us, their thorns tearing at our skin as we fought our way through.

"Jump!" he shouted, barely giving me time to comprehend what he was saying before he shoved me roughly over a gully.

I yelled as I fell, plunging into icy water that stole my breath away. The swirling waters engulfed my gown, the layers of fabric turning to lead to drag me down. My lungs screamed…

I broke the surface with a shattering cry, grasping at Laphaniel while he held me up. I fought the urge to give into panic, and instead focused on kicking my legs to keep my head above water. Laphaniel dragged us to the riverbank, his grip on me relentless.

We clawed our way out, coughing and spluttering, shivering. I whirled on Laphaniel as he tried to catch his breath, smacking him sharply in the shoulder.

"Don't ever launch me over a cliff again!"

"I thought you could swim," he panted, and stepped closer to drag me into his arms in an embrace that was far too brief.

"You try swimming in a corset and a hundred foot of silk," I retorted, turning to eye the swirling waters we had just climbed out of. I couldn't see the wolves.

I could hear them though…

"Keep moving," Laphaniel said. "They won't be far behind."

"Wait." I grabbed a handful of sodden silk and ripped it so it hung in rags just above my ankles. "Can you loosen the stays on my dress? I can barely breathe."

He worked quickly, and I took a huge gulp of unrestricted air before we started running again, the baying of wolves echoing just across the river.

Laphaniel slowed to keep pace with me, dragging me on and on and on until I thought my lungs would give out, my body using the desperate fear flooding it to power me onwards, because I had nothing left.

A dry, broken sob gurgled from my lips when the trees finally thinned out, revealing the faded golden gates of the Seelie castle. Dropping Laphaniel's hand, I slammed into them, my fingers curling around the handle desperately. I pulled and I pushed and I rattled the bars, shouting at them to open. I begged, but they only creaked slightly and refused to give way.

Laphaniel swore beside me, taking the bars in his own hands and forcing them forwards. They gave an inch more for him, a tormenting gap and nothing more.

"Climb up," he said, grabbing me by the waist to push me up against the bars, just as the wolves burst through the clearing. "Quickly!"

I scrambled up and clung to the bars, leaning back to reach for Laphaniel. His fingers barely brushed mine before snapping jaws caught his leg and snatched him away. I felt him slip from me, a gasp of pain rushing from his mouth as he tried to hold on. The monstrous wolf released its hold, only to throw its head back and lunge forwards again, dragging Laphaniel further down the gate.

Without thinking, I slid down and using every bit of my strength, kicked it hard enough to force its mouth open, releasing Laphaniel's leg in a burst of blood and spittle. I grabbed his hand again and forced him upwards.

The bars were so cold, numbing my struggling fingers as I hauled myself up. I clung on tightly, my hands cramping, knowing that if I slipped and the fall didn't kill me, then the wolves would.

I reached the top before Laphaniel and swung my leg over to clamber down the other side, my hands sliding over the frost-soaked bars. I jumped the final couple of feet, rolling onto the unforgiving ground and away from the snapping jaws of the wolf pack outside. Laphaniel followed, hitting the floor beside me with a grunt.

I dragged him away from the gates, where the wolves snapped and flew at the bars in a furious attempt to get to us. The foam at their mouths turned bloody as they ravaged the gates, the metal shrieking against the onslaught, but they couldn't get to us. They knew that.

They stopped, watching us with too much intelligence behind their feral eyes, then they backed away, hackles still up, black lips still curled to show off their teeth. As one they lifted their heads and howled up at the sky, their echoes ringing through the trees as they vanished back into the shadows.

Turning my attention to Laphaniel, I pulled up the soaked

remains of his trouser leg, wincing at the torn flesh just below his knee. "Can you walk?"

"I think so." He grimaced as I pulled the fabric away, ripping strips off my dress to form makeshift bandages. "It will heal in a few days."

"Will it scar?" I asked, tying off the scraps of silk, relieved the blood didn't seep through much.

"Would you be willing to stitch it up?" He gave a small smile as I felt the blood drain from my face. "No? Then it'll probably leave a mark."

I helped him up, taking some of his weight as he tested his leg. He winced but was able to walk with only a slight limp.

"Why did you choose this?" Laphaniel looked up at the twisting towers of the castle.

I followed his gaze, taking in the ruined splendour of the former Court of Seelie, the court of Light.

"Because it was too late to choose you."

Laphaniel closed his eyes, his hand coming up to shove the wild hair away from his face. "You have finally reached the castle," he said sadly.

The castle loomed over us like Disney on meth, and it was exactly like something out of my nightmares. I counted six towers that rose high above us, their peaks disappearing into the cloud overhead. Tattered flags snapped against the breeze, ruined by age so I couldn't tell what colour they had once been. Huge windows stretched over the stone, all black...all void of any light. The drawbridge was down, the chains that once held it up, shattered. Nothing swam within the moat, nothing lived. The earth below was dry and cracked, even the weeds creeping over the edge had withered and died.

Laphaniel was right, it was a forsaken place.

"Thank you," I said, turning away from the sprawling nightmare, "for everything. I wouldn't have made it without you."

Laphaniel continued to gaze up at the castle, his expression unreadable, "Perhaps not."

"Where will you go now?" I asked, not knowing if I could say goodbye to him again. "Please don't go back to Luthien…if she finds out you helped me…promise me you won't go back to her."

He looked at me strangely before drawing me close, his lips brushing the top of my head. "I promise."

"I didn't mean for it to end like this," I whispered against him, listening as his breath caught.

"I'm coming with you Teya."

I pulled away at his words, hardly believing the ones that tumbled from my own lips. "You can't, I made a bargain with Luthien. You have to go, she'll kill you."

Laphaniel took my hand, closing his fingers around mine. "Luthien won't look for me here, it would be incomprehensible to her that someone would return to this place. It's cursed, Teya, remember? Can't you feel it? No one comes here except to lock away the new human Queen, in compliance to Sorcha's curse."

"Luthien will know…"

He shook his head. "No, she won't, because she has never sacrificed anything for someone she loves."

So very gently, he brought his hands up so they cradled my face, his fingers lightly brushing against my skin. I squeezed my eyes closed, not daring to hope for anything more than a few more moments in his arms.

"You'll have to search for my replacement when the time comes."

"Don't," he said, touching his head to mine. "Don't find

reasons why I can't come with you. If we can't have forever, Teya, I'll take whatever I can get to be beside you."

"I love you," I breathed, as quiet tears trailed over my cheeks. "More than I can bear."

He nodded, though there was something that looked like regret behind his eyes, as if he were giving up what happy ending he had once wished for us. But if it were to be my ending, I would take it with grateful arms and be content with the few years fate had granted us.

CHAPTER TWENTY-NINE

*T*he great doors of the castle screeched open, protesting after so many years of disuse. Cobwebs broke over us as we entered, our feet making trails in the dust on the floor, revealing the swirl of colours hidden beneath. Blues, greens and violets all trailed together in the marble, flecked with hints of gold that would have once shone beautifully. Age and neglect had darkened it, coating it all in a film of misery and despair.

Candle stubs flickered in dusty alcoves, ancient webs hanging from the wicks so I had to wonder how they burned at all. Tattered scraps of cloth hung from the windows, swaying along the floor like ghosts. It smelled of damp, of lost things. It was little more than a bitter memory, and it was suffocating.

"Did you ever live here?" I asked, my echo stealing away my voice and rebounding it off the walls.

"No." Laphaniel turned around slowly as he took in the decay around us. "Luthien's sister ruled here, and as we never won the war against Sorcha, I never got to see anything but the tower where she placed the curse on the Seelie."

"It must have been breathtaking once." I craned my neck to take in the two spiralling staircases that wound around each other, leading up into darkness. "Wait, I thought you were one of Luthien's knights? Didn't you stay at the castle before the war broke out?"

"I never said I was a knight," he said, taking a step onto the staircase and looked up. His fingers swept over cobwebs clinging to the faded gold, sending spiders scurrying down the steps. "I was born a long way from this place."

"With Nefina?" I pressed, skipping aside as the spiders fled by my feet. I realised then how little I knew of his past. "You grew up with your sister? Where is the rest of your family now? Your mother and father?"

"My past is something that I do not wish to dwell on, Teya," he answered. "Leave it be."

"Why does Nefina hate you?"

He turned, stepping down so that he was level to me. "Because I abandoned her."

"Laphaniel..." I began, as he sighed, brushing off the look of regret with a quick shrug.

"She was with Oonagh tonight. She was always gifted at potion making, so much so that Luthien accepted her as an apprentice. She made the antidote to the Goodnight Kisses, and they covered my escape."

"What will happen if Oonagh and Nefina are caught?" I asked, and Laphaniel shook his head.

"I don't know."

I reached for his hand, entwining my fingers with his, relieved when he squeezed back. "I never meant for this to happen. I don't want anyone to get hurt because of my mistakes...my choices."

"There's unrest amongst Luthien's fey," he said. "They're

bored. You just made their lives more exciting for an evening. You made a few of them rather reckless."

I felt a small smile tug at my lips. "I hope they're safe."

"I do too," he said, turning back to look up the stairs. "You are stalling."

"What would happen if I walked out now?" I asked, feeling the subtle tug on my hand as he inched me closer to the stairs. "If I ran away..."

"The curse is holding you to the castle, Teya. You can't walk out of those doors. Try if you want, but it's done now. All that's left to do is free Niven from it." Laphaniel took a breath, and I glanced at the great doors before turning back to him. "Without our Queen, the Unseelie would sniff us out and slaughter us all."

"Are they a stronger court?"

"At the moment we are at a stalemate. Their barren queen is dying and she leaves behind no heir."

"I thought faeries were immortal," I said, moving away from the staircase to walk around the gloomy hall.

Laphaniel followed me, as curious as I was. "No one lives forever, Teya."

His words reminded me of what Luthien had told me, how love was fleeting, that it had an ending like all things. I couldn't help but wonder what would happen if that were true, if Laphaniel would one day wake up and decide he no longer wanted to be locked away within a nightmare for me. Would he just leave? Would I awaken one day to find no trace of him, or would he stay as he promised, until resentment set in? Perhaps he would stay until there was nothing left between us but a memory of a love that had never stood a chance.

"Stop that." He startled me out of my dark thoughts. "I know what you are thinking, Teya."

I gestured around the gloom, at the frost sprawling over the far side, inching in from a shattered window. "You didn't choose this, Laphaniel. You wanted endless dancing and drinking and laughter…a relationship, not a prison."

"I chose you," he said softly. "I'm not going anywhere."

"You have no idea what it means knowing I don't have to do this alone," I said, and he gave me a small smile.

"I have a faint idea," he answered. "I've witnessed your nightmares, Teya. I couldn't bear to leave you alone in the dark."

I echoed his smile. "You say that now, but just you wait until I need the bathroom at three in the morning and drag you down endless corridors, because there is no way in hell I'm walking around this castle without you."

He laughed, the echo filling the hallway with a displaced note of happiness. "The bathrooms will be joined to the bedrooms, Teya."

"Even so, I'll need you to light every single candle."

He kissed me, soft and gentle. "I won't ever let them go out."

I leant against him. "I don't want to go upstairs, Laphaniel."

"I know," he whispered back. "But you may as well get this over with, you cannot sit out the curse in the hallway. Send Niven home, and let her go."

I took a breath, allowing it to blow through my teeth before I broke away from Laphaniel. I picked up the tattered silks of my skirt and forced myself up one of the staircases, making no sound at all upon the polished stone. I clung to Laphaniel's hand, watching him limp each time he put weight on his injured leg. He gave me strength when he had little left to give, coaxing me through the darkness as he gave up the light, and I had nothing to offer him but myself.

The stairs opened up to a wide corridor, the dusty floor twisting and splitting off into three different directions, each one dark and gloomy. We chose left, and I followed Laphaniel as he guessed it led to the highest tower.

Delicate tables lined the walls beneath windows that were thick with grime, and vases were cobwebbed to the surfaces, holding the long dead skeletons of flowers. Black, foul water pooled from cracks in the china, spilling thickly onto the already ruined carpets.

The scraps of fabric billowing at the windows trailed along the filth, spewing up the mildew and dust that heaped along the floor. It was hard to imagine the castle being anything but dank and forgotten. I couldn't picture anyone ever being happy within its walls.

I paused when we reached a winding landing, stone steps circling up and up and up, shining smooth with age. I shivered, a sense of dread seeping into my very bones.

"She's up there," I breathed. "I can feel it."

"Teya..."

Laphaniel reached for me as I pushed past, my heart a hammer at my chest. I took the steps two at a time, my hand scraping over crude stone. Echoes spiraled back down the twisting stairs.

"She's in there," I said when Laphaniel caught up with me, his hands coming tightly, almost possessively around me. "Niven is in there, Laphaniel."

My voice was a breath, small and frightened, yet oh so determined. There was no doubt though, that I would ever have summoned the courage to go any further if he hadn't been holding onto me.

"This is what you wanted," Laphaniel said softly. "You've waited ten years for this; let it stop defining who you think you are."

I took a breath and it trembled past my lips. "You put her in there; maybe you should tell her she can leave."

I felt his laugh rather than heard it, a warmth against my neck. "If I could, Teya, I would."

Strengthened by his simple words, I moved forwards, and with shaking fingers, I reached for the door, which swung open as if it were waiting for us.

"Niven," I choked out, stepping through the thin veil of cobwebs and into the lonely room, my eyes darting to the hundreds of candle stubs flickering over the floor. "Niven...it's me..."

She sat upon a filthy chair in the middle of the room, her head bowed so the black of her hair fell over her face. If it were not for the slow rise and fall of her shoulders, I would have believed she was dead.

I didn't dare touch her. There wasn't a nerve in my body that wasn't screaming at me to run.

In a flurry of broken spider silk, she was standing in front of me, her gloved hands rising up as if to touch my face. She hesitated, fingers curling, head tilting, before allowing her hand to drop to her side.

"I know you," she began, her voice a nightmare splitting past her pale lips. "I know you."

"Yes," I breathed. "It's me, Teya...your sister."

Her eyes flickered up to meet mine, the blue dulled by darkness. Any innocence they had once possessed wiped clean by so many years alone. She fumbled with the holes in her gloves and stared at me, a droplet of blood gathering at the cracks in her lips as she tried to smile.

"I've come to rescue you, Niven."

"I... waited for... you," she said, her words jarring as if she had forgotten how to speak them. "You didn't come."

"I was so frightened, Niven," I began, knowing my fear

was nothing compared to what she had endured. "I'm here now...I'm here."

"Yes, you are."

She stopped looking at me, cocking her head with a terrifying malice to stare at Laphaniel. "I know you..."

I stepped forwards, holding my hands out, moving slowly as if she were a rabid animal and not my sister. "I'm here to take your place, Niven. You can go home."

"Home?" she echoed, her lips curling slightly in a chilling parody of a smile. "Tell me of home, little sister."

I swallowed. Niven ran her hands over her dress, disturbing the creatures that lived within the torn fabric. "Mum hasn't been coping well."

Her smile widened, a spark igniting the blue in her eyes.

"Dad passed away, Niven. I'm sorry."

"And you?"

I flinched when she touched my cheek, her fingers cold beneath the ruined silk of her gloves. "I've had my share of nightmares."

"Good," she breathed. "I can smell him on you, little sister."

"What?"

"I waited years," She reached for the hairpin that secured some of her tangles, causing it to fall in knotted clumps around her shoulders and release spiders that had taken refuge within the black curls. "You made me wait for years, and you come to me reeking of him."

"It wasn't like that..."

"You forgot me."

"No..."

"Liar!" she spat, twirling the pin in her hands, and I saw it wasn't a hairpin at all, but a knife. "I can see the regret on your face. You would leave me here to rot."

"Does it matter now?" I asked, eyeing the blade and feeling Laphaniel come closer behind us. "You have your freedom; surely it makes you happy that I have to suffer for it?"

"It does, Teya." She smiled and lunged towards me with madness in her eyes. The fabric of her gown rippled around her feet, sending a mixture of scents into the stale air. The smell of nutmeg and mould hit my face as she moved, striking out with a grace I had only seen before in faeries.

Pain exploded through my shoulder as I fell to my knees, dragging from my throat a cry that reverberated around the room like a personal eulogy.

"You do not get to be happy here," Niven whispered, kneeling beside me. I could still smell the odd mix of spice and age on her; it was bitter in my mouth, warm against my skin. I closed my eyes at her words, the ache in my shoulder stretching down to my chest, everything I had once been, ebbing away and dying.

I felt the curse holding Niven dissolve, and watched as her face blurred in front of me, her fingers ghosting to little more than mist as she was pulled away from her nightmare. I knew then that I was plunged into mine.

Without a whisper, she was gone.

"No!" The single word fell from my lips, both meaning-less and pointless. I crawled to where Laphaniel had fallen, my shoulder throbbing where he had shoved me so hard it had bruised instantly. Niven had found a target; but it hadn't been me.

Laphaniel fought to sit up, arching his back while his feet scrabbled against the marble. Blood trickled from him in a steady flow, cutting through the dust on the floor as easily as water.

"Out..." he gasped. "Pull...it...out..."

He fumbled for the knife, the flesh on his hands scorching when he touched the metal, and I realised with a cold dread what it was made of. He dropped his hands with a cry, his body twisting around as the iron poisoned him.

"Out..."

With a sickening twist I pulled it free. Red bloomed against his chest. He fell back against the floor with a sigh, his eyes fluttering closed.

"Laphaniel!" I grabbed his hand, squeezing his fingers, bringing them to my lips. My other hand pressed against his chest, feeling the almost gentle pump of warmth spread over my skin. "Open your eyes. Look at me."

"Teya..." The word bubbled in his mouth, but his eyes found mine, his beautiful, lovely eyes, shining a shade of pale lilac I had never seen before, and I knew he was fighting to keep them from closing again.

"You should have stayed behind," I cried, and brushed the hair away from his face, leaving a trail of red. "This isn't what was supposed to happen. Why didn't you stay behind?"

"I would have followed you to the ends of the earth," he said softly, blood on his lips. "And back again."

"Stay with me," I pleaded, a desperate echo. "Please."

He blinked, his eyes closing for too long before he opened them again, they fell into a pattern, staying closed a little longer each time.

"Stay with me," I pleaded again, my hand slick against his chest. "Please don't leave me here on my own."

"There was a moment when I nearly turned away from you," he said, his voice lost and far away. "At the marketplace, you were tied to the table leg, and I thought you were already gone. If it were not for Lily calling me back, I would have left you there." He squeezed my hand. "You have no idea how much that thought terrifies me...how close I came to losing you."

"Laphaniel." My voice broke as he fell quiet. "Laphaniel?"

I kept hold of his hand as his eyes closed and didn't open again. I pressed my head against his chest to hear the song of his heartbeat, my own screaming out for it.

It sang twice for me, and then there was nothing, nothing at all.

CHAPTER THIRTY

I lay beside him, my hand still clinging to his, and waited for tears. They wouldn't come, though grief ached through me like a physical force. My body wouldn't let me weep. I felt something deep within me break completely, the pain something I had no way of dealing with...a feeling that was beyond reason and beyond tears.

I let go of his hand so gently, biting my lip as I uncurled his fingers from mine. I brushed the hair from his face and then placed my lips to his, silently wishing a kiss would wake him and that he was only sleeping. Just like a fairy tale.

The candles flickering on the floor mocked me with their light, joyfully sending shadows dancing over the walls, coaxing out the spiders that nestled within the cracks. Cobwebs hung over every surface, thick and fragile with age. They clung to the curled black bodies of those that had withered with the castle as I had clung to Laphaniel.

I pressed my hands hard against my eyes, an image of Laphaniel covered in spider silk forcing its way uninvited into my mind. I moved my hand to my mouth, screaming around my fingers, startled by the inhuman misery that echoed back. I had wondered if I should move him to the bed, subconsciously trying to take control of something I couldn't change...couldn't fix.

I wondered if I should bury him...cremate him...set fire to the entire damned castle—myself included—and be done with it? I didn't know the burial rights of faeries; it had never crossed my mind to ask. Why would it? I had no idea what Laphaniel believed could be waiting for him after death, if there was anything at all. I didn't know what I believed...I had listened to the words spoken when we buried my father, but they hadn't really meant anything. I could only grasp onto a distant hope that one day our souls would find each other again...I would cling to that until the end.

The desiccated spiders in the corners seemed to twitch, forcing me to look up. My breath ghosted in front of me, the room suddenly chilling as the temperature dropped. I shivered and watched the frost prickling at the windowsills, crackling across the glass. One by one, the candles sputtered and died out, casting the room in eerie moonlight. It shone through the clouds and the rain and the bleak autumn night to my lonely little room, like a beacon.

Within broken vases, beneath the moonlight, the flowers began to stretch and bloom, yawning to life as if woken from sleep. Frost clung to their leaves, glistening on their petals, but they stood strong against the chill and awakened at the cold as if it held the promise of spring. They were the brightest blooms I had ever seen, standing tall and proud in the chaos and ruin of the castle.

I turned from the flowers when a shadow spread over the far wall, abandoning my grief as fear crept over me. It was blacker than pitch, bringing with it a coldness and dread I had never felt before. It exuded anger and swept up over the walls and ceiling until it had enveloped the room with its wrath.

Shadowed fingers coiled outwards, reaching to the far corners of the room to settle against the dead cobwebs. They lingered for a moment, duskiness wavering over the mass of webs, stirring the silks until they moved on their own. A soundless shriek broke past my lips as the bloated bodies twitched and jerked, legs uncurling until they scuttled back into the beams far above me.

Murky tendrils moved down the wall, creeping over the floor and back again. Hesitant. It settled over my leg, cold and angry...and so, so old. I felt its ancient mind, its unavoidable presence...and I felt it see me... Curiosity clouded its wrath, piquing its interest, stilling its fingers. Fingers which lingered on me, a caress with a whisper.

Not yet.

Shadows splaying, it withdrew its hand and lunged forwards, through me, plunging instead straight into Laphaniel with a scream of rage. I screamed with it, my echo resounding around the room long after it had gone.

Laphaniel's body started to buck beside me, rigid and convulsing. His head thumped against the marble, his limbs twisting and tensing, his fingernails dragging along the ground until they snapped back.

"Laphaniel!" I grabbed at him and cradled his head in my lap as he writhed against me. "Laphaniel? Can you hear me?"

Bloody foam dribbled over his lips, his mouth open in a strangled howl that froze my blood. It was otherworldly, filled with only pain and nightmares, and he wouldn't stop.

His eyes rolled back to the whites, his hands clenched so tightly on my arms that his broken nails raked at my skin. I called his name, not knowing if he could see me or something else entirely.

I moved my shaking hands to his face when he finally stilled, his chest heaving, his skin ashen. "Open your eyes."

He blinked, panting and terrified and pushed away from me. Tears streamed down his face.

"It's okay," I said, reaching for him. "I'm right here."

He raised himself up on one elbow, then fell against me with a sob. His body shuddered and he completely fell apart in my arms. We clung to each other as if we were drowning.

I wanted to see his face, make sure he was real and alive and breathing, hoping to hear the sound of his heart beating. But I didn't let him go, couldn't be the one to break away first, not when I could still feel his tears seep into the fabric of my gown.

Even when he had calmed his breathing, he didn't stop shaking.

"Say something," I pleaded, pulling back only slightly so I could look at him. He looked awful, ghostly white and frightened, as if he had seen hell itself. He ran a hand over his face, streaking it with blood and dirt. He took a breath and it caught, then he swallowed and shook his head.

"I think I'm going to be sick."

I pushed his head gently between his knees and rubbed his back while he sucked in a few gasping breaths, his body sagging against mine.

"Don't you faint on me." I propped him up as his head lolled against my shoulder. I was deeply concerned about the amount of blood he had lost, terrified he would pass out and not wake up again. "I won't let you forget it if you do."

A smile...a small one, ghosted over his too pale face as he took a steadier breath and held it, before allowing it to shudder past his lips. He looked around the room, eyes narrowing at the flowers standing proudly in their cracked vases, shining with a life that had no place within the castle walls.

"What...what did you do?" Laphaniel asked, his words

quiet and shaky. His hand moved to his chest, touching the wound that only moments before had left him dead.

I blinked. "I didn't do anything."

"Something isn't right here..." He pushed himself up so he stood over me. I rose, watching him warily. "You must have done something..."

"I watched you die, Laphaniel... Hey...whoa! Sit back down please." I caught his arm as he swayed, forcing him to stay down when he tried to stand back up again. "Lie down, you've lost too much blood to go waltzing around the room, wait a minute."

"What happened?"

I closed my eyes at the thought of him lying dead in my arms. "You don't remember?"

"Has Niven gone?"

"Yes," I replied, reaching for his hand again, but he shook me off. "Not before she stabbed you in the chest."

"I died."

I nodded.

"Are you sure?"

I stared at him, words failing me, and I wondered if he was going into shock. "Yes, I am sure," I bit out. "Your heart stopped, I heard your last breath. I felt your hand go cold in mine Laphaniel."

"The flowers and spiders were dead too," he said, almost to himself, his words distant. "I think the castle is coming back to life, bringing everything else with it."

"Why?" I grabbed at him, forcing him to look at me. He blinked, as if only just remembering I was there. He narrowed his eyes at me and leaned closer to run his fingers through my hair.

"I love you," he stated, turning away and looking at the roses blooming in the windows.

"You're frightening me."

"No, don't you see what's happening here?" he asked, his gaze darting around the room, sensing something in the darkness that I could not.

"What's going on?"

"We need to leave," he said, his voice urgent. "Now."

"I can't leave, Laphaniel. You know that."

"You have to help me up," he said, ignoring me. "We have to get away from here."

"What about the curse holding me here, or have you forgotten about that?"

"It's broken."

"How?" I mouthed the word, my hands tight on his.

"Because I love you."

Images of sleeping princesses, poisoned apples and stolen maidens swam through my mind, each one ending with a happily ever after. Stories where the wicked queens were vanquished, evil banished, curses broken, and true love endured against impossible odds.

I looked at the velvet soft petals of the flowers, thriving after death, and watched the scuttling of the spiders overhead, no longer broken husks. I looked at Laphaniel, alive and breathing and mine again, hardly daring to believe that after everything, amongst all the darkness and fear, after so much pain, that love could simply conquer all.

"You gave your life for me," I said, not daring to believe he was right and that I wasn't bound to the damned castle. "Can love really break a curse? Doesn't that sound just a bit too Disney to you?"

Laphaniel pushed himself to his knees, ignoring my request for him to stay still. "All curses can be broken, Teya, every single one of them. For years, we have left young girls up here to suffer alone, no one spoke to them, no one befriended them..."

"No one loved them," I finished, my heart breaking at the thought of all those forgotten girls.

"Sorcha knew the coldness of her fey when she made her curse. She knew we would abandon the castle and not look back. It would have been never-ending."

"But then I came along."

"And then you came along." He smiled faintly, his hand coming up to cradle my face. I leaned into him, his touch warm against my skin. "Luthien will know the curse has been broken. It's not safe to linger here, Teya."

He rose to his feet, his eyes darting to the pool of blood on the floor. I stood up beside him, forcing him to look away and at me instead.

"But she can be queen again," I said, hope a beacon in my chest as I dreamed of life with Laphaniel outside of the castle walls, away from darkness and death.

"You are still the Seelie Queen, Teya. You took it from Niven: the mortal bloodline ends with you."

"Then I'll give it to her..."

"It ends with your life!" he snapped, his voice terrifying in the darkness. "Luthien will take the throne the moment she takes your life."

"She will never stop chasing me, chasing us," I said, exhausted. I glanced around at the room that should have been my prison, not feeling the relief I should have, knowing I was free to leave. I was free to go...but not free to live. "What do we do now?"

"Get away from the castle," Laphaniel said, searching the dusty cupboards for anything useful. He pulled a moth-eaten cloak from a rotten drawer and shook it off in a cloud of dust. "Get as far away from here as we can."

"And then?" I asked, taking the lump of fabric from him and shrugging it on, thankful for the warmth.

"I don't know."

I took a breath and searched the room with him, busying my hands so my mind didn't focus too much on the future. There was nothing else to take, nothing that would aid us as we ran for our lives, again. Nothing, nothing, nothing. I really didn't know what I was expecting. Warm clothes beside the mangy fur cloak? Hiking boots? A canteen of food and water? A weapon?

"Come on." Laphaniel outstretched his hand to me and led me down the corridor, down the stairs and out of the castle.

It let me leave without a whisper. Only the uncurling blooms moved as we walked past them, creeping up the cracks in the walls as if claiming the castle for their own. We moved through the gardens; with Laphaniel unable to scale the gates, it was our only way out.

Frost had begun to settle over the grass, lush and sparkling beneath the moonlight. Flowers and buds crept up, ignoring the signs of winter, to bloom from frigid earth. The trees themselves shook their branches awake, igniting long dead wood into blossom that rained down upon our heads, showering us in a hope that didn't belong to us.

The garden rejoiced in its awakening, stirring not just the flowers, but also decaying birds that lay shattered against the paths. Feathers bloomed where rot had set in, growing smooth and strong and bright, until the songs of the wind touched them, and they took flight.

We left the garden behind and stepped back into woodland, winter once more nipping through the tattered remains of our clothing. Laphaniel leant against me, his steps staggering and clumsy, his breaths uneven. I knew we would only get so far before we had to stop and rest, and that it wouldn't nearly be far enough.

"Is there anything I can do?" I asked as he forced us on. "Is it healing?"

I made him stop, lifting up his shirt to look at the wound on his chest. Beneath the blood there was already a scar, raised and shining white. It looked miraculously healed, except for the blackish veins that snaked outwards from it. I moved my hand to trace them, but Laphaniel caught it, pulling me away.

"It doesn't hurt, it just feels cold."

I closed my fingers over Laphaniel's. "I thought I had lost you."

"So did I," he answered, his body tensing at the thought.

"What was it like?"

"Dying?"

I winced. "Sorry, you don't need to talk about it if you don't want to."

He closed his eyes and took a breath. "I don't remember dying, Teya, just being dragged back, and that it hurt more than the knife to my chest, and..."

Laphaniel stopped, voice catching. He opened his eyes and focused on something far away, something that didn't belong to me.

"And what?"

He shook his head, shrugging me off. "Nothing."

"And what?" I pushed, remembering the sense of anger and discontentment that had come from the shadows. The reluctant ghostly fingers, the reluctant surrender of a possession that was rightfully won. I squeezed my eyes shut at the realisation. "You didn't want to come back."

Laphaniel sat down awkwardly, his head bowed. "I don't know."

I sat beside him, drawing him close. He rested his head against my chest. I wanted to cry, his words breaking yet another part of me so that I feared there soon would be nothing left. I didn't cry.

I didn't want him to comfort me, I wanted and needed to be there for him, to be his rock after he had been mine so many times before.

"Do you want to talk about it?"

He shook his head. "No."

"It dragged you back from somewhere. Where did you go?"

Laphaniel buried his head in his hands, his fingers gripping his hair as he shook his head again. "Don't."

"Okay," I soothed, hating how broken he seemed. "That's okay. Just understand that I'll listen if you ever need to talk to me. Please don't shut me out."

He kept his head in his hands, his body rigid and I longed to comfort him. I placed a hand on his shoulder and he flinched.

"We should keep moving," he said, still sounding a little bit lost.

"I think we should camp here for the night," I replied. "Beneath those rocks, it's sheltered back there, we'll be fairly well hidden."

"It's too close."

"We need to rest..."

"Teya..."

"You need to rest," I snapped, frayed nerves causing me to lash out. "You can't keep limping through the forest until you pass out."

"I don't know what to do," he said quietly. "I don't know what to do next."

I could see how much it was troubling him not to be in

control, to not be able to fix the mess we had found ourselves in. He looked as frightened as I felt.

"Shh, get some sleep," I whispered, pulling him close. "We'll stay here tonight; a few damned miles are not going to make much of a difference, are they?"

"No," he said finally, giving up. "I suppose not."

We hid amongst the rocks, shivering in the cold, not daring to light a fire. I sat with my back against the stone and watched the black forest, stroking the dark hair off Laphaniel's face as he slept fitfully with his head in my lap.

I didn't dare fall asleep, but allowed my mind to wander instead, taking me to a place where I had been completely safe and loved. I wanted to forget, for just a moment what dangers lay ahead of us, and what it would have been like if I had said yes...if I had stayed with Laphaniel in the first place.

Away from the cold and the fear and the unknown, I daydreamed, imagining myself as once I had been, held tight in Laphaniel's arms, dancing beneath the cherry blossom with every whispered promise of forever.

SNEEK PEAK

Continue reading for the first chapter of book two of The
Wicked Woods Chronicles:

Hush, the woods are darker still

OUT NOW

CHAPTER ONE

*G*et up, Teya, we need to go."

I blinked as Laphaniel shook me awake, then stretched out my aching limbs until they cracked, willing warmth back into them. The skin over my hands split; the chill bit into the wounds, making them sting.

For a moment, I lay on the cold ground, staring up at the stalactites dripping from the cave roof. The early morning sun peeked into the cave enough to illuminate them, casting an eerie glow, so they looked like giant teeth.

Wincing, I shoved myself to my feet and bit into the strip of dried meat Laphaniel handed me, the last piece we had. We had been fortunate enough to stumble across a travelling merchant, purchasing some warm clothing and scraps of food. The food was mostly stale and the clothing old and threadbare, nothing more than a small bundle of roughly woven shirts, trousers, and cloaks with holes in them. We would have likely perished without them though, and the merchant had taken in our desperate state and had charged us extra for it.

Winter had stopped nibbling at the edges of Faerie and

now crept further in until everything was blanketed in unforgiving snow and ice. It was too cold for us to sleep outside, forcing us to seek shelter in caves, if we were lucky enough to find one, or shallow hollows if we weren't.

It was too barren for Laphaniel to hunt for food. He would lay traps deep in the snow, and we would wait. Days crept by, but they remained empty.

The wolves were quicker than us, hunting, unburdened by the snow and cold, to pick off the last straggling animals. Everything else had hunkered down for the winter. The howling would keep me from sleep, always sounding too close to us, despite Laphaniel assuring me we were downwind.

But we had more to worry about than the wolves. Luthien had sent her fey to hunt us down.

Three weeks had passed since Laphaniel and I had broken the curse, binding all the Seelie Court to a mortal queen, broken it when we fell in love, just like a human fairy-tale.

My sister Niven had been chosen to be the next mortal queen, bound to the ruined Seelie castle for fifty years where she would wither and die, and then another girl would be chosen. Again, and again and again, for all eternity. Until, on the evening of my father's funeral, I had walked into the woods and demanded my sister back.

But found Laphaniel,

And fell in love.

I gave up the chance to spend forever with him, safe and loved beneath the branches that stretched throughout his home. Instead, I traded my life for my sister's, bargaining with Luthien, the rightful Queen of Seelie, to spend the rest of my life in a dark, abandoned castle alone. I thought it would fix the ruins of my family.

It didn't.

Years spent alone in the castle had ignited a darkness within Niven, a darkness that had lingered in her. She had always been cruel, cold…wrong. The girl I had found in the mouldering tower of the Seelie Castle was a nightmare in ruined silk. I would never forget the look of ecstasy on her face as she plunged a knife through Laphaniel's chest.

Laphaniel had not let me come alone.

He had died in my arms. He died for me, a mortal girl, which broke the curse on the Seelie Court—doesn't love always conquer all?

"Did you sleep at all?" I asked Laphaniel, noting the bruise-like shadows beneath his eyes. His face, like mine, was streaked with dirt, his hair matted with it. Stubble darkened his chin, a stark contrast to the pale skin beneath the filth and blood.

"A little."

I narrowed my eyes as I helped to roll up the thin blankets we had, tying them tight as we readied ourselves to move on from the damp cave we had stumbled upon. I knew he barely slept. Every night he tossed and turned ever since we had ended the curse. Something had dragged him back from the dead, a colossal shadow of fury and rage that had descended upon the castle and brought everything inside back to life…husks of flowers in long dry vases… desiccated spiders in the rafters…trapped birds, and Laphaniel.

I no longer woke screaming from my nightmares, but every night Laphaniel was dragged from sleep by his.

I woke with him each time, reaching out while he clamped a hand to his mouth to force the scream back down his throat. He would wake, shaking, drenched in sweat until the chill caught hold, and he would tremble. He wouldn't tell me what he was dreaming, but I could guess, as sometimes the shadowy fingers that had hauled him from death still plagued my dreams.

With the curse on the Seelie broken, it made me the last mortal queen, with my reign ending upon my death. Luthien had no plans to allow me a long and happy life.

"You can't stay awake forever," I said, taking his hand.

Laphaniel curled his fingers around mine before shrugging. "I can try."

Staring out of the cave mouth, I noted the fresh snowfall and the heavy skies, thankful at least that our footprints had been erased.

"You can talk to me," I said as he shoved a hand through his filthy hair, making it stand on end. I doubted mine looked much better. "I just wanted you to know that."

He nodded, his voice cracking as he spoke, "Every time I close my eyes, I feel like I'm dying all over again."

The words came out in a quick rush as if they had been pressing against his lips for too long. He wouldn't look at me, staring instead at the hostile landscape before us. I reached for him again and hesitated, terrified he would pull away, but he wrapped his arms around me and held me close.

"I wish I could take your nightmares away like you once did for me," I said against him, not letting go until he pulled away.

"This helps," he answered. "Thank you."

"The talking or the hug?"

He gave me a small, wonderful smile. "Both."

"Can I ask you something?" Laphaniel nodded, so I continued, "If you had the choice and you found me again in the woods, would you force me to turn back, knowing where it would end up if you helped me? Or would you still take Niven, knowing this is where it would all end?"

Laphaniel said nothing for a few agonising moments, but

then he leant forwards, his lips moving close to my ear so I could feel each word he whispered back at me. "I would choose you, Teya—for every day of forever, it will always be you."

I closed my eyes against the words, knowing how much choosing me had already cost him. In the days following our flight from the castle, we had circled back to Laphaniel's house for supplies...only to find it engulfed in flames, fire licking the dark clouds like they were trying to set the sky alight.

I could smell it burning before I saw it, could hear the dying trees as they were forced away from the walls, turning to kindling as the fire consumed them. Glass shattered...nothing was left but the stone, a cold and brittle shell that offered only helplessness.

It hurt more than I thought it would, to know we would never make a home there together.

"Are you ready to go?" Laphaniel asked. "We need to keep moving."

I took his hand and followed him out of the cave, wincing as the wind hit me. The snow crept over my boots, soaking the hem of my cloak. The surrounding trees offered no shelter, all the branches stripped back, so they resembled spindly naked limbs. The lakes were frozen too, some of the ice so deep in places, we could walk across it.

Laphaniel kept trying to summon a flame in his hands, flicking his fingers until they were raw. Nothing came, nothing had come for the past week.

He was too tired,

too hungry,

too cold.

"We're not going to last the winter," I said.

"We just need to keep going."

"Until we can't go on anymore?" I asked, eyeing the heavy white clouds overhead. "We are either going to freeze or starve, Laphaniel."

"Then what do you want me to do?" he snapped, turning to me. Against the blinding white of the snow, his eyes were as black as coal. They were always black. "Luthien has hunters everywhere. If we stop, she will find us. And you're right. If we go on, we'll likely starve, so what do you want me to do, Teya?"

"I didn't mean…"

"No," Laphaniel interrupted. "I'm really asking you, what do we do?"

I shook my head. "I don't know."

Laphaniel sucked in a breath. "There is somewhere we can find food, somewhere warm we could stay until we think of something."

I knew he would never suggest such a place if we had any other choice if death wasn't chasing us down.

"No."

"Then we are going to die."

"No, Laphaniel. I am not going back there."

"I haven't found food for days," he said, exhaustion hissing through his voice. "Luthien won't need to catch us soon; she'll just need to wait until winter finishes us off."

I stepped away from him, wrapping my arms around myself as the bitter wind tugged at my ragged clothes, biting the raw skin beneath. I wanted to scream at the unfairness of it, at knowing he was right and that we had no other choice. I had to go home.

The thought of it would have once been a relief to leave the chaotic world of Faerie behind and return to my quiet village. Now it only filled me with dread.

"Niven killed you."

"Luthien wants to kill us," Laphaniel answered, bringing his cloak up over his face to ward off the wind. "I have been thinking about it for the past few days, trying to come up with another plan, but there's nothing. We need food, Teya. We need warm clothes, a night spent away from the frozen ground so we can think of what we're going to do next. If there was any other choice..."

"There isn't," I said, knowing he was right. "I'm sorry."

"What for? This isn't your fault."

I shrugged. "I should have chosen to stay with you."

Laphaniel caught my arm, his hands coming up to rest against my face, his touch icy cold. I could feel the calluses as he stroked my cheek, his fingers as raw as mine. "That wouldn't have made you happy, I made sure of that. But I'm right here now, I'm not going anywhere."

He pulled me closer, his mouth pressing against mine in a moment of warmth that made me remember how wonderful it felt to be alive. I moved my hand beneath his ruined shirt, searching out the miraculous thump of his heartbeat. My fingers stilled over the smooth scar tissue, and he tensed at my touch, his hand coming up to pull mine away.

"I just want to feel your heart beating," I said, and his hand stilled. He moved mine back over his chest so I could feel his heart thump against his ribs, beating the same wonderful song I had fallen in love with. I swallowed a sob, leaning my head against our entwined hands.

"Don't cry," Laphaniel breathed, pressing a kiss to the top of my head. "Your tears will freeze."

I smiled, not moving away. "What's the going rate for frozen tears?"

"In winter? I think they're pretty worthless." He kissed me again. "So, stop."

Even now, I could barely believe he was mine, that I

belonged to someone who would follow me through death and darkness and still be eager to hold me...to know he was mine as much as I was his.

We walked and walked, on and on. Even when the skies above darkened and let loose a storm made of snow and despair, we carried on. We walked even when the blisters on my feet popped and my boots squelched. When Laphaniel fell, his feet slipping from beneath him on black ice, I dragged him up, and we kept on moving.

"Where's the edge of the wood?" I called out over the relentless storm. "How far until we leave Faerie?"

"There's a path this way that is rarely used," Laphaniel called back, the wind snatching away his voice. "It should take us near your home town...if we're lucky."

"And if we're not?"

"Then I don't know where we'll end up, or when."

I skidded to a stop. "When?"

"If I misjudge the path, Teya, we may end up in China a hundred years from now."

"You didn't think to mention this to me until now?"

Laphaniel shook his head, grabbing my hand to help me through the snow that was piling up around our feet. "If we don't find shelter from this storm, then it won't matter."

I understood why he hadn't said anything. Our future was measured in hours...days if we were fortunate. There was no use in finding something to worry about too far ahead; it was a bleak outlook, but an honest one.

"Teya, look," Laphaniel said, quickening his pace as he hauled me uphill. "There's a house up there."

"Who on earth would live all the way out here?" I asked, squinting past the storm to see the dark outline of a crooked hut shrouded by twisted trees.

"I think that was the home of the Harp Witch," Laphaniel

answered, wiping the snow from his face to get a better look.

I stilled, remembering all too clearly the last time I ended up in the house of a witch. "Please tell me she was a nice old lady who just loved her music."

Laphaniel gave me a grim smile. "She strung her harps with heartstrings, so when she played them, they would reveal the secrets of those she had butchered. Don't look so worried—she's long dead."

I followed Laphaniel up the narrow, winding path to the witch's house, torn between the desperate need to find shelter, and the terror of what might still linger in the Harp Witch's home. Even though Laphaniel said it was empty, I could still sense the horror that had taken place within its walls, the terrible deeds so dark they left an echo that had bled into the eaves and timbers and begged to be left alone.

We reached the gate, and I placed my hand beside Laphaniel's on the railing, noticing too late it wasn't made from wood, but bone. Bones surrounded the cottage in a grotesque parody of a fence, all yellow with age, all picked clean. I couldn't fathom how many lives had been snuffed out to create it. Atop each post sat a skull, the tops cracked open to allow a candle stub to be wedged within.

"Those are too small to belong to an adult," I said, recoiling as Laphaniel swung open the gate and walked into the courtyard.

"That's because they don't."

I hurried after him, ducking under the low doorway as we entered the cottage, my heart hammering against my chest at the darkness within it. Laphaniel grabbed hold of my hand, pulling me close.

"There is nothing here but bad memories," he said softly. "It's a horrible place, but I won't let anything happen to you, I promise."

I nodded, taking a breath to calm the fear that threatened to overwhelm me. I had faced worse than a dark room and had come out fighting.

"I need to light a fire," Laphaniel said, rubbing his hands together and blowing into them. I took them in my own, trying to warm them up. "Grab one of the candles."

I did as I was told, plucking a candle stub from a nearby table. Slimy, yellow wax squelched over my fingers, but I held the wick under Laphaniel's hand and hoped. He clicked his fingers over it, furiously blowing into his hands to get some warmth behind them. A flame flickered and faltered. He clicked again as I cupped my free hand around the candle to ward off any breeze.

Flame finally danced over Laphaniel's fingers, weak and stuttering.

"Go light the rest, don't let it go out."

I ignited the rest of the half-melted candles around the cottage, collecting a small handful to take back to the table. After lighting them, I took Laphaniel's hands and held them over the flames.

"Do you think you'll be able to get a small fire going after you warm up?"

He nodded, "I think so."

Brittle light cast shadows against the stone walls, glittering against the cobwebs that hung so thickly overhead I couldn't see the beams. Spiders scurried back into the eaves, huge and bloated, disturbing the carcasses of long dead birds so they dropped to the floor with a dry thud.

"I think I preferred the dark," I half joked, not daring to look up again. I glanced around the room, noting the macabre harps that lined the walls. "On second thought-"

"Don't touch them," Laphaniel said, filling the fireplace

with old, dusty logs. "Unless you're curious as to what they have to say."

"I'm really not."

I took a step closer anyway, to look at the delicate etchings that had been painstakingly carved into the wood. I didn't dare touch the strings which were knotted and red and still impossibly wet looking. Even though I hadn't touched them, I could hear a faint hum that quivered through their strings, as if they were singing to themselves. I moved away, swallowing my disgust.

Against the far wall stood an ancient bed, the wooden headboard so rotten, chunks of it lay crumbled around the base. I pulled off the mouldering covers and blackened pillows, replacing them with our blankets. There was nothing I could do about the mattress.

Laphaniel managed to get a meagre fire crackling, and for the first time in ages, I began to remember what it felt like to be warm.

I sat on the edge of the bed, its creak echoing around the room, and watched as Laphaniel pulled his knife from his belt and disappeared outside. He was gone only moments, and my heart sank at what he brought back in to roast over the fire.

"Is there no bacon running around out there?" I asked, eyeing the long tails that dangled from his fingers.

Laphaniel smiled, a quick quirk of his lips that did nothing to lighten the shadows in his eyes. "The place is infested with them."

He readied himself to clean them, but I stopped him, holding my hand out for the knife. "Can I help?"

"You don't have to, Teya," he replied but handed me the knife when I didn't back down.

We prepared the rats together, some of the tension lifting ever so slightly as we worked. Laphaniel's skilled fingers showed me how to skin them whole, how to take out the bits we didn't want, and then how to skewer them over the fire.

"They didn't teach this in the Girl Guides," I said, as the fat bubbled and dripped from the tiny carcasses making the flames hiss.

"It is a privilege to teach you, Teya," Laphaniel replied, turning the meat, so it blackened and cooked. "Despite the circumstances."

"It seems a shame to waste these." I held up the skins, each of them looking like empty glove puppets. "Maybe we could sew them together and make a really small blanket?"

His laugh was wonderful and too brief. Any fragments of joy we managed to scavenge between us were always too fleeting and too few.

"I never thought I would be so hungry I would look forward to eating rodents," I said, as Laphaniel passed me one. "But, these look like the most delicious things in the world right now."

"Try not to get too excited. They're mostly skin and bone," Laphaniel answered, watching as I sunk my teeth into my food before starting his.

The feeling of having hot food was almost overwhelming, and before I knew it, I had a pile of little bones in front of me. Laphaniel picked his clean also, snapping the bones to suck out the marrow inside. He did it with such practised skill, one only someone who had known true hunger could possess.

"How was your first rat?" he asked, a smile dancing against his lips.

"Better than roast chicken," I said, reaching for another. "Which is something I thought I'd never say about eating rodents."

We finished eating and crawled under the covers of the bed, trying to ignore the reek of mould and damp that rose from the ancient mattress. Laphaniel had covered the fire, so only the embers glowed, barely giving any warmth but not sending smoke up the chimney like a beacon.

It was still cold inside the cottage, and my breath fogged in front of me as I wrapped the blankets tight around myself, but it was still a much more forgiving chill than what we faced outside.

"Close your eyes, I'll keep watch," Laphaniel said beside me, his head resting against mine as he ran his fingers along my arm.

"You need to get some sleep," I answered, turning to face him. "We both do."

He looked set to argue, but he said nothing as he ran a hand over his face, breathing out a heavy sigh I recognised as defeat. He closed his eyes, exhaustion dragging him under as if someone had flipped a switch.

I stayed awake a while longer, listening to the faint murmurs of the harps as they whispered in the shadows, the cold breeze teasing their strings as it crept through the cracks in the walls. I was just drifting off when Laphaniel kicked out, his hands tense on the mattress as he struggled with whatever dark dream had hold of him. He gasped, a frightened and broken sound that rasped through his lips, he took another breath, and it caught and another...the sound scraping against his throat as his nightmare choked him.

"I'm right here," I whispered to him, catching his hand as he made to lash out. "You're not alone, I'm right beside you."

The blankets twisted around him as he struggled, his breaths almost barking up past his lips. I pulled him closer, my lips at his ear.

"I love you," I breathed. "I love you, and I'm here, and I'm not going anywhere."

With a shuddering sigh, he opened his eyes, blinking at

me in confusion before swiping a hand over his face.

"Teya?" My name slipped strangely from his mouth, his black eyes not quite looking at me. "Can you close the window, it's cold."

I had missed him rambling in his sleep, the feel of him mumbling incoherently in my ear as I slept. He seldom did it anymore. Stroking the dark hair back from his face, I watched as his breathing settled, the nightmare retreating elsewhere for a while.

I wished I had Glamour like a true Queen of Faerie should. I would have loved nothing more than to weave threads of dreams from starlight just for him, to have the wind sing a lullaby. To hold the nightmares at bay simply because I willed them away. Like he had once done for me.

But I didn't have Glamour because I was a human girl. The mortal Queens held no true power but were merely figureheads...something to hold the Seelie crown and to be hated from a distance. I would have gladly given it up to Luthien if I could.

If the price for losing the crown wasn't my life.

Snuggling closer to Laphaniel, I closed my eyes, keeping my arms wrapped tight around his body, my forehead to his. Sometimes... just sometimes, it was enough to keep his nightmares away, a tiny fragment of magic only I possessed.

I fell asleep to the sound of his breathing, accompanied by the almost gentle plucking of strings.

HUSH, THE WOODS ARE DARKER STILL IS AVAILABLE IN PAPERBACK, EBOOK AND IS AVAILABLE IN KINDLE UNLIMITED.

MYBOOK.TO/HUSHWICKEDWOODS

ACKNOWLEDGMENTS

Where on earth do I start with these?

I guess, first of all, I must thank my mum and dad for raising me in a haunted cottage surrounded by dark and wonderful woodland…which was full of faeries of course.

Thank you to my beautiful, unwavering best friend forever, Cheryl Solman, for not only standing by me while I dream up worlds, but for also braving the woods with me… maybe one day we'll explore them again?

To my so very patient editor, Lynne Raddall, who has transformed this world of mine into something I am immensely proud of. You are so very awesome!

To Jorge Wiles for the tremendous original cover for Darling, there are wolves in the woods, it will always hold a special place in my heart. Thank you for all your enthusiasm and your humour.

Thank you, Suzie Kellaway for all your wonderful advice and all the wine…oh, especially the wine!

To my Beta readers, who tore the early drafts to well-deserved shreds. Thank you.

To one certain Beta…keep that stick sharpened.

For this new edition, I would like to say a massive thank you to Chesney Infalt and Katherine Macdonald, two wonderful authors that I am now lucky enough to call my friends. You two are keepers!

The beautiful new interior is all down to Nicole Scarano, you are magic!

This book could not have been written without the hauntingly beautiful music by Evanescence...Amy Lee, you are a true Faerie Queen.

To my readers, obviously! All of you who took a chance on an indie author and helped her dreams come true...I love you all.

To my husband, Matters. For all the support...the coffee...the hours spent ignoring you so I could just finish one more chapter! Thank you, thank you, thank you.

And lastly to my little changelings...my imps...my girls. This book is, and always will be, for you.

ABOUT THE AUTHOR

Lydia Russell grew up on a farm deep in the Dorset country-side alongside her three elder brothers, using the fields and woodland as their playground.

As an adult with two young children, she has used the memories of the wild woods of her youth to write The Wicked Woods Chronicles.

Stories of lost sisters, whispering oaks and dark romance.

Oh, the woods are dark and wicked.

Intothewickedwoods.wordpress.com

Join my free newsletter for updates, exclusive short stories, and bonus content.

https://mailchi.mp/762a54899973/join-my-mailing-list

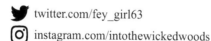

twitter.com/fey_girl63

instagram.com/intothewickedwoods

Printed in Great Britain
by Amazon